"What about my

The doctor consulted [...] anytime." He eyed his patient. "Or never," he continued as he turned to leave.

Once alone, Robert shut his eyes and his thoughts drifted. Then he sensed that someone had entered his room. A whiff of perfume and the muted click of her heels warned him that she wasn't one of the nuns at the hospital.

Robert glanced toward the door. The woman was dressed in white and was half-hidden in the shadows. She wore a wide-brimmed hat and dark glasses. An odd sensation stirred inside him, but it was gone before he could analyze it...like a dream.

"Robert Minardos?" she whispered in a low, husky voice. "I have come for you."

ABOUT THE AUTHOR

Tina Vasilos has successfully written romantic suspense for many years. She has traveled widely around the world, and she uses her trips to research her novels. Tina and her husband live with their son in Clearbrook, British Columbia.

Books by Tina Vasilos

HARLEQUIN INTRIGUE
68—UNWITTING ACCOMPLICE
101—WOLF'S PREY
132—PAST TENSE

Cry of the Peacock

Tina Vasilos

Harlequin Books

TORONTO • NEW YORK • LONDON
AMSTERDAM • PARIS • SYDNEY • HAMBURG
STOCKHOLM • ATHENS • TOKYO • MILAN
MADRID • WARSAW • BUDAPEST • AUCKLAND

Harlequin Intrigue edition published July 1993

ISBN 0-373-22235-1

CRY OF THE PEACOCK

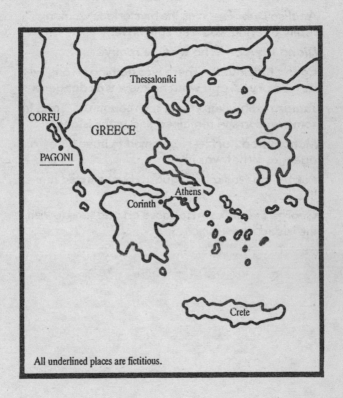

Thessaloníki

CORFU

GREECE

PAGONI

Corinth

Athens

Crete

All underlined places are fictitious.

CAST OF CHARACTERS

Robert Minardos—Could he regain his memory on a haunted island?

Analise Dubois—Was the mysterious woman really offering Robert a safe haven?

Diana Taylor—Who was she really?

Cedric Blackwell—There was nothing wrong with *his* memory . . . and what he knew was dangerous.

Tamara—She was young and beautiful . . . and for some reason she remained tied to the island.

Mohammed Kurtz—He seemed to have his own agenda. What was it?

Petro—He was a bodyguard, but he acted more like a spy.

George Leonides—He chose an odd time to visit the island.

Chapter One

Thomas lifted his head from the cloak that he had wrapped around himself. Dewdrops lay beaded on the thick black felt, sparkling coldly in the starlight. Around him the flock of sheep and goats slept, their bells silent in the depths of the night. He rose to his feet and emerged from the shelter of the thicket, skirting a huge boulder that lay on the hillside as if tossed there and forgotten by a playful giant.

Below him, the road was a ribbon of asphalt wrapping the mountain. He cocked his head, listening. Some sound not normally part of the night had awakened him.

The light breeze shifted, and he heard it again, a low, grinding roar. The growl of a car laboring up the hill. Glancing at the stars, he estimated that it was an hour before dawn. A frown tugged his brows together. Cars seldom used this old road anymore, with its potholes and its eruptions of weeds from cracked pavement. And certainly not at this hour of the night.

Firmly grasping his shepherd's crook, Thomas started down the path to get a better view. The car was a large black one. French, he thought, or German. What did he know of cars? He was a simple man, born and raised on the island. And likely to die here. He had no desire to go anywhere, not even to Athens. His brother had worked in the city for a while and had come back with stories of large department stores and a million cars that scurried through the streets like demented mice, day and night. Thomas had decided he was better off here in his mountains, tending his flock.

Thomas had reached the edge of the pitted asphalt by the time the car came up. He crouched in the shadows next to a hedge of overgrown oleanders and watched its laborious ascent. Two people sat in the front seat, a woman driving, a man beside her. The woman's long hair blew in the draft from the open window.

He recognized her. She'd driven into the village square shortly before the siesta hour. He and several of his friends had watched from their table in front of the coffee shop as she stepped out of the black car, shaking the creases from her yellow dress. Her hair was long, the color of sunshine, hanging loose down her back. Used to the dark, sturdy women of his family, Thomas had wondered if she was an angel sprung to life out of the icons in the church of Saint Spiridon.

The man must be the one he'd seen in the morning, arriving on the bus. During the hot, idle afternoon, the strangers had been the subject of avid discussion. Tourists rarely came to the village. Two in one day was unheard-of.

The tall, dark stranger had sat in the church garden for most of the day, alternately reading from several thick books and writing on a pad of yellow paper. His absorption in his work and his aura of self-contained solitude had been such that no villagers dared approach him.

Late in the afternoon, as Thomas was going down to relieve his cousin with the flock, he had seen the man and woman together in the coffee shop. The man was lucky they'd met, for it meant he didn't have to take the noisy, stinking bus back to Kérkyra—or Corfu, as the tourists called it—an hour to the north.

Thomas frowned, wrinkling his nose against the acrid smell of exhaust fumes. At the moment, the car was headed away from the city, toward the remote southern tip of the island. What business could they possibly have down there?

He shrugged. Perhaps they'd mistaken the road in the dark. Why should it matter to him what the mad tourists did, driving all over the desolate countryside in the middle of the night?

He was about to return to the flock when he heard another car. It rushed past, headlights boring white tunnels into the night. Thomas saw it clearly, an old steel-gray Mercedes like the one his brother had driven for years. Unlike the first car, this one seemed to have no trouble maintaining speed on the steep incline. Too much speed.

Sweat breaking out on his skin, Thomas sprang out of the shadows. The curve ahead could be lethal for someone who didn't know the road. Only last month a man on a motorcycle had been killed.

He ran out onto the fragmented pavement, waving his arms frantically and giving a shrill whistle through his teeth. But the sound was lost in the howl of the powerful engine as the second car accelerated up the crest of the hill.

The first car, slowing prudently, had just entered the curve when the Mercedes caught up to it. Thomas watched in horror as the heavy German car swerved wildly. Its brake lights flashed, but Thomas knew it wouldn't be able to slow down enough to negotiate the hairpin bend. Not without endangering the black car taking up most of the narrow road ahead of it.

With a shriek of tortured brakes, the Mercedes slammed into the other car. The crash of impact resonated over the valley as the black car skidded out of control on the gravel shoulder. It careened down the slope, lurching wildly left and right. Two wheels lifted off the ground, and for an instant the car hung suspended, on the point of rolling over. By some miracle, it remained upright, coming to rest at a crazy angle against an outcropping of rock almost hidden in dense shrubbery.

The Mercedes shuddered to a stop off the pavement on the inside of the curve. Dust settled slowly around it as the driver opened the door.

Thomas was about to call out, but the shout died in his throat when he saw the gun in the man's hands, a hunting rifle with a telescopic sight. Heart pounding, he shrank back into the bushes. Something was wrong here, something violent and evil.

The man ran to the edge of the road. Thomas could see his silhouette as he lifted the rifle. The wrecked car's headlights were still on, pointing a twin shaft of light toward the sky. The rifle fired, its snarling report echoing off the mountainside and startling the sheep into a plaintive bleating. Several more shots followed the first. Then an explosion shook the ground and a massive fireball flared into the night sky, briefly eclipsing the stars.

The gunman lowered the rifle and stared at the column of acrid smoke rising from the wrecked car before striding back to the Mercedes. He backed it up and turned it, then drove down the mountain in the direction from which he'd come.

Cowering in an oleander thicket, Thomas listened with ringing ears until the sound of the engine faded into the distance. Satisfied that it wouldn't return, he stepped out, brushing the fragile petals from his shoulders with shaking hands. The flock stirred in the brush, their bells clinking hollowly. Thomas hesitated, his eyes skittering from the mountainside where the sheep waited to the road, which had carried violence into his mundane life.

His sheep dog barked sharply as it brought a couple of strays under control. The bells fell silent. Thomas nodded in satisfaction. The dog would take care of the sheep, settle them down.

Quickly he strode down the road toward the curve. The cliff below was not steep, but the impact of the explosion had driven the car down the sudden drop past the rocks. Thomas crossed himself. Even if the people in the car had survived the crash, they would not have survived the further tumble into the deep ravine, or the fire that was consuming the car.

His eyes narrowed as he surveyed the surrounding brush. In a dry season, fire spread quickly. Luckily, it had rained the day before, and the shrubs were green like a wet spring. The damage would remain limited to pungent smoke and blackened wreckage.

He was about to turn away when a movement near the outcropping of boulders caught his eye. Someone from the car? Or only an animal disturbed by the crash? The sky was graying as dawn approached, but it was still too dark to see details.

Thorns tore at his clothes as he scrambled down the slope. He ignored their claws, long inured to the hazards of the mountains. Twisted pine trees clung to the meager soil at the edge of the ravine. He prodded the shrubbery with his stick, gently, as he would have in searching for a lost sheep in the dense shadows.

Wait. Was that a groan? He stilled, straining to hear over the renewed sawing of crickets now that the fire had begun to die. He heard it again, a low moan and a rustling of brittle leaves to his right.

Swinging around, he pushed through the prickly scrub, coming upon the man so suddenly that he almost tripped over him. He groped in his pocket for a match, lighting it and holding it high between callused fingers. The man had a gash on his forehead that was seeping blood. His mouth moved as he muttered words unintelligible to the shepherd.

Thomas ran his hands quickly but thoroughly over the man's body and limbs. His cotton shirt and jeans were ripped in numerous places, but he didn't seem to be seriously injured. From the broken twigs and trampled grass around him, Thomas surmised he'd crawled away from the car before the explosion.

There was no sign of the woman. She must have been caught in the fire. He crossed himself again.

Squatting back on his heels, Thomas considered his next move. The man was tall, but lean. He could carry him to the village easily, but was that wise? The Mercedes would have reached the village by now. Instinctively he knew the driver wouldn't want witnesses. The shots had been deliberate, cold-blooded. The gunman had meant for the couple in the car to die.

Thomas's mind slowly digested the problem. He got up, his face set in resolute lines. If he took the old mule track cross-country, he would reach the main highway in twenty minutes. He would leave the injured man at the side of the road. It was well traveled at all hours. Someone would find him almost at once and take him to a hospital.

And no one would know what Thomas had seen.

EVERY BONE in his body ached. As well as every nerve, every joint, and every sinew. He tried to get up and almost screamed with pain as his muscles twisted into knots of agony, refusing to obey him. He lay still, panting, trembling, waiting until his brain was once more capable of thought.

How much pain could a man endure and still be alive? Slowly, with agonizing care, he lifted one eyelid. Needles pierced his brain, and he snapped his eye shut, restoring the darkness that was marginally less painful than the light that lay beyond it.

Light. And silence. New sensations seeped through the pain. Maybe he was dead. How did one tell? An agonizing throb drilled into his temple as he struggled to think. Giv-

ing up, he tried to turn on his side. If he could find a cool
spot to rest his head, the throbbing would stop.

A soft rustling sound came from somewhere nearby. He
attempted to hold on to it, drawn by its nebulous familiar-
ity. The sound came again, and a smell that somehow conjured up an image of a steamy room and hot linen.

Starch. That was it. His mother had starched his father's
shirts when he was a child. It had been years since he had
smelled that pungent aroma.

He cautiously forced his eyes open again, millimeter by
excruciating millimeter. A blinding light seared his retinas,
but as he blinked he could see a shadow between him and
the source of the light. Again he heard the familiar rustling, and again he smelled the starch. Clothing. A volumi-
nous white garment.

Closing his eyes briefly, he fought to dislodge the pain in
his head. It remained, a restless dragon unfurling lacerat-
ing claws. He licked his lips, feeling the dry, cracked skin.

Progress, he thought. He could make his lips move,
though no sound emerged. He opened his eyes again, sheer
determination compelling his lids upward. The shadow was
still there, surrounded by a nimbus of light, and in its center gleamed a gold cross. *I've died,* he thought with grim
irony, *but at least I've gone to the right place.*

He should be relieved, he supposed, but a question
nagged at him. If he was in heaven, he shouldn't be feeling
pain. He would have left his broken body behind and would
be soaring on a celestial plane, free of gravity, headaches,
and all the other little inconveniences of life.

One inconvenience was making itself an insistent nui-
sance. He needed to go to the bathroom, and he wasn't at
all sure that any of his muscles were in a condition to take
him there.

Gritting his teeth, he dragged his hands onto his chest.
Both were bandaged, leaving only the fingers and half of the

palms free. He stared at his fingers and realized he must have been burned. The little hairs above his middle knuckles were singed off, although the skin seemed intact.

He'd obviously been in some kind of accident. Searching his mind, he tried to picture it. Nothing.

He clenched one hand into a fist. The skin felt as if it had shrunk, but his muscles obeyed him. The bite of his nails digging into his palm gave him an inordinate satisfaction. So far, so good. He wasn't paralyzed.

Unless his legs—

He flexed his knee experimentally, throwing it to one side. His foot slid off the mattress and swung above the floor, or at least where he assumed the floor must be.

Before he could follow up on this small victory, two gentle hands tucked up his leg and wrapped the sheet around him. "Hurt," said a low voice in accented English. "No move. Call doctor."

Yes, call the doctor. Sweat wrapped his body in a clammy embrace. He lay on the bed, shaking. His eyes fell closed as exhaustion enfolded him in a woolly blanket that momentarily blocked out the pain.

"Well, Kyrie Minardos, you're awake." The cheerful greeting jolted him.

"It's no pleasure, believe me." His voice sounded alien, grating harshly on his ears.

The doctor lifted each of his eyelids in turn, shining a light into his pupils. He wanted to scream. The beam felt like a skewer. "We'll put you on a medication for the pain," the doctor said soothingly as he picked up his patient's wrist and timed his pulse. "We were waiting for you to regain consciousness. I'm Dr. Nakos. Can you tell me your name?"

His name? "Minardos."

"Come, come, Kyrie Minardos. You'll have to do better than that. Your Christian name, please, and your place of residence."

"Rob—Robert." Memory flooded back, a confusion of images—airplanes, city buildings, a house with trees and wide green lawns, and, oddly, a newsstand displaying colorful magazines. "I live outside of London, and I'm a writer."

"Very good, Kyrie Minardos." Turning his head, Dr. Nakos spoke to someone at his side, and a moment later Rob heard a sound that he interpreted as the window blind being adjusted.

Cautiously he opened his eyes once more and found himself staring at a white starched bosom on which resided a gold cross. A wimple framed the woman's round, good-natured face. The angel he'd seen was a nun. Not much difference, he thought tiredly as he swallowed the tablets and sipped the water she held to his lips.

What happened to me? he wanted to ask, but he couldn't summon the strength to form the words.

"Bathroom," he mumbled, although how he would make it there, he didn't know. Nodding, the nurse took care of the problem with matter-of-fact efficiency, without moving him from the bed. Too exhausted to feel embarrassed, he was conscious only of relief and the easing of the pain as sleep overcame him.

When he woke again, it was night. The blind was up, the window dark. A lamp cast a soft light from the corner of the room.

Rob stretched his legs, turning onto his back. Except for his headache, and the pain in his ribs when he moved, he felt almost human again. He ran his hands over his body, lifting the sheet to examine his bare chest. Bruises everywhere, some of them blue, others already turning a lurid greenish yellow. The skin on his back stung in odd places, and he wondered if he had minor burns there, as well.

He was hungry, he realized. An IV tube ran into his arm, feeding a clear liquid into his vein from a plastic bag on a pole. Nourishment? His stomach growled, making its preferences clear.

He groped under the pillow, finding a device he recognized as a call button. Pushing the end of it, he waited.

A moment later, the cheerful nun bustled in, carrying a tray covered with a white napkin. The doctor followed close behind her. "Ah, Kyrie Minardos, I see you're looking better." He went through his stethoscope-and-blood-pressure-cuff routine. "How do you feel?"

"Better," Rob managed to say. His throat was still dry, and it burned when he talked. "How did I get here?"

"A motorist found you by the side of the road and brought you in. You'd been in an accident."

"In a car?" he asked, forming the words with difficulty. "Yes."

Rob moved his head slowly back and forth in denial. "I didn't have a car."

"You must have borrowed or rented it."

A new pain stabbed through Rob's head. He didn't remember a car. Blankness filled his mind. It hurt too much to think, and he was too tired to make the effort. It would all come back, in time. "Hungry," he croaked, with a grim economy of words.

Nakos nodded. "That's a good sign." He glanced at the IV pole. "I think we can dispense with that."

Rob winced as the doctor yanked off the tape that held the needle in place. "A quick jerk hurts less than peeling it off slowly," Nakos said with a grin.

"If you say so." His mouth felt like an old sock. He thought longingly of fruit juice, his eyes straying to the tray.

"In a moment," the doctor said. "We'll just crank up the bed a little."

The room spun crazily for a second as the nurse helped Rob to sit up. "Okay?" she asked, her eyes crinkling merrily at the corners.

"Fine." He swallowed down his faint nausea, realizing that the churning in his stomach was doing nothing to diminish his hunger. Lifting the napkin, he stared at the tray. A glass of orange juice, a slice of toast, and a bowl of unadorned rice pudding.

"Soft foods for now," Dr. Nakos said, his smile sympathetic. "If that doesn't cause any problems, we'll get you something more interesting for lunch tomorrow."

To his chagrin, Rob could barely keep his upright position long enough to finish the juice, the pudding and half of the toast. With gestures and her limited English vocabulary, the nurse offered to help him, but he pushed the tray away, suddenly too weary to speak, even to tell her he knew her language. He closed his eyes and slept.

HIS RECOVERY WAS RAPID. The bandages were removed, and the burns, mainly superficial, healed quickly. The cut on his forehead had closed, a thin line bordered by neat stitches that would fade in time. By the third day he could walk the length of the hall without feeling as if his legs were encased in cement.

He'd learned he was in a clinic on the outskirts of Corfu town run by one doctor with a staff of nursing sisters. The nuns made much of him, enjoying the novelty of caring for a foreigner and admiring his fluency in Greek. They asked him innumerable questions about his work, his home and his income, questions that he answered or evaded with good humor.

He found out he'd been in the hospital for two days before he regained consciousness, which meant he'd lost not one, but three, days of his life. Every time he tried to remember, his head ached. The doctor assured him that none of his symptoms were unusual in the aftermath of concussion and severe trauma.

"But I didn't even have any broken bones," Rob protested. "What severe trauma?"

"The car exploded and burned," Nakos said, in a soothing tone that only increased Rob's frustration.

"Was anyone with me? Anyone else hurt?"

Nakos shook his head. "Apparently not. But you were lucky to escape with your life."

ON THE MORNING of his sixth day in the clinic, Robert was seated by the window when a short, slight man dressed in a drab gray suit came into his room.

"Kyrie Minardos, my name is Venetis. I'm with the police. You speak Greek? Good. My English is very bad." He extended his hand. His smile was fleeting, and his dark eyes were watchful.

Rob felt a little chill of apprehension creep up his spine, although the man's handshake was cordial enough. "I suppose this is about the accident. Unfortunately, I don't remember it. Dr. Nakos says it wasn't my car. I went up to the village on the bus. After that, everything's a blank."

Opening a small notebook, Venetis pursed his lips. "I can fill in some of the blanks. You spent the day reading and making notes. In the evening you had dinner with a blond woman, also a visitor to the village. She drove there in a black Peugeot. Just before dawn, the car went off a sharp turn on what they call the old road, exploded, and burned."

Rob closed his eyes as his stomach lurched sickeningly. "She wasn't in the accident?" he asked, his voice cracking.

Venetis shook his head. "It appears that you were alone. Do you remember borrowing the car?"

Rob swallowed, his ears humming nastily. "I don't know. I don't remember." He wet his dry lips with his tongue. "Who was the car registered to? That might tell me something."

Venetis turned a page in the notebook, running the tip of his pen down the lines. "The registered owner is a company called Media Consulting. The company doesn't have an office in Corfu, but they keep the car for employees here on business or vacation. It was kept in a parking facility. The fees were always paid on time." He looked up. "We haven't been able to trace the woman who met you in the village."

The woman. A black car. A vicious pain stabbed Rob's head. "I don't remember any woman," he said tiredly.

He closed his eyes, then blinked as the policeman touched his shoulder. "Kyrie Minardos, are you all right? Shall I call the doctor?"

An icy chill shuddered through him. Slowly, as if he were in a trance, he rubbed a shaking hand over his face. "No, I'll be okay. Doesn't the parking garage know who took the car?"

"I'm afraid not. The cars aren't closely monitored, especially during the day. Anyone who has a key to their car can take it out."

"What does Media Consulting say? I presume you contacted them."

Venetis consulted the next page in his notebook. "Their office is temporarily closed for vacation."

"In other words, a dead end," Rob said, wishing the man would go away and leave him alone.

"The fact remains that you met a woman in the village," the policeman persisted. "You had dinner. She drove off in the car. You went to the room you'd rented for the night."

"Then how did I end up in the car?"

"A question we'd like the answer to. She must have brought the car back later, when everyone was asleep."

Clawing his fingers through his hair, Rob let out a long breath. "If you say so. I can't remember."

Venetis stared at him so intently that Rob could barely restrain himself from squirming. "Nothing, Kyrie Minardos?"

"Nothing. Why? Are you accusing me of something?"

The man's gaze didn't waver. "Should I be?" The corner of his mouth turned up in a half smile that Rob didn't trust at all. "No, Kyrie Minardos. There is no evidence that the woman was in the car or that the crash was anything but an unfortunate accident, too much speed on a mountain road. And no one has filed a missing-person's report. There's nothing more to be done, at least for now." He eyed Rob closely. "You're sure you don't remember the woman? The villagers got the impression you knew one another."

Rob clenched his teeth. "I don't know anyone here, except in the most superficial way."

"Nevertheless, many people know you, Kyrie Minardos. Your picture was in the newspaper two days before the accident. You attended a banquet where you received an award for your article on the arson fires that have been devastating Corfu's forests. You must remember that."

"Of course I remember the banquet." Sudden insight flashed through the fuzz in his brain. "Wait a minute." He groped in the drawer that held his belongings, pulling out his wallet. He extracted a note. "This is why I went to the village. It says to go there on a certain day, the day I went, if I wish to discuss an interesting story. But I can't remember anything."

"Perhaps you'll be contacted again. The story of the accident has also been in the newspapers."

Rob shifted in his chair, his energy dying rapidly. "What did you say this woman looked like?"

Venetis leafed through his notebook once more. "The villagers describe her as tall, beautiful as an angel, with long blond hair. She wore sunglasses."

Rob's head began to ache again. The pain slicing into his temples sharpened sensations. He could hear Sister Angela singing down the hill, and cutlery clanging against a metal cart as she arranged the lunch trays. Venetis's after-shave surrounded him with a cloying sweetness, although he'd barely noticed it earlier.

The smell changed, becoming the fragrance of hyacinths as a nebulous veil seemed to lift. He was back in the past. Paris in the spring. Diana Taylor.

He shivered as the years peeled away to reveal a mental picture of a tall, vital young woman with short auburn hair and owlish spectacles. There had been promise, even magic, between them during that springtime weekend when they had met at an art opening in Paris. Scarcely six months later, when reality intruded, they had known the truth. Wrong time, conflicting goals. Their lives had never truly meshed.

Ten years had gone by since they'd agreed to dissolve their marriage, a brief marriage contracted too soon on a youthful impulse that had quickly died.

Ten years.

After all this time, he rarely thought of her, except for odd moments filled with nostalgic regret. What had reminded him of her now?

Venetis finished writing, closed his notebook and slowly replaced it in his pocket. "If you remember anything, could you contact me, Kyrie Minardos? And please let me know when you leave the island, in case we find anything else that may help us reconstruct the circumstances of the accident. I'm sure that, as a writer, you'll be interested. Good day, Kyrie Minardos."

Good day to you, too, Rob thought bitterly. Venetis had spoiled his, raising more questions than answers. He slumped back in the comfortable chair they had provided for him. Who was the woman, and why had she lent him her car?

After lunch, he lay down on his bed, drowsy in the heavy midday heat. The blinds were closed, filtering the light to a hazy dimness. Outside his window, even the birds had fallen silent. He'd dropped into a light doze when he sensed that someone had entered the room. A drift of perfume and the muted click of heels warned him that it wasn't one of the nuns.

He glanced toward the door, his eyes half-closed. A woman dressed in white stood there, half-hidden in the shadows.

"Robert Minardos?" she asked, in a low, husky voice. "I've come for you."

Chapter Two

Come for him? For a crazy moment Rob was transported back to the day when he'd recovered consciousness and seen the nun by his bed. But no, this woman was as real as Sister Angela had been.

Her heels tapped faintly on the tile floor as she came toward him. She sat down in his chair, her back to the window. The wide hat she wore cast her features in shadow, and dark glasses hid her eyes.

"I've come to take you to the island."

She spoke quietly, her voice piquant with an accent he couldn't quite place. Her hands lay folded over a small clutch purse on her lap. Only the lower part of her face was visible—smooth, lightly tanned skin, a narrow, straight nose and a firm chin. She had the most beautiful mouth he'd ever seen, with luscious coral-pink lips apparently unadorned by cosmetics.

An odd sensation stirred inside him, as if a warm hand had touched his heart. It was gone before he could analyze or interpret it, like a dream forgotten when one wakes, leaving only a pleasant memory. And a curiosity to know if those lips would taste as soft as they looked.

"How did you find me?" he asked, distracted by the heat that tingled in his veins. Shouldn't he have asked who she was, and what island? Somehow it didn't seem important.

Her shoulders rose and fell, the loose white cotton of her dress momentarily pulling taut to outline her breasts. "We have our sources," she said, opening her purse to withdraw a card. She extended it to him, holding it lightly between two fingers.

Rob pushed himself to a sitting position on the bed. When she bent forward to hand him the card, he caught a trace of her perfume. Gardenia. Sweet, and at the same time sensual.

The rectangle of heavy embossed paper was printed with a name and a telephone number. Paul Joubert. Rob recognized the number as Swiss by the area code.

Recollection stirred. "Yes. I called that number." Rob frowned. "I'm not sure when. Couple days before the awards banquet, I think. His office was supposed to contact me."

Joubert was a wealthy industrialist who had business interests in most of the European countries, and who was known as an openhanded supporter of the arts. He was also known for his reputation of being pointedly antagonistic toward any kind of media attention. Had he consented to see Rob?

Wait a minute, he thought suddenly. "You don't know anything about a message a waiter gave me at the banquet, do you?"

The woman's face was shadowed by the brim of her hat, making it impossible to judge her reaction to the question. But her reply was prompt and direct. "No. Was the message about Mr. Joubert?"

Rob clenched his fist in frustration. "Actually, no. It was ambiguous, promising a story if I would go to the village."

"And you went. And you were in the accident." She sounded sympathetic.

"Yes. Was it you I talked to on the phone when I called Joubert's office?"

"At the Swiss office?" She gave a light laugh. "Hardly, Mr. Minardos. I work with Paul on his island here."

"I knew he lived in the area," Rob said. "That's why I thought I'd take the opportunity to ask for an interview. So Mr. Joubert is expecting me?" he added, reluctant to reveal his loss of memory. "I'm afraid I lost my appointment book."

"It doesn't matter. We read of a car crash involving a Canadian writer and assumed it was you."

She shrugged again, the movement of her shoulders graceful and negligent, as if the accident were a minor inconvenience easily dismissed. "Mr. Joubert would like you to come to Pagoni to recuperate. It's very peaceful."

"I'm sure it is," Rob murmured, still a little stunned by the offer. "But I haven't been released yet."

"Tomorrow, I believe."

"You're well-informed." Rob's tone was dry.

"Mr. Joubert tries to be."

She lifted her fingers to adjust her dark glasses, and he noticed her hands. She had blunt nails and well-defined tendons, as if she were no stranger to work. Somehow her hands seemed at odds with the impression of pampered elegance he received from her clothing and manner.

"Let's see," she said. "You are thirty-three. Canadian by citizenship, but you own a house near London and spend most of your time either in England or on the Continent. You have a reputation for insight and honesty in your articles, and you write thrillers that sell in the millions. How am I doing, Mr. Minardos?"

"Correct so far," Rob allowed.

A smile crossed her lips so quickly he might have imagined it. "Mr. Joubert is a fan of your books. He's looking forward to meeting you."

As I am him, Rob thought, his anticipation nonetheless mixed with a degree of caution. He'd heard Joubert could be a ruthless man, although nothing illegal had ever been proved against him. But rumors persisted, and Rob didn't believe rumors materialized in a vacuum.

Suddenly he felt like laughing out loud. The best he had hoped for when he'd called Joubert's office was a brief telephone conversation. He actually had an interview with the man? Hundreds of writers would sell their mother for this chance, and Rob certainly didn't intend to turn down the opportunity that had unexpectedly been tossed into his lap.

The woman rose from the chair, extending her hand to him. "I will be here at ten tomorrow morning, if that is convenient."

"Fine. I should be ready."

He took her hand. Her cool fingers gripped his briefly before letting go. With a supple twist of her tall, long-legged frame, she turned and walked to the door, pulling it open.

"Wait," Rob called. "I don't know your name."

She paused without looking around. "Analise Dubois," she said. She went out, closing the door gently behind her.

THE TALL YOUNG WOMAN turned the corner of the deserted hall, then paused, dragging in a long breath. Leaning against the wall, she closed her eyes in relief. She'd gotten away with it. Wise or not, her course was well and truly set from here on in.

Diana Taylor, alias Analise Dubois, was playing a dangerous game that involved tweaking a man-eating lion's nose. And she had no choice now but to drag Rob into it.

He hadn't recognized her—not that she expected him to. The plastic surgery she'd had to repair the broken nose sustained in her escape from a Middle Eastern prison five years ago had guaranteed her anonymity, especially since Rob hadn't seen her in ten years. Her voice was different, as well, lower, huskier. And his amnesia, combined with the disguise she'd affected that day, ensured that he wouldn't know her as the woman he'd met in Makrino, a village she'd picked for its isolation and relative difficulty of access.

The car couldn't even be traced back to her.

Pain swamped her briefly. She shouldn't have left Rob on that mountainside. But she'd seen he was alive, and that the shepherd would take him to safety, and she couldn't take the chance that anyone would see them together. And see through her disguise. The blond wig, the pale makeup, the huge dark glasses—the villagers would remember those, rather than any details of her real appearance. And they would also assume that she and Rob had been two strangers who had met by chance and parted at the end of the day.

His memory loss would work in her favor. He wouldn't inadvertently give away her true identity. She'd revealed it to him in the village only in order to buy time. After the call from Switzerland, when she'd recognized his name, she'd known she had to head him off by whatever means she could. She couldn't have him coming and stirring up Joubert when she was so close to success.

Rob had been surprised to see her after all these years, and startled by her altered appearance. "Joubert likes your work," she'd told him. "And he's mentioned that he may give you an interview. If he does, can you find some excuse to put him off for a couple of weeks? I need that time." She'd promised him the story afterward, an exclusive, and he'd agreed to wait for her call.

But the accident, and Joubert's sudden demand to see Rob, had changed all the rules. And the amnesia placed an unexpected wild card in the deck. His memory wouldn't return any too soon, she hoped. A week or two should be enough time to finalize her job.

In the meantime, she would keep an eye on him, just in case he'd been the target of the gunman. In the end, when he had the story of his life, Rob would forgive her deception.

How extensive was the amnesia? she wondered. He'd lost three days, Sister Angela had told her. Three days, two due to concussion and the other, more critical one apparently from the trauma of the car crash. But were there gaps elsewhere?

It didn't matter. The important thing was that she'd succeeded. Paul would be pleased. She could congratulate herself for that, too. Paul was not easily pleased, and it was crucial that he remain complacent and off guard.

Three days ago he had called her into his office, his face creased in a smile. With a sinking heart, she'd recognized the significance of that smile. It meant he was up to something. He'd quickly enlightened her by thrusting a newspaper across the desk and into her hand.

The Greek headlines had screamed the news of a prominent Canadian writer injured in a flaming car crash. "Robert Minardos. Didn't you tell me he phoned about an interview? I've decided I'll indulge him. I want you to go and bring him here."

"Bring him here?" Diana had echoed in disbelief. Joubert shunned publicity as if it were a virulent disease. She'd told him about Rob's earlier call, but, as she'd expected, he'd flatly refused to talk to a journalist.

"Yes," he'd said impatiently. "I've been thinking that some positive publicity would be a good idea. I don't like the interest Interpol has been taking in my business lately. Those impressionist paintings I'm donating to the museum in New York should show my good intentions. Minardos's byline on the story would only increase its impact and credibility."

"What if he doesn't want to come?" Diana had asked, grasping at any objection that might carry weight with Joubert. She couldn't count on her cover holding if Rob came here. She hadn't known then of his memory loss, the fact that he'd forgotten their meeting in Makrino.

"He'll come," Paul had said, lighting a cigar that sent a cloud of pungent smoke to the ceiling. "Any journalist would kill for an interview with Paul Joubert."

"He might not be in any condition to leave the hospital."

"I've done my homework, Analise. He's apparently suffering from partial amnesia, but he'll be released soon." His smile had been almost gentle. "Get him to come, one way or another."

At least it had been easy. Rob hadn't known her. And he'd readily agreed to come. Paul had known what kind of man he was dealing with. As usual.

Not for the first time, she wondered if her boss was beginning to suspect that she wasn't what she appeared to be. A chill ran up her spine. The main computer, from which Paul controlled his extensive commercial empire, had been down ever since she'd returned from her last business trip to Paris.

Then she'd met Rob.

Before the next dawn, both of them had nearly been killed. She might have dismissed the nudge of the Mercedes against her Peugeot as an accident, but the gunman had aimed the rifle with cold-blooded intent. Who was the sniper? And who had sent him?

Joubert? She doubted it. She knew him too well by now, and his manner toward her hadn't altered. And his invitation to Rob seemed to confirm his innocence.

Which meant that the danger lay elsewhere.

Danger to her?

Or to Rob?

She would have to be doubly on her guard. The accident, added to the mysterious failure of the business computer, gave her a very uncomfortable feeling. And she knew from past experience that it was prudent not to ignore the prickling of her caution sensors.

Just a couple of weeks more, and the case would come to a head, if her projections were on target. Joubert had another deal brewing, and this time she would have the proof, adding it to bits of information she'd given her superior when she was in Paris, ostensibly arranging the shipment of the donated paintings. The game would be over.

The strident blast of a car horn sent her running across the foyer of the clinic and down the steps to her waiting taxi.

"You said fifteen minutes, miss," the driver grumbled as she climbed into the battered old Mercedes. "It's hot out here."

"I'm sorry," she said, still distracted. "Please take me back to town."

Muttering, he set the car in motion.

Diana paid little attention to the lush subtropical gardens that lined the road, her thoughts returning to the man she had just left.

He'd changed. Grown and matured. But then, so had she. She was now a far cry from the silly girl Rob had married and with whom he'd shared a home, a home from which one or the other of them had been absent most of the time.

She almost laughed as she thought of Joubert's assessment of Rob. "He's clever, but naive," Joubert had said complacently. "He'll make me look like a generous philanthropist. Which, of course, I am."

Clever Rob certainly was. Always had been. Diana remembered the idealism that had driven him when he was twenty-three. He'd defended causes with the same passion he gave to their lovemaking. Had he been hurt when their marriage failed? He'd put a good front on it, generously offering her a settlement, which she'd refused. He'd told her that if she ever needed him, she had only to call.

She hadn't wasted time on regrets then, throwing herself into her studies and then into a career with the European Fine Arts Commission, an organization that investigated art disappearances and smuggling, often in cooperation with insurance companies. Few outsiders had heard of the EFAC, since the results of its underground work remained hidden until arrests were made by law-enforcement authorities.

She'd followed Rob's career over the years, since it often paralleled her own work. Now and then, when she saw his name on a particularly incisive article about the state of the art world and those who influenced it, or on the cover of one of his thrillers, she felt a twinge of guilt, mixed with fond remembrance. If she hadn't suggested they go their separate ways, would they have worked out their differences and be together still?

She certainly wouldn't have been bored with him. Even when he was half asleep in his hospital bed, the vibrant force of his personality could not be ignored. His eyes, a startling silver-gray against his tanned skin, had been sharp and intelligent as they examined her. She had been aware of his curiosity, the questions he must have been burning to ask. He hadn't even hesitated before accepting her invitation.

Impulsive still, and capable of instantly sizing up a situation and making the most of it. They were qualities she admired. Not for the first time since this had started, she was sorry that she couldn't recruit him as an ally.

But the risk was too great, both for him and for her.

She phoned Paul from her hotel. "He's coming."

"Excellent. Excellent." She could picture his smile, the display of very white teeth that reminded her of a shark's. "I knew I could count on you." He paused as if debating whether to ask the next question. "What do the police say about the accident?"

A cold frisson feathered up her spine. She recalled the gunman standing on the road, coolly shooting at the car. Again she wondered if Paul had sent the man. But there was no indication that he'd been aware of the accident before he read about it in the newspaper. No hint that he knew of her involvement in it.

This morning, before going to the clinic where Rob was recuperating, she had visited the police station to see Venetis, a man she knew she could trust with her life. He was also a man who was interested in seeing an end to the wholesale disappearance of Greece's greatest treasures. When she had asked about the accident, he had shrugged philosophically and said it was an obvious case of a tourist, unfamiliar with mountain roads, taking a curve too fast. No witnesses. Case closed.

After much thought, she had decided not to tell Venetis about the man with the rifle, nor about the shepherd. Stirring up questions could risk her own position, and that was the last thing she wanted.

"The police blame excessive speed and poor road conditions," she told Paul now. "Why?"

"No reason, my dear. Just curiosity. When will you be here with Minardos?"

"He should be released tomorrow. We'll be there in time for lunch."

"Good," Paul said. "Everything will be prepared."

An odd note in his voice made her bite her lip. Why did the simple statement sound ominous? She shook her head. She was imagining things. The "accident," and meeting Rob again, had unsettled her.

"Till tomorrow, then," she said, in a calm voice that gave no indication of the butterflies fluttering in her stomach.

"Tomorrow," he echoed, and again she heard that peculiar intonation.

She must be crazy. Her double life was finally getting to her. "Au revoir, Paul," she said, and rang off.

She slept badly, her dreams full of images of Robert Minardos and a menacing Paul Joubert. In the morning she did her best to banish the sense of foreboding, chiding herself for the attack of nerves. She couldn't give up. She was in too deep, and the game had to be played out to its conclusion.

SHE SEEMED NERVOUS, although she covered it well. Rob wondered why. Snapping the locks shut on the suitcase that his hotel had delivered the night before, he lifted it from the bed. He set it on the floor, his mouth twisting at the discomfort as he put inadvertent pressure on his bruised ribs. "Guess I'm not as strong as I thought," he muttered. "What's the name of this island where Joubert lives?"

"Pagoni. It means—"

"Peacock. Yes, I know. Are there peacocks?"

An odd look, almost of fear, crossed her face. "Yes. Mr. Joubert has a large garden."

He'd made a call last night to his agent, asking him what he knew of Paul Joubert. Not much, only that he was reclusive, mysterious, and hostile to questions about his life, both personal and professional. Sean's congratulations at the opportunity had been tempered by a warning not to antagonize the man, and not to let him dictate what Rob should write.

That, coupled with Analise's elusiveness, should have told Rob to exercise caution, perhaps to postpone the meeting until he received the information Sean had promised to send. Instead, as usual when a juicy story was within reach, excitement had fueled his adrenaline and made him even more eager to proceed.

"Shall we go?" he said to the woman who stood by the door, silent and grave. As she had the day before, she wore a hat and dark glasses. Her dress was navy blue, with large white buttons, a chemise that skimmed her slender body. "Will you call a taxi?"

She moved abruptly, as if her mind had been far away. "I have one waiting. I'll ask the driver to come and get your case."

He scowled at the case as she went out, his hand massaging the tender place over his ribs. Take it easy, the doctor had said. That wouldn't be difficult, with various parts of his body reminding him of their condition whenever he did anything even mildly strenuous.

Outside, he squinted against the sun. The sky was intensely blue, as only a Greek summer sky can be. The brilliant orange and purple of the trumpet vines and bougainvillea climbing on the wall struck him as almost garish after a week of living with the unadorned pastels of the clinic. He breathed deeply, inhaling freedom. It wasn't that his confinement had been arduous, but he was not used to having his hours circumscribed by a nurse, however kind.

Joining Analise in the taxi, he grinned and waved to Sister Angela, who was calling a final goodbye from the clinic steps.

"Are you that popular wherever you go, Mr. Minardos?" Analise asked as the car pulled onto the road.

He glanced at her, saw the pure, classic lines of her profile silhouetted against the bright light from the window. The quiet set of her features told him nothing of her thoughts. "I try," he said lightly. "And call me Rob. I don't think we need to keep formality between us. After all, you've seen me in bed."

The corner of her exquisite mouth twitched, as if she were about to smile. But the face she turned toward him was serious. "And I'm Analise," she said. "But you'll probably see very little of me once we get to the island. I've been away on business for Mr. Joubert, and I have a lot of work to catch up."

"What is your position, Analise?"

"I'm Mr. Joubert's executive assistant. He rarely leaves the island, so it falls to me to see to any of his business that requires personal attention."

"What's the island like?" Rob asked.

"It's small. The terrain is much like Corfu. There's a village with a few shops, but almost everything except produce has to come from Corfu or the mainland."

"Don't you get bored out there, isolated?"

She shrugged. "He pays generously. If I get tired of it, he'll give me a good reference."

"To limani," the taxi driver announced. The harbor.

They were bypassing the long line of cars waiting to be loaded onto the Igoumenítsa ferry. Analise leaned forward and gave the driver directions to the slip where Joubert's boat was docked.

The boat was a sleek cabin cruiser with a powerful inboard engine, captained by a burly man who looked like a former wrestler. "I've stowed away the supplies, Miss Analise," he said.

"Thank you, Petro. Would you please take Mr. Minardos's suitcase?"

Stooping, she removed her sandals. "Paul is rather fussy about the decks." She glanced at Rob's rubber-soled sneakers. "Your shoes are all right."

She tossed her purse and sandals onto the deck of the boat. Before he could give her a hand, she'd hiked up her narrow skirt and hoisted herself up after them. He caught a glimpse of tanned thigh, but with quick agility she straightened and smoothed her dress over her hips. Very much her own woman, he thought, strong and independent, expecting help from no one.

A bemused smile curving his mouth, Rob stepped carefully onto the deck, mindful of his bruised ribs.

He joined her at the low rail, watching the activity in the harbor while Petro went forward to the controls. Moments later the engine throbbed to life beneath them and they were on their way, carving a lazy arc in the oily water.

On the open sea, the wind was just brisk enough to tug at their clothes and tease the surface of the water into a million sparkles. Analise tilted her face up toward the sky, one hand holding her hat in place. Sunlight cast a golden glow on her flawless skin, and she smiled as sea spray beaded on her cheeks.

For the first time, Rob saw her display unreserved emotion, the pure joy of being alive on a perfect day. The rush of pleasure he felt startled him. He wanted to share it with her. He reached for her hand.

"I love the sea," she said, turning toward him. "So free and open. Beautiful."

Suddenly it became imperative that he see all of her face. He stepped close to her and flipped off her hat and her glasses. Her hair uncoiled down her back like a bolt of black satin, its iridescent highlights gleaming in the sun. But he barely noticed that, or her startled gasp, as he fell into the deep blue pools of her eyes.

They were fringed by long, curling black lashes that fluttered closed as he continued to stare at her. "You shouldn't have done that," she murmured, turning her head aside and reaching for the glasses in his hand.

"Why not?" He frowned, concerned by her obvious distress. "I wanted to see you."

She raised her eyes. The incredible blue was suddenly dark and opaque, the color of an approaching storm. "Look at me, then," she said, almost angrily. "Look at me."

Chapter Three

Rob's eyes didn't waver. A long moment ticked by. Then he smiled. It was a gentle smile that held such sweetness that she felt her heart do a slow somersault. Her breath hissed out silently in relief. She'd passed the final test. He didn't know her.

"I'm a man, Analise," he said softly. "You're a beautiful woman. I can't ignore you any more than I can ignore the blue in the sky or the fresh scent of the sea."

He lifted her hand and brought it up to his mouth, placing a light kiss in the palm, as if bestowing a gift. "I won't push, but I can't pretend you don't exist, either."

Pulling her hand free, she turned her head aside. "It's better if you do. There are things you don't understand. You wouldn't like me if you knew."

"Let me be the judge of that."

Diana bit her lip, wishing she could confide in him. Already on this, their third meeting, she was impressed by the man he'd become. He wasn't the Robby she'd known. She smiled faintly. Robby—it had been her private pet name for him. It didn't fit him now.

She couldn't help speculating on how he would react when this was over and he learned the truth. Would he be angry? No, he hadn't been angry in the courtroom when they parted forever, only a little melancholy, as if he regretted the death of their marriage. She'd reminded herself that he was young, only twenty-three. At that age, men, driven more by their hormones than by their hearts, rarely formed deep attachments.

At twenty, she had been overwhelmed by his ardency. Afterwards she had gone on, mourning lost love for a month or two. She'd convinced herself that it was sentimentality and buried her heart and mind in her work, getting her degree almost a year earlier than she had planned. She'd built her life and succeeded in a career that, despite its frustrations, she found fulfilling.

She hadn't expected to meet Rob ever again, and especially not under these circumstances. In spite of her altered appearance, she had to remain constantly on guard lest some look or gesture give her away.

Staring down at her hands, which were gripping the rail, she searched her mind for something to say, some way to dispel her edginess. Her hair blew around her face, and she pushed it impatiently back. A long black strand clung to Rob's shoulder. He lifted it away, tucking it into the swath that hung down her back.

"I'm sorry," he said. "I should have realized the wind would tangle your hair."

"It's all right." Facing the front of the boat, she raised her hands and deftly braided her hair into a long plait. She coiled it on top of her head and jammed on her hat to anchor it in place. She stepped back and sat down on the bench seat, out of the wind. Out of his space, the space that was permeated with memories and possibilities she could not allow herself to consider.

She'd read most of his work. He had astute powers of observation, and, even more critical for a writer, a knack of delving beneath the surface. She would have to avoid him as much as possible while he was on the island. He was a threat, both to her mission and to her peace of mind.

For an instant she considered leveling with him, trusting his discretion and self-control. But no, it was out of the question. She couldn't afford any slipups.

"Have you been to Greece before, or is this your first time?" she asked, in an effort to restore a polite social distance.

He hesitated, and for a moment she thought he might not pick up her lead, but then he shrugged lightly. "I've been many times. It's my heritage, after all."

"Oh, yes, I'd forgotten. But you grew up in Canada?"

"My father was Greek, and even when he took Canadian citizenship he kept up his business interests in Greece. We came over often when I was a child. I guess that's why I finally moved to England. I've always felt an affinity for Europe." He'd been watching the horizon, the barren rocks they passed, jutting out of the sea like beached whales. He suddenly turned those silver eyes on her. "What about you?"

She was silent, debating whether to evade the question or to use her fictional background. She settled for the bare minimum, since as far as that went, the cover and the truth were similar. "I went to school in Paris and London, but my work takes me to many countries. I came here after Paul hired me."

"Parents?"

"Dead since my teens." Her last foster parents. She had never known her real parents.

"I'm sorry," he said sincerely.

An island loomed ahead of them, rising into a cliff that loomed several hundred feet above the waves that lashed hungrily at its base. Relief mixed with dread as Diana recognized the far side of Pagoni. The roar of the boat engine echoed off the forbidding rock face, the sound thrown back as if the island were warning them to stay away.

Diana glanced at Rob's profile. He was frowning. Could he, too, feel the oppressive atmosphere that was raising goose bumps on her skin, despite the heat of the sun straight overhead?

"Does Joubert live on the island year-round?" he asked.

She didn't take her eyes off the rocky coast. "Most of the time. He goes away on business sometimes, but I've done most of the traveling for him in the past year."

The boat cleared a headland composed of tumbled boulders and circled into a sheltered bay. Standing up, Diana moved to the rail, balancing expertly against the sway of the craft. "There it is," she said, lifting her hand to point at a cluster of pastel houses with brightly painted doors and shutters. "Pagoni."

Rob had gotten to his feet, too. "Odd name, isn't it?" he said with a grin.

"From the air, the island's shaped roughly like a peacock. The cliffs we passed earlier are the tail, that row of boulders the neck and head." She shivered. "And, of course, Paul keeps peacocks as pets."

The boat lurched as Petro cut the throttle. Rob, close to her side, almost fell, and his body pressed against hers briefly before he recovered. The subtle sandalwood scent of him surrounded her, dark and evocative, hinting of hot, moonlit nights and black magic. Even though he hadn't used that scent in the past, some elemental sense in her recognized the underlying essence of his body. A woman never forgot her first lover....

"Sorry," he murmured. "I still feel a little dizzy. Especially when I get up too fast."

Again she felt the softening inside her. Again she suppressed it. "The doctor said that would happen. You can rest when we get to the house."

With a determined set to her jaw, she stepped back, stooping to pick up her purse and sandals. Taking her sunglasses from the bench, she put them on, hiding her eyes, and whatever expression Rob might have seen in them.

The engine died with a discreet cough. Petro jumped onto the stone jetty and secured the line around a worn iron cleat. This time Diana accepted Rob's hand as they stepped from the boat. Balancing first on one foot and then on the other, she slipped on her sandals, letting go of him the instant she finished. Firm palm, warm, dry skin, strong fingers—the impression lingered with her as she gave instructions to Petro.

"There's no rush to bring up the supplies, Petro. Go home, have lunch, and take your siesta. Early evening will be soon enough."

He nodded. "Fine, Miss Analise."

She turned back to Rob. "My car is just over there."

"You mean there are roads?"

"One road that's paved, and a couple of dirt tracks branching off it. The agriculture is quite extensive here, orchards and vegetable crops."

"That's why you didn't have crates of tomatoes on the boat."

"Yes. We can buy them here from the farmer who grows them."

Groping in her purse, she produced a key that she inserted in the lock of an acid-yellow Deux Chevaux. Hot stale air rushed out of the little car when she pulled the door open.

"Wait a moment until it cools down." Diana placed her hand on Rob's arm, and immediately wished she hadn't. The fine, silky hairs under her fingertips seemed strangely intimate. Heat stole into her veins, and she felt her skin flush. Without even intending to, he had the power to make her aware of him as a man, an attractive man to whom she was drawn, more than before, even against her will.

She quickly dropped her hand, surreptitiously wiping the feel of him off on her skirt, wishing she could wipe him out of her mind as easily. Going around to the driver's side of the car, she tossed her purse inside, then manipulated the clip that would release the sunroof. She rolled back the canvas covering, securing it in place.

"You don't mind a little wind, do you?" she asked across the top of the car.

"In this heat? Of course not." He opened his shirt another button, revealing the beginnings of a mat of rich, dark brown curls.

Her fingers tingled as she remembered how she'd delighted in the feel of him, his soft hair, his damp skin, his excitement.... Angry at herself, she got into the car. "Let's go. It'll cool off as we drive."

She wanted to squeal the tires as she steered out of the parking area, but the small engine lacked the power to make that childish but satisfying gesture. Instead she vented her frustration by speeding up the rolling hill outside the village at a rate that nearly caused the car to lift from the ground as it careened down the other side.

When she hit a level stretch, she hazarded a glance at Rob. He sat in his seat, safety belt in place, apparently as relaxed as a man on his way to church in a limousine. Irrationally disappointed, she slowed, and she was glad she had when a flock of goats ran across the road, barely giving her time to brake.

HEAT CONDENSED in the car as they waited for the goats to pass, setting up a pounding in Rob's head. He'd seen the tension in Analise's jaw and wondered about its cause. But her reckless driving suited his mood, the sense of freedom he felt at being alive and out of the hospital. He supposed he should have been nervous at getting into a car again after the accident. But his memory of the crash was still mercifully blank, and no fear entered his mind. Obviously amnesia had its advantages.

The goatherd waved as he chased the last, impudently staring goat out of their path. Analise continued at a still-brisk but more reasonable speed.

In an effort to ignore the pain in his head, Rob concentrated on the countryside. As Analise had said, the terrain was similar to that on Corfu: forests of stunted pines on the heights, orchards, farm fields and vegetable gardens at lower levels. Not that the heights were great, although he had the sense that they had been climbing steadily since leaving the village behind. He estimated that they must be almost at the far end of the island, where steep cliffs formed massive ramparts above the sea, the tail of the peacock.

Analise took a turn to the right, through an open iron gate that combined ornamental elements with function. Closed, the gate, and the high stone wall it was set in, would make the estate impervious to all but an army.

Joubert's house was a low, sprawling structure built of local stone and surrounded by extensive gardens. The cream and honey tones of the walls made it blend into the land-scape as naturally as if it had grown there. Multilevel, clay-tiled roofs formed a pleasing contrast to the green back-drop of palms, olives and fruit trees behind it.

Rob surveyed the house with intense interest as Analise sent the car up the driveway and around to the garages in back. Its single story clung to the uneven terrain, setting al-most every room on a different plane from its neighbor. The walls were interspersed with many deep-set windows that could be closed off with shutters. Wide verandas further shaded the interior from the heat.

As he stepped out of the car, he could hear the roar of the sea. They must be close to the cliffs, although the lush vegetation created the illusion that the land went on forever.

The ultimate in privacy, Rob thought. Walled on one side, inaccessible cliffs on the other.

A palace? Or a prison?

He shook his head, wishing he had some water so that he could take one of the tablets Dr. Nakos had given him. The dizziness had returned in earnest, along with a throbbing ache in his head. He swayed on his feet, grabbing the roof of the car to keep from falling. He had a sense of unseen eyes watching them, an uneasy feeling that, even though Analise had invited him, he wasn't welcome.

Then again, the weakness in his body might be making him fanciful. Still, he realized that if there was trouble, he wasn't yet fit enough to handle it.

"You're very pale," Analise said, taking a clinical look at his face. "I think Dr. Nakos was right. You'd better lie down at once."

He couldn't argue, but he did draw the line at leaning on her and entering the house like an invalid. Gritting his teeth, he walked across the neatly raked gravel courtyard to the door.

Inside, the marble-tiled hall was cool, with a dimness he welcomed after the piercing glare of the sun. Analise led the way to a large room where a woman was dusting furniture with a lemon-scented polish.

"Maria, would you show Kyrios Minardos to his room while I report to Monsieur Joubert?"

"Maliste." The woman nodded affirmatively.

Analise turned to Rob. "I suppose you can manage without your suitcase for now. I'm sorry I didn't think to bring it along in the car." She hesitated, adding, "I can give Petro a call if you need it sooner than this evening."

He shook his head, and regretted the motion at once. "I'll just lie down. My head—"

Her ocean-blue eyes darkened with sympathy, and Rob felt a momentary easing of the pain. A man would gladly bear a little suffering if he had a woman like her to soothe it away. "I'll tell Paul you can't make lunch, shall I? He'll understand."

"Thanks." His smile felt like a grimace as he turned to follow Maria.

He barely noticed the luxurious bedroom before rushing into the adjoining bathroom and turning on the tap. Taking the small bottle of pills from his pocket, he shook one out and ran water into a glass. Lying down on the bed, he closed his eyes, willing the painkiller to work.

WHEN HE AWOKE, he could tell by the faded golden quality of the light that it was early evening. The long nap had revived him, eliminating both his dizziness and his headache. He got up and went to the window, lifting the roller shutters.

This wing of the house was higher than the rest, offering a commanding view of the garden, a jungle tangle of green vines and purple bougainvillea tumbling over stone-paved terraces. The heady fragrance of unseen blossoms drifted into the room, reminding him of tropic Islands. He inhaled deeply, grateful he was no longer breathing the pungency of antiseptic and pine cleaner.

A raucous shriek from somewhere on the lower terraces made him jump. He leaned out, laughing when he heard the flutter of wings and saw the peacock land on the roof of a small building that might have been a potting shed or a pool house. The bird fanned out its flamboyant tail, its tiny head bobbing as it preened its wings.

The peacock suddenly stilled, its head lifting. *Scree, scree, scree.* The bird folded its tail and dropped into the lush shrubbery. Above the cliff, a falcon wheeled off into the distance, searching for easier prey. Rob shivered, without knowing why. Something about this place bothered him.

Turning away, he saw his suitcase near the door. He unpacked, his thoughts going back to Analise. He'd dreamed about her, he realized. And in his dream, she'd been open to him, responsive. Only her eyes, eyes the deep, rich blue of twilight, filled with shadows, had kept their secrets.

He frowned suddenly, recalling his phone call to Venetis early that morning. The feeling that he hadn't been alone in the car had haunted him during every day of his stay in the clinic. The police had assured him there was no sign of a body. Even in a fire, where temperatures could reach over a thousand degrees, there was usually some residue if a body had burned. The car had been examined; nothing had been found.

"But the woman who met me in the village couldn't just vanish into thin air," Rob reminded Venetis.

He'd heard the rustle of papers as Venetis consulted a report. "I had someone go up to Makrino and check on that. A bus going to Corfu town passes through there at six in the morning. A blond woman was seen getting on the bus at the stop near the village cemetery. By now, she could be anywhere."

Relief had sped through him. Whoever she was, at least she was alive.

The memory loss was causing him greater frustration the longer it lasted. Who was the woman? And why had she met him? That loose end would nag him until it was securely tied up.

He showered and changed, conscious of the silence of the house. Except for the occasional cry of the peacock, the only sounds were the rustling of the trees in the light breeze and the distant tinkling of sheep bells. Even the sea was calm, a flat burgundy line on the far horizon, the dying rays of the sun bleeding into it.

Opening the door of his room, he paused, orienting himself. The hall, lined with closed doors, was dim in the twilight. At the far end he could see an illuminated space he vaguely remembered passing through on his way to the bedroom. Earlier, held in the grip of pain, he'd had only an impression of wide, sun-filled rooms and starkly modern decor.

He moved down the hall, entering a spacious living room softly lit by fixtures embedded in the ceiling. The chrome and leather furniture was arranged in solitary islands on a glossy marble floor, incidental to a stunning and eclectic display of art and artifacts.

The room was dominated by a large abstract painting. Its expanses of bloodred, saffron yellow and blue contrasted luridly with the cold gray walls. But Rob's eyes were drawn to a sculpture of a young girl that stood in a backlit alcove.

About a meter high, the work appeared perfectly preserved. The stone the artist had used was an unusual pink marble that appeared to have the qualities of living skin. The maiden wore a self-absorbed smile as she poised at the edge of a tub, a robe dangling from one hand. Her eyes were raised, as if someone had just entered the room, someone who was obviously welcome at her bath. The overall effect was erotic and yet virginal.

"Beautiful, isn't she?".

Rob was barely able to keep from starting when the man spoke behind him. He turned, hiding his sudden uneasiness under a polite social expression. "Yes, she is," he said quietly. "A Roman copy of a classical Greek work, isn't she?"

Paul Joubert smiled, showing even, exquisitely capped white teeth. "My dear fellow, she is the original. Almost all my treasures are originals."

Eyes narrowed, Rob glanced around the room. The artifacts and paintings he could see would have been worth a tidy fortune even if half of them were reproductions. If they were originals, their value would be equal to a small country's entire national budget.

He turned back to his host. The man was tall and muscular, in his fifties, with bold, handsome features. His thick black hair was liberally threaded with gray. He surveyed Rob with chocolate-brown eyes that should have been warm, but instead appeared opaque, and strangely lacking in animation. Rob again felt the cold finger of caution walk over his skin.

Joubert reached out and touched the statue's shoulder, smoothing his fingers over the marble with a sensuous pleasure that struck Rob as faintly obscene.

"I search the world for art treasures and bring them here, where I can enjoy them."

And no one else can. Rob heard the unspoken implication as clearly as if the man had shouted it. Joubert's hand slid lower, to the maiden's small, pointed breast. As his eyes flared to life, Rob felt sweat break out on his spine. It wasn't lust he saw in those eyes, it was a more chilling quality. Greed.

Rob had heard of collectors like Joubert, had even interviewed some of them, although they tended to be a reclusive lot. Acquisition and ownership were everything to them. A normal person took pleasure in showing off his possessions, but certain collectors wanted to keep the treasures for themselves, locked out of sight. Which was why they rarely had scruples about how they obtained the works they coveted. Most of the art stolen from museums and private collections ended up in the hands of these men, never to resurface in public.

"You're very isolated here," Rob said, his bland tone hiding the anger that surged through him. "Isn't security a problem?"

Joubert laughed. It was a low, sibilant sound that indicated little humor. "Not at all. An island forms its own fortress. And the villagers are fiercely loyal to me. My family has lived on this island for over a century, and we've taken care of them."

Rob's brows climbed. "The feudal system, in this day and age?"

"Come, come, my dear Monsieur Minardos. The villagers live their own lives in complete freedom. They own the land they cultivate. I demand nothing from them except their loyalty and respect."

"I'm relieved to hear it," Rob said dryly. "You won't mind if I interview some of them for my story?"

Did he imagine it, or did the man stiffen? The moment passed, and Joubert reached into the pocket of his white dinner jacket for a cigar. He lit it, smoke briefly hiding his face. He inhaled deeply. Smiling with pleasure, he took the cigar out of his mouth and held it between his fingers. "I take it you don't smoke, Monsieur Minardos?"

"No, but you go ahead." Rob moved away from the alcove and began to circle the large room, pausing before a horse's head he would have sworn he'd last seen in the Greek rooms of the British Museum. "A fine piece, that," he commented, wondering where Joubert had stolen it. Although it might not be one of the Elgin Marbles, it was from the same period.

"Thank you. It's one I'm very fond of."

"At least you don't have to worry about anyone walking off with a piece of marble that size," Rob added, deliberately baiting the man. He suddenly realised that, despite being in Joubert's territory, he was in a position of power in this mild duel of personalities. Joubert had summoned him here; therefore he must want something.

Joubert's eyes narrowed ever so slightly, although his urbane smile remained firmly in place. "Nothing leaves this island without my knowledge, Monsieur Minardos. Nothing."

Chapter Four

Dinner was served in a cavernous dining room, at a round table that stood in the middle of a threadbare but obviously valuable Persian rug. At least his host believed in using his possessions, Rob thought. Most people would have hung the intricately patterned rug on the wall, protecting it but denying its function.

Joubert directed Rob to a seat on his left, next to a young woman he introduced offhandedly as Tamara. Rob glanced curiously at her as he sat down.

Masses of dark curls framed her expertly made-up face. Her features were angular but striking. She had the thin, lanky figure of a fashion model, except for her breasts, which were full and round, barely confined in a black leather bustier. Her matching skirt was so short and tight Rob wondered how she could sit down. She didn't respond to his greeting, beyond regarding him briefly from under kohl-darkened eyelids. Her gaze slid away as Analise came into the room and took the chair on Joubert's right side.

Maria, the housekeeper, entered the room from another door, which presumably led to the kitchen, and set a tureen of soup on the table. Joubert served himself, then offered the ladle to Tamara.

She shook her head, pushing the heavy china container toward Rob.

Joubert frowned. "You should eat, Tamara. You're getting much too thin."

She shrugged but didn't look at him, keeping her eyes fixed on a point just ahead of her plate.

As he passed the tureen across the table, Rob met Analise's gaze. Anger turned her blue eyes to a chilling cobalt. She masked it quickly, and he couldn't tell if it was directed at Joubert or at Tamara.

APPLYING HERSELF to her soup moments later, Diana cursed her slip. Once again she had let Rob read her thoughts. A little more of this, and Paul, with his sharp eyes and suspicious mind, would start to wonder what was going on. Not to mention Rob. The relationship between Joubert and Tamara was none of her business anyway.

Joubert rose from his chair, raising his wineglass and smiling as he glanced around the table. "I'd like to propose a toast to our honored guest, Robert Minardos. However brief our association will be, I'm sure both of us will benefit from it."

Pasting on a smile and avoiding Rob's eyes, Diana drank from her glass. Tamara gulped the entire contents of hers, holding the glass to her mouth with both hands, like a child drinking milk. She hiccuped delicately and patted her lips with her napkin. Diana held her breath, waiting for an outburst from Joubert, but after a brief look at Tamara he sat down and turned to Rob with every appearance of affability.

"When I heard you were in Corfu, I thought this would be an opportune time to meet you. I've enjoyed reading your novels."

"Thank you," Rob said, hiding a wry smile. Joubert hadn't mentioned Rob's original call, but that wasn't surprising, considering the man's monumental ego.

Joubert inclined his head as if he were an emperor conferring a favor. "I don't know if you're aware that I'm donating a number of impressionist paintings to a New York art museum. I trust I can depend on you for a favorable report in this matter."

Rob's hand jerked as he halted his spoon halfway to his mouth. Arrogance had been invented with this man in mind. "I write the story the way I see it. I don't make judgments about the subject."

Joubert waved his hand in a dismissive gesture. "I had no intention of belittling your work. In fact, my admiration for what you've done was what prompted me to ask you here. I know you'll be fair and unbiased."

Rob was not willing to be mollified so easily. "Then perhaps you'll give me the inside story on where one obtains some of the art you have here." He indicated the statues that lined one wall of the dining room, nude young men and elaborately dressed maidens from the archaic Greek period, standing like silent sentinels, their faint, secretive smiles eternally frozen in place.

He waited tensely. If that recklessly flung gauntlet didn't get him kicked out, the man was more tolerant than his reputation suggested.

To Rob's surprise, Joubert threw back his head and laughed. "Monsieur Minardos—Robert. I may call you Robert? I can see I chose well. You're not one of those insipid reporters who stand in awe of those they interview."

Rob let out a long, inaudible breath of relief. "I hope not," he said, with an answering grin. "I write the truth."

Joubert sobered as he pushed away his soup bowl. "Truth is sometimes found where we least expect it, and eludes us when we seek it."

A teenage girl Rob assumed was Maria's daughter came in to clear away the bowls, and returned with the main course—roasted potatoes and a crisply browned loin of lamb neatly carved into servings, accompanied by a salad of sliced tomatoes sprinkled with finely shredded basil.

"Wonderful," Rob said as he tasted the salad. "I haven't had tomatoes like these in years. And the basil is the perfect seasoning."

"Basil isn't used much in Greek cooking," Joubert said. "It's grown for good luck. But then, I expect you know that, don't you, Robert, with your Greek heritage. I understand you're fluent in the language, too."

"I manage," said Rob.

The language of choice in the household seemed to be English. Joubert had even addressed the maid in that language. A thought struck Rob. Perhaps Joubert didn't speak Greek?

"What about you, Mr. Joubert?"

Joubert took a second helping of potatoes. "I, too, manage. I grew up here. Naturally I learned the language. But Tamara—" He glanced at her as she silently ate her potatoes and a small portion of meat, smiling with the indulgent affection one would extend to a pampered poodle. "Tamara only speaks French, and a little English. She hasn't had our advantages. Our Analise, though, is fluent in four languages, which is a great advantage in her work, since she is able to translate my correspondence."

Diana applied herself to her meal, letting Joubert and Rob carry the conversation. At times she could barely restrain herself from kicking Rob under the table. She didn't like the way he kept baiting Paul, especially about the art treasures.

The last thing she wanted at this point was for Paul to become edgy. Her investigations indicated that Joubert was a critical intermediary between thieves and collectors. A long prison term for him would seriously hamper the world trade in illegal art. She needed him to pull off this last deal he had brewing so that she could catch him in the act.

Which was why she had gone to Makrino to ask Rob to hold off until she had the case ready to wrap up. By asking too many questions, Rob might just throw off the delicate balance she had maintained, and all her work so far could be wasted.

For an instant she debated seeking him out after dinner and taking him into her confidence. She discarded the idea at once. It was too risky, not to mention completely against agency policy. Although in Makrino she'd asked him to delay the interview, she hadn't revealed her true position, merely asking him to accept her word that it was important. He had readily agreed. Now that he was here, however, there was little point in trying to influence him. It was safer to avoid him as much as possible.

After dinner, Joubert left them, saying he had work to do in his study. He'd given an Oscar-winning performance as the gracious host, inviting them to stroll in the garden, drive to the village in his car, or walk down to the beach.

With her usual vague air, Tamara went down the hall toward her room, in the section of the house that also contained Paul's studio. Diana shrugged as she left the dining room. One never knew what went on in Tamara's head. She'd been Paul's model nearly as long as Diana had been his executive assistant, and they were as much strangers now as they'd been the day Tamara had arrived.

Pausing in the softly lit living room, Diana glanced down the hall where her room was, across from Rob's. It was tempting to hide in there, but after the tension at the dinner table, she needed some fresh air, a few moments alone in the open, where she could breathe without feeling she had to watch every word and action. What made her hesitate was the possibility that she would run into Rob.

As if she'd conjured him up out of her troubled mind, he appeared in front of her, coming down the hall from his room.

"I decided to change before going for a walk," he said. Instead of the suit and tie he'd worn at the table, he had on a white cotton T-shirt and jeans softened by years of wear. He put out his hand to grasp her elbow courteously. "Would you join me? There are a few things I have to ask you."

Just what she'd been afraid of: questions. "I'm tired," she murmured. She needed more time to plan her strategy, to decide how to handle him.

He must have heard the halfhearted note in her protest, for he steered her gently but firmly toward the front door. "I won't keep you long. I need to get out of this mausoleum."

She couldn't help the smile that tugged up the corners of her mouth. "Don't you mean museum?"

He closed the door behind them and led her down the steps and onto the path that wound through the jungle of subtropical foliage. Hidden spotlights cast pools of discreet illumination that emphasized rather that distracted from the untamed ambience. "The house has the most marvelous architecture. It should be wonderful, but instead it depresses me. How do you stand it?"

"I have my work," she said. On impulse, she added candidly, "Every so often I hike to the other end of the island, stand on a cliff above the sea and scream. Amazing how therapeutic a good scream can be."

Rob looked at her with approval and new respect. "Amazing. And more amazing that you admit to frustration. When I first saw you, I found your formidable self-sufficiency intimidating."

"Self-sufficiency in a woman is a virtue, don't you think, Rob?"

"Maybe, but it can be taken to extremes. Then it's scary."

Diana laughed. "Do I scare you? I should hope not. I'm really very ordinary."

Stopping suddenly, Rob turned to face her, his free hand coming up to cup her cheek. His breath feathered her face, faintly wine-scented. She could see his teeth gleaming in the dim light. "You're far too beautiful to be ordinary, Analise."

A harsh scream sliced through the crickets' song. Diana jumped, her heart pounding. Her fingers tightened on Rob's arm, digging into the hard muscle. "Those damn peacocks."

"You mean there's more than one?"

"There are about half a dozen. Stupid birds. Sometimes they wake me up at night. I wish Paul would get rid of them."

She was suddenly aware of how close she stood to Rob, her breasts pressed against his chest. His heart beat steadily, unlike hers, which was still racing. She chided herself for her edginess. She should be used to the stupid peacocks, but they seemed to take a perverse pleasure in shrieking when she least expected it.

Looking up into his eyes, she saw laughter, but also a tenderness that made her breath catch in her throat. The dark sandalwood scent of him spun through her brain like a narcotic. He bent his head, and her heart skipped with dismaying excitement at the thought of him kissing her. But again he surprised her by merely dragging his thumb slowly across her bottom lip. "I'd like to..." he whispered. "But not yet. Not just yet."

When? cried a traitorous voice inside her. Against her better judgment, she was seized with an urgent need to know whether his kisses would taste as sweet as her newly resurrected memory of them.

Too dangerous, common sense warned. *Both for him and for you. It's impossible, so there's no use wishing.*

She pulled her arm free and continued down the path after a brief argument with herself about fleeing back to the house, where she could hide from temptation. Keeping pace with her, he said nothing. She sneaked a glance at him and saw that he was frowning, but not with frustration or disappointment. No, he looked thoughtful, as if he were sifting through the questions he intended to ask her.

"Analise," he said when they reached a little clearing where a herb garden grew in an intricate pattern around an antique sundial. "What is Tamara to Joubert?"

The finger she had been trailing along the carved edge of the sundial platform paused in its circuit. "Tamara? She's his model. He paints, you know. Impressionist stuff, and abstracts."

Some quality in her voice must have betrayed her. He gazed at her intently with those disconcertingly clear silver eyes. "You don't like his work."

It was a statement, not a question. She answered anyway. "No. I particularly dislike that monstrosity in the living room, over the fireplace." She shuddered. "All those bloodreds. It looks like a slaughtered animal."

Distracted by the statue in the alcove, Rob hadn't given the painting more than a passing look. "I'll have to study it further. All I remember is that the colors are rather overwhelming. How does he paint Tamara?"

"I haven't seen many of them—he doesn't like people poking around in his studio unless he's there—but they all seem to have an undertone of violence." She shrugged. "I can't explain it. The pictures make me uncomfortable. But obviously I'm in the minority. They sell well all over Europe."

"Then why isn't he listed in art reference books? I looked him up in the few books I had in my luggage. No mention of his name as either a collector or a producer of art."

"He paints as Paul Lepine. Few people know."

"Do you think he'd mind if I write about it in my article?"

"I don't know. But I'm sure he'll tell you." She sat down on a wrought-iron bench, shaking back her hair so that it rippled down her back. Rob pushed his hands into his pockets, clenching them into fists to keep from running his fingers over the black satin swath. He couldn't take his eyes from her.

"Why did you ask about Tamara?" Her low, musical voice broke through his thoughts. "She'd never talk to you about Paul."

"Would you?"

She considered, her teeth worrying her bottom lip. In Makrino, she had, but of course he didn't remember that. "It would depend on what you asked."

"Oh?" He walked away from her to the sundial, gazing down at the zodiac figure as if seeking inspiration. Then he turned, leaning back against the platform and crossing his legs at the ankles. "It occurred to me that Tamara might be Joubert's daughter."

Diana's gasp was loud against the backdrop of crickets sawing in the shrubbery. "His daughter? No wonder you write fiction. Your imagination is frightening. His daughter? A man would hardly have his daughter posing for him in the nude."

"Is that what she does?"

"Well, not exactly. In the paintings I've seen, she's always partially dressed." Diana got up and paced impatiently around the knot garden of lavender and thyme. "But the paintings are very erotic."

"Maybe Paul has a vivid imagination, as well." He reached out and caught her hand as she passed him, bringing her to a stop. "Analise, how did he get all those artifacts?"

He felt her body tense, heard the sharp breath she dragged in. The question didn't please her. But that was to be expected, wasn't it, after the look she'd quickly hidden when he'd asked Joubert the same thing at dinner? As if she were warning him that he was on dangerous ground. Unfortunately, warnings had the effect of making him even more eager for answers.

"If you're wise—" Her voice was trembling very slightly. "If you're wise, you'll restrict your questions concerning art to the impressionist paintings he's donating. Paul does not discuss his collection of ancient works."

Rob drew her along the path, walking farther away from the house. The scent of mint sprang up around them as their feet crushed low-growing mentha plants. "And no one knows he has it, do they?"

"No one knows much about Joubert at all." She spoke more firmly now, as if Joubert, the man, were a safer topic than art. "That's why I was surprised when he asked me to bring you here to interview him."

"I didn't have an appointment, did I?"

"The Swiss relayed your request. Paul didn't tell me he was granting you the interview until he read of your accident."

A significant fact? Rob wondered. "Does Joubert know about my memory loss?" he asked.

She nodded. "Of course he does. All I had to do was talk to the nuns for five minutes and I had all the details."

Rob's mouth tightened. The accident, Analise's appearance, Joubert's invitation, like a dangling carrot—there had to be a connection between all these occurrences. He couldn't believe that Joubert would risk his closely guarded privacy simply to gain publicity for his art donation.

One thing was clear, though. Analise did not like Joubert. Still, for whatever reason, she did his bidding.

In spite of her secrets, however, Analise was plainly the most normal person in the household. Not only that, but Rob sensed she felt the attraction that had spun a rapport between them from that first afternoon at the clinic. She let things slip with him. She forgot to guard herself. He could take advantage of that from a professional standpoint. Or he could simply let it develop along an ordinary man-and-woman-getting-to-know-one-another path.

Except that his feelings for her were not ordinary. In fact, they almost frightened him with their intensity. He felt a physical buzz in his hormones when he was near her, but more than that, he felt a need to know her secrets, to discover what caused the shadows in her eyes. Against all logic, he wanted to be the man to banish those shadows forever.

Pausing again and turning her to face him, he decided to take the plunge. "If you dislike Joubert so much, why do you work for him?"

They were standing in a pool of light cast by a lamp marking an intersection in the garden paths. Although she tried valiantly to control her expression, he saw several emotions cross her face, the most telling one being dismay. He thought he also saw fear, fleeting and undefined, and finally an odd desperation that she swiftly buried under anger.

"That's none of your business, Mr. Minardos," she snapped.

He snatched her arm as she moved away from him, her muscles tensed for flight. "I'd say it is my business. You brought me here."

"Paul told me—"

"Against your better judgment," Rob continued relentlessly, as if she hadn't spoken.

"Then why don't you leave?" she burst out. With a twist of her arm, she threw off his hand, stepping back a couple of paces.

"Because, damn it, I want to know what's going on. You can help me."

Her eyes flashed. "Why should I? You're nothing to me."

"Because you're not like your boss, without a conscience," he shot back. "I don't know what your part in this is, but I know that whatever it is, you have a reason for it. You tried to warn me this morning, didn't you?"

The realization hit him suddenly that it was her presence that had made him accept the invitation, not simply impulse and journalistic curiosity.

Sure, he would have been a fool to miss this opportunity, but he could have taken more time. He rarely did interviews without a good deal of preparation. He liked to study what others had written and said about the person, to prepare his approach and make it unique. Even with the unexpected invitation from Joubert, he could have done that. Pleading a need for a longer period of recuperation would have bought him a couple of days to do his research.

Instead, he'd fallen into the shadows of Analise's midnight-blue eyes. He hadn't wanted her to disappear from his life without giving him the chance to explore the mystery that hung around her like an aura. He'd followed her instead of his own judgment.

Not that he felt regret. Only an immense frustration. She was more elusive than moonlight, and just as intriguing. Woman or phantom? He had to know.

SEEING THE SUBTLE CHANGE in his face, Diana knew she was in trouble. He was even sharper than she had given him credit for. But it might not be too late to backtrack. "You're mistaken, Mr. Minardos," she said coldly. "But you should be careful. Paul isn't always a nice person. But I'm sure you've figured that out for yourself."

"With Tamara, you mean? She seems to handle it by ignoring him. What gets me is, Paul doesn't seem to care at all what anyone thinks of him." He laughed shortly. "His total arrogance must be unique in the entire human race. No matter how confident we are, most of us have some regard for conventions and how other people perceive us."

Diana stared at him, her desire for escape forgotten. A man who had been in the places she knew Rob had visited should have become an utter cynic. He hadn't. Still, he was far too nosy—not to mention perceptive—for his own good. A ruthless man like Joubert could swallow Rob for breakfast, which meant she had to protect him, and handle him like the professional she was.

"You are innocent, aren't you, Mr. Minardos?" She deliberately used formality to emphasize the impossibility of friendship, much less anything deeper, between them.

"If you believe that, you're not much of a judge of character, *Miss* Dubois. And if you call me Mr. Minardos one more time, so help me, I'll—" He broke off, grinding his teeth. He wanted to shake her, to make her open up and talk to him. He wanted to kiss her and find out if those strawberry-pink lips tasted as sweet as they looked. He hated himself for both urges, hated the lack of control they indicated.

"You'll what?" she said, with a cooly arched brow. "Somehow, whatever it is, I don't think you will. You're not a violent man."

"How would you know?"

Because I've known violent men. The stark truth jumped into her head. But her words remained deceptively mild. "Despite what you may think, I am a good judge of character. I've had to be, the way I've lived."

"Why don't you tell me about the life you've lived?" he said, more calmly. "I'd like to know."

For one wild instant, she was tempted. During their brief marriage, she'd never volunteered any information about her life before they'd met. And he hadn't asked. Enthralled as they were by passion, living for the moment, it hadn't seemed important.

She wondered what his reaction would be if she told him now. He would either understand, with that empathy she'd seen in his writing, or he would reject her, and she would regain her peace of mind.

"I'm tired, Rob," she said, taking the easy, prudent way out. "Good night. I'm going in."

Rob watched her go, her white dress a ghostly beacon, until she had almost reached the house. More confused than ever, he walked in the garden until the return of his headache and the rubbery weakness in his limbs forced him inside.

Tomorrow. Tomorrow he would be stronger. Tomorrow he would get some answers.

Chapter Five

Rob emerged from his room at nine the next morning to find that his host had gone to Corfu for the day. Maria informed him that Joubert would return by dinnertime.

"What about some breakfast, Kyrie Minardos?"

"Maybe a little later."

Wishing he'd gotten up sooner and gone with Joubert, if only to check out a library while the man did his business, Rob sauntered through the silent house. For the first time since the accident, he hadn't woken with a headache, and the pain in his ribs bothered him only if he twisted his body sharply. He felt almost normal again, ready to get to work, and frustrated that the source of his work was unavailable.

Pausing in the living room doorway, he cast a long look at the painting over the fireplace. Analise was right. Between the swirls of yellow and Prussian blue, the slashes of crimson did resemble a freshly killed animal carcass.

An undertone of violence? Probably. And that wasn't surprising. If Joubert had acquired his artifacts by the route Rob suspected, ruthlessness, a lack of scruples and a propensity for violence were almost a prerequisite for success.

He wondered where the telephone was. In Joubert's study, no doubt. He started down the hall toward the wing that also held the studio and Tamara's quarters. A door that stood slightly ajar drew his attention. As he neared it, he could hear the faint clicking of a keyboard. He pushed the door open. Analise sat at a desk, typing into a computer.

She paused, read what was printed on the screen, made a change and resumed typing. Absorbed in her work, she hadn't heard him.

He glanced around the room, taking in shelves of books and art objects. Besides the printer and the personal computer Analise was using, Joubert had a fax machine and a larger computer that was presumably hooked up to his business empire. Communication obviously wasn't a problem, despite the isolation and the otherwise primitive aspects of the island. However, if he wanted to send a message to anyone, he wondered how secure it would be from Joubert's scrutiny.

It might be wiser to contact his agent and a couple of people he knew in the art trade by phoning from Corfu. But that could wait until he'd assessed the situation a little more thoroughly.

DIANA SAW A SHADOW cross her screen as Rob came into the room. She swung around in the swivel chair. "Good morning." She kept her voice even and cool, although the sight of him did crazy things to her equilibrium. "Paul asked me to apologize on his behalf. He had to go up to Corfu to take care of a problem."

"A problem?"

"Nothing serious. He said to take it easy, as the doctor suggested, and make yourself at home. If you want to swim, I'll show you the path to the beach."

He propped his hip on the corner of the desk, his blue-jeaned thigh close to her arm. "I thought you were Joubert's assistant. And here I find you typing."

She glanced up at him, smiling. "Don't you know that half the time *executive assistant* is just a fancy name for a secretary? And I don't mind. There's hardly enough typing to keep someone else employed."

"Will this take you long?" He gestured at the screen, where he saw she had just typed "Yours truly" at the end of a letter.

"I'm almost finished. I only have to print out the letters I've done and take them to the village to mail. Why? Did you want to use the computer?"

Rob shook his head. "I've got a portable. And I haven't decided on an angle yet, so I'm not ready to start the article. I was wondering if you wanted to come with me to the beach, or maybe show me around the island."

She bit her lip. She'd decided she should stay aloof from him. On the other hand, a little harmless sight-seeing might take the edge off his curiosity about her own purpose on the island.

"I do have work to do." Even to her own ears, the excuse sounded feeble. She'd finished what Paul had left her. And the main computer was still down, which meant she couldn't work on retrieving the shipping lists that had given her the first real break in this case.

"Work? I thought you just said you were almost finished." He added, on a coaxing note, "I'll buy you lunch, unless you're needed to baby-sit Tamara."

Diana couldn't keep from smiling. "Never mind the impression you got last night. Tamara is moody, and maybe Paul is a little hard on her, but she's quite independent. Anyway, she's not here. She went down to the village with Paul. She often goes there when Paul doesn't need her."

"What does she do?"

Diana shrugged. "I don't know. It's a pretty village. She sketches, I believe. I don't know what she does the rest of the time. Probably goes swimming or has coffee with other people her age."

"But she doesn't even speak Greek."

Frowning, Diana turned her attention back to the computer, typing in commands to the printer. "Most of the young people in the village speak English. Tamara speaks it better than Paul seems to think. I've heard her on the phone."

The printer came to life with a high-pitched buzzing. "Go and get some coffee from Maria. I'll find you in the kitchen as soon as this is done."

She let out an exasperated sigh when Rob was gone. Tamara kept such a low profile, Diana hadn't given much thought to what she did or even why she stayed on the island. Maybe she was in love with Paul, but if public body language counted for anything, Diana didn't think so. Paul treated her with exactly the same urbane courtesy he used with all his employees, except for those odd times when he took almost cruel digs at her. But that happened rarely, although when it did, Diana wanted to scream at Tamara to fight back instead of just sitting there.

Tamara had been a successful model before she'd come. Full-color ads in fashion magazines had featured her angular face and body, and she'd appeared on several covers. She'd made a lot of money, to judge by her luggage and the quality of the clothes she wore. Diana wondered why she'd given it all up, why she seemed to be hiding from life.

A disastrous love affair, perhaps? Or maybe she was a relative of Paul's. His daughter, as Rob had suggested, or a niece. Since Tamara hadn't made overtures of friendship and knew nothing about Paul's business, Diana had virtually ignored her. It was unlikely she could contribute anything to Diana's investigation.

Entering the kitchen with the envelopes in her hand, she found Rob sitting at the table, drinking coffee and making serious inroads into a freshly baked walnut cake Maria was urging on him. "You're too thin. And you have to build your strength back up." She pushed the plate closer. "Eat."

"You'd better do it, Rob," Diana said, laughing. The scene was so domestic, so normal, she felt her spirits lifting. Would it be so bad to pretend she was just an ordinary woman spending time with a personable man who attracted her? Just for one day. Tonight, when Paul returned, the game would begin again.

THE VILLAGE WAS BUSTLING with Saturday-morning activity. Farmers had come to town to sell their produce in the market, and peddlers from the mainland hawked shoes, pots and pans, toys and trinkets. Diana's first stop was the post office, where she bought stamps and sent the letters off.

Afterward, she and Rob pushed their way through the crowd in the outdoor market, Analise acknowledging the greetings of several of the villagers.

"Joubert told me—warned me?—that the people here are loyal only to him." Rob threw out the statement like a challenge.

Her heart gave a little leap, although she managed to control her expression. "What possible bearing could that have on anything you're doing here?" she asked, her eyes wide and guileless.

"Just what I was wondering."

She made herself laugh lightly. "Oh, Paul often likes to be dramatic. He was probably joking. He's very proud of his ancestors, who came here from Marseilles. Seafaring traders, he says they were. Pirates, more likely. Although the island has been in Paul's family for generations, they didn't actually live here until Paul's great-grandfather started using it as a summer retreat."

"He didn't build the house, did he? It looks too new."

"It is new. Paul had it built ten years ago, when he decided to make Pagoni his permanent home." She stopped at a fruit stand and bought a couple of pears, handing one to Rob before lifting the other to her mouth.

She bit into it, laughing as the juice spurted over her teeth and almost ran down her chin. Plucking a folded handkerchief from her pocket, she wiped her mouth. "They're good, aren't they?"

"Delicious," Rob said, his eyes fixed on her wet, parted lips. The pear was sweet, at the perfect point of ripeness, resisting the teeth but melting on the tongue.

"Where did you grow up?" he asked, wanting to know about her, to understand what had made her the woman she was. Wanting to know why, as he focused on her radiant face, he again felt as if he'd lived this scene before.

"Everywhere." She shrugged as she bit off another chunk of pear. She chewed it slowly, hoping he'd forget the question she hadn't answered. He waited until she swallowed, then laid his hand on hers before she could take another bite.

"Where, Analise?"

IIis hand was firm, reassuring rather than threatening. She was torn between wanting more of his touch and wanting to play it safe by stepping out of his reach. She remained where she was, the two of them forming an island around which the other shoppers eddied like the current of a river. "In Athens for a while. Then in France. Later in England, where I went to university."

He stared at her. "Analise—"

She looked at him, her eyes troubled. "What is it?"

He scrubbed his hand across his face. "Nothing. Except . . . just for a moment . . ."

"What?" Her pulse was hammering so loudly in her ears that she wondered if he could hear it.

He shook his head. "We haven't met before, have we? Every once in a while, I think I should know you."

Diana forced a laugh. "I'd remember if I'd met you."

"Well, maybe there's something to this reincarnation business. I must have known you in a former life."

"Or I look like someone you knew." Best to defuse the situation by not overreacting.

"That's probably it," he agreed, although a trace of a frown remained, etching a line between his brows.

REINING IN his frustration, Rob carried Analise's net shopping bag as she continued through the market. With her shadowed eyes and evasive answers, she was more of an enigma than Paul Joubert. Just when he thought he was making progress, she would withdraw, with a maddening dexterity that was beginning to infuriate him.

Reaching the village square, she stopped at the public fountain to rinse her hands, splashing water on her face with the unselfconscious abandon of a child. Little wet tendrils of hair clung to her temples, framing her heat-flushed face. Again Rob felt a gut-deep need to kiss her.

To distract himself, he said, "I don't see any castles here. Didn't Paul's ancestors stick around long enough to build one?"

"They were pirates, remember? I suppose they were too busy pillaging. And when the Venetians took over these islands, the pirates must have found it prudent to pillage elsewhere."

"The family tradition," Rob muttered.

"I beg your pardon?" Her brows lifted. For the first time he noticed how thick they were. The sooty eye shadow she wore gave an exotic cast to her deep blue eyes. He wondered what combination of genes had produced that haunting beauty.

And haunting she was. In restless dreams last night he'd seen her eyes, unaccountably reproachful, lit by flames that seared his throat and nostrils. He'd awakened, sweating, heart pounding. He'd told himself he was probably reliving the fire that had consumed the car after the crash. It had taken him a long time to fall asleep again.

"Nothing," he said. "Just a thought that passed through my mind. It's not important."

Not important. Merely crucial. Who was the blond woman who'd sought him out in the village on Corfu? Not for the first time, he wondered if she had a connection to Paul Joubert. He'd always been skeptical of coincidence. And in this affair there were several coincidences, all too convenient to be explained away easily.

A dull throbbing began in his temple, and he brought his hand up to touch the fading scar. For a moment, the village square shimmered before his eyes. The sweat breaking out on his upper lip tasted bitter. He picked up Analise's bag and took her arm with his other hand. "I think I could use a cold drink."

She was instantly concerned. "Is it your head?"

"Just a bit," he muttered, annoyed at his weakness. "It'll be all right."

THE TART, ICY LEMONADE slid down his throat like a blessing. "Ah, that's good." Leaning back, he gazed up at the dappled shadows playing through the canopy of grapevines that shaded the courtyard of the coffee shop. "This place is paradise."

"Some people think it is." Diana let her gaze wander over his face as he closed his eyes. Even in repose, his features showed strength and character, and the lively intelligence that made him a keen observer and a brilliant writer.

If only the timing were more propitious. The scenario she had envisioned for the future was success in her work and a contented solitude. All her life she'd had to depend on her own wits. The last man she'd trusted had betrayed her, almost gotten her killed.

Not that that would happen with Rob. With him, she had the past, the indisputable fact of his integrity. No, the only danger with him was that he distracted her. He touched a deeply feminine core of feeling in her that she had always found it expedient to deny.

She sat up straighter, squaring her shoulders. She would do well to remember why she was here. After that? Time would tell. And Rob might well hate her for her deception.

However, at the moment, the sun-dappled patio did indeed seem the paradise Rob thought it. He opened his eyes and, seeing her gaze on him, smiled tenderly. She felt a delicious warmth shimmer through her body. His eyes were molten silver, with tiny laugh lines crinkling at the corners. His tanned skin was clear again, without the underlying pallor of a few minutes ago.

Dropping her gaze, she stared at the table as she rolled her glass between her palms. The condensation was wet and cold against her skin, a jolt of reality against the enervating heat that seduced her senses and her will. It would be so easy to trust him, perhaps even to ask for his help.

In that thought lay potential disaster, yet she found she couldn't pull away when he lifted her chin with his forefinger. "Come on, Analise. It can't be that bad. As my grandmother used to say, sufficient unto the day—"

"Is the evil thereof," she finished for him. Seeing the question in his eyes, she added, "Even orphans get sent to Sunday school."

"You were an orphan?" he asked. When she didn't respond, he continued, "What deep thoughts were making you look so melancholy?" he asked, making his tone lighter, but with an edge of seriousness that told her he wanted an answer. "Or am I boring you?"

"No, not at all," she assured him. "I was just thinking that life is unpredictable. I couldn't have guessed that I would meet someone like you."

"It hasn't made you happy, though."

His perception was uncanny. She was right to have misgivings about this—this thing—between them. To be with a man who always seemed to know what she was thinking could soon become very uncomfortable. She took refuge in superficiality that nonetheless had an inner core of truth. "Maybe I find you too intense. And too nosy. Isn't that the word you use for someone who puts his nose where it doesn't belong?"

Her faint accent had grown more pronounced, and he was charmed anew. He wanted to be as intense, and as nosy as she accused him of being.

With an effort, he curbed his urgency, sitting back and taking a swallow of his lemonade, which was rapidly warming in the heat. "How about if I buy you lunch? Is there some place to eat around here?"

Lunch. Normal, mundane. Conscious of having been granted a reprieve, Diana silently let out her breath. "Spiro can fix us a pizza if we wait."

Squinting against the glare, Rob surveyed the street, which was beginning to quiet as the siesta hour approached. The white sunlight sending waves of heat up from the flagstones contrasted almost painfully with the inky-black shadows of the grape arbor where they sat. He turned back to her. "Fine by me," he said lazily. "I don't mind postponing another bout of heatstroke."

Diana laughed. "Want me to go in and order it? Or will that offend your masculine ego?"

He waved his hand. "What ego? Go ahead. I've always had a fantasy of having a woman wait on me hand and foot."

A patent lie, she guessed, and laughed again. He was much too self-confident to expect anyone to supply his comforts or his necessities. Still smiling, she got up and headed toward the coffee shop. As she approached the open door, she could see over the stone wall to the patio of the tavern next door. Petro sat at a table, by himself, nursing an ouzo in a shot glass.

She frowned. Hadn't he gone with Paul early this morning? She was sure she'd heard him joking with Maria in the back garden, and Paul telling the housekeeper they would be back in the evening. They—he and Petro.

But maybe she'd jumped to a conclusion.

"*Kali mera,* Petro," she called.

He jerked as if she'd touched him with a live wire, but recovered at once. "Uh, *kali mera,* Miss Analise," he said. "Showing Kyrios Minardos the village, are you?"

"Yes." She glanced at the crowd sitting at the tables that surrounded Petro. They were young, mostly in their late teens and early twenties, and they were noisily arguing politics. "This isn't where you usually drink, is it?"

His eyes slid away from hers. Tapping a cigarette out of its package, he busied himself lighting it. He drew deeply, blowing twin spirals of smoke from his nostrils. "I thought I'd give it a try. Change my habits, so to speak. Man gets old if he gets in a rut."

"I suppose so." She hesitated, then plunged on. "Didn't you go with Kyrios Paul to Corfu?"

Again he didn't meet her eyes. "No. He took the small motorboat."

She nodded. On the surface it all seemed logical, but she couldn't help wondering if there was something going on beneath that placid exterior. Was it possible that Joubert knew of her connection to the car crash, and had asked Petro to keep an eye on her and Rob? If so, was Petro supposed to protect them, or spy on them?

Saying a polite goodbye to Petro, she went into the building to order lunch. When she came out, he was gone. The cigarette he'd only half smoked lay twisted in the ashtray. From its tip, a curl of blue smoke rose into the still heat.

"Did you see someone you knew?" Rob said when she sat down.

"Pardon?" she asked, distracted. "Oh, just Petro." Her frown deepened. "I don't know what he was doing there. He usually sits with his friends at the coffee shop across the square."

"Maybe Joubert sent him. Maybe he was worried about leaving you alone with me." His mouth turned up in a parody of humor.

Diana saw no reason to hide her own suspicions. "I think he was following us. And I don't think it was out of concern for my safety with you."

Chapter Six

Rob's brows drew together. "But why?"

"Exactly what I've been asking myself." Diana stared off into the distance, wondering how much she could tell him. She kept getting a very uneasy feeling about the situation, as if Rob's presence on the island were creating a turbulence that hadn't been there before.

He remained silent, waiting.

"You know," she said at last, "I've wondered about this whole thing from the beginning. Paul inviting you here, for instance. He could have gotten favorable publicity through a simple press release. This is the first time he's sought out a reporter."

"I'm not a reporter."

"But you write articles about interesting people. And Paul Joubert would be an interesting person to many of your readers."

His mouth quirked in amusement. "You flatter me, Analise. But I agree. It is odd about Joubert. What else?"

"I don't know. Just a feeling I have—" She glanced up as the rotund and cheerful Spiro laid cutlery and china on the table.

"The pizza will be ready in half an hour," the man said in passable English.

"Thank you, Spiro." After Spiro had gone, Diana sat back, a thoughtful frown on her face as she traced a pattern on the white paper tablecloth with her fork.

"The woman who met me in Makrino," Rob said suddenly. "According to the police, she was tall and blond, with very pale skin. Have you ever seen anyone like that around?"

Experience allowed Diana to keep her voice steady. "No, I haven't, but that doesn't mean much. Corfu is a large enough place, and in summer there are plenty of blondes around, given its popularity with the British. Do you remember what you were doing in the village? Was there something you were writing about?"

"That's just the trouble." He slammed down his lemonade glass, as if it were to blame for his amnesia. "I can't remember anything about that day."

"Didn't you have any notes, anything you'd written while you waited?"

"If I did, they must have burned in the crash." His face drawn and white, he clenched his hand into a fist. "I keep thinking someone was with me in that car."

Diana placed her hand over his. "The police did a thorough investigation, even called out an expert from Athens. There was no sign of anyone else."

He glanced at her sharply. "How do you know this?"

Her throat tightened. How did he make her feel so guilty about lying? The ability to spin a believable cover story was the first skill an undercover investigator perfected. Anyway, this wasn't a lie. It was the truth, as far as it went. "I asked. I could see how not knowing bothered you."

"Yeah, but what about the car registration? What's Media Consulting?"

She shrugged lightly. "A Paris-based firm. Something to do with the marketing of olive oil." And one of the many

small businesses her employer, the EFAC, had set up to
provide a base of operations in other countries.

"Legitimate?"

"Of course. The car was kept for the use of its sales-
people. Anyone with a set of keys could use it."

"What about the parking-garage attendants? Did they
have keys they might lend to someone?"

"Not in that facility. The individual owners keep their
keys. And the insurance company that had the policy on the
car will take care of the loss."

"So it's a dead end," Rob said flatly.

"I suppose so." She looked up in relief as Spiro set down
a pizza, crisp and hot from the old-fashioned brick oven.
"Here's our food. Thank you, Spiro."

Tapping her fingers on the table, she gazed out at the
waves of heat shimmering over the street in the midday sun.
Could she take the chance? Yes, she had to. Although not
naive, Rob was far too trusting. "Rob, are you sure the car
crash was an accident?"

Rob looked startled, then thoughtful, as he separated the
slices of pizza. "The police seemed convinced it was," he
said slowly.

"But are you?" she persisted.

"I don't know. Logically, they're probably right, but I
can't help wondering. Every now and then I've had dreams
or flashbacks, and I keep feeling there's something I'm
missing."

"Do you have enemies?"

His laugh was short and humorless. "There might be an
odd person who didn't like what I wrote about him, or
someone who took exception to one of my books. But on
the whole, no, I don't have enemies. Or if I do, they're
keeping a very low profile."

He clenched his fist again before slowly releasing it.
"That woman. She seems to be the key to this whole thing.

If we could only find her... But I wouldn't know where to start. It's as if she vanished off the face of the earth." He placed a slice of pizza on her plate. "Here, eat it while it's hot."

The aroma of oregano, tomato sauce and melted cheese tickled Diana's nostrils, and she realized she was hungry. Picking up her knife, she cut off a small section and chewed it, swallowing hastily when the crust burned her tongue. "Good," she said, fanning her mouth and downing a gulp of water. "But hot."

"In Canada we always ate pizza with our hands."

"But you're using your fork," she pointed out.

"When in Rome—or, as the case may be, Greece. I don't want people to think my mother never taught me any manners."

"Are your parents still alive?" she asked, momentarily startled to realize that she didn't know.

"Sure. They're retired, living in Victoria, on the West Coast. It's called the banana belt of Canada. Of course, bananas don't really grow there, only rain forests."

The fondness in his voice touched her, and for an instant she felt a pang of envy. He had never known what it was like to be without a family, while she had been essentially alone all her life. Her adoptive parents had been kind enough, but too involved in their careers to give a little girl the warmth she needed.

"You're doing it again."

She jumped. "Doing what?"

"Going off to that place where you disappear from me. Why do you do it, when it makes you look so sad?"

Forcing herself to smile brightly, she cut another bite of pizza. "I'm afraid you wouldn't understand, even if you knew."

A muscle in his jaw tightened, a hard knot under his tanned skin. "Try me. You might be surprised."

Still smiling, she shook her head. "Not today."

And Rob heard the echo: *Not today, and probably not ever.*

ON THE WAY HOME, under a white sun that glared like a malevolent eye from a pale saffron sky, they stopped for apricots. With a brief word to Rob, Analise turned onto an unpaved side road that snaked through olive orchards. The gnarled trees clung to the hillsides with a tenacity that made Rob wonder if their twisted roots were all that held the island together. It was as if the rocky soil would disintegrate and dissolve in the sea without their support.

As the little car climbed higher, olives gave way to peaches, apricots, apples and kiwi. The air was cooler than on the flats, fragrant with the perfume of ripening fruit and the green scent of freshly irrigated alfalfa beyond the orchards.

She braked in front of a small whitewashed house covered with bougainvillea and grape vines. The windows were shuttered against the heat, but the door stood open, a bead curtain serving as a barrier to insects.

The light slam of the car door brought two children, dressed in rumpled pajamas, running out of the house. The curtain clicked and swayed wildly in their wake.

"Analise, Analise, you came," they yelled, flinging themselves at her legs.

Rob watched in amusement as Analise bent and kissed first the little girl, who looked about three, and then her brother, who was probably a year or so older. Reaching into the back of the car, she pulled out a couple of chocolate bars, which the children proceeded to devour with all the finesse of starving lion cubs.

"*Yassou*, Analise," a voice called from the doorway. A sturdily built man with the leathery skin of one who worked outdoors came down the path, followed by a small woman with delicate features, evidently his wife.

They had obviously been interrupted in the middle of their siesta. The woman had on a crookedly buttoned housedress, but from under its hem peeked the lacy edge of a nightgown. Placing her hands on Analise's shoulders, she stood on tiptoe and kissed her cheek. "You should have come sooner, eaten with us."

"I was showing Rob the village," Analise said with a warm smile. "Rob, this is Nick and Eleni, my dear friends. Nick takes care of Paul's garden. And those chocolate-covered rascals are Vasso and Dino."

The adults shook Rob's hand, Nick with robust exuberance, Eleni with shyly downcast eyes. "You are from America, Kyrie Rob?" Eleni asked diffidently. "I have a brother in New Jersey."

"No, I'm Canadian, but I live in England," he answered in Greek.

"Rob is only here for a week or two," Analise said. "He's a writer."

They looked as impressed as if Analise had announced he was a film star. Rob felt his face grow hot with embarrassment. "Are these your orchards?" he asked. "The crop looks good."

Nick pursed his lips. "So-so." He flipped his hand back and forth in a gesture that suggested thousands of trees were not worthy of notice by an outsider.

"We've come to buy some apricots and tomatoes, if you have them," Analise said to Eleni.

"Of course. Come with me. I've got some fresh-picked in the storage shed."

The two women went off, leaving Rob with Nick, who hitched up his trousers and contemplated a low bank of clouds forming on the horizon. From the height on which they stood, the sea was visible, a deep indigo ruffled by a breeze that kicked up little whitecaps.

"A man makes many journeys in life," Nick said contemplatively. "And finds his happiness close to home."

Rob, always interested in a story, recalled Joubert's comment about the islanders. "Were you born here?"

"No. I was born on Corfu, in Makrino." He turned his deep brown eyes on Rob. "I believe you had a misfortune there."

"You might say that."

Nick pushed gnarled fingers through his graying hair. It struck Rob that he was a good twenty years older than his wife. "Those mountain roads can be treacherous. Danger often appears where you least expect it."

He walked to the doorstep and picked up a small pair of pruning clippers. Turning his back to Rob, he lopped spent blossoms from a rosebush and dropped them into a bucket.

Rob watched, hearing the sleepy twitter of starlings in the fig tree and Eleni's tinkling laughter as she and Analise appeared from around the back of the house. Nick picked up the bucket of clippings, grinning at Eleni and Analise as if the conversation with Rob had never occurred. "I trust my Eleni gave you the best of the fruit."

"Yes, thank you. It's lovely. I'll be back in a few days, when you've got more ripe pears."

Nick laughed heartily. "I'll let you have as many as you want if you'll show Eleni how to make the chocolate sauce that's so good with them."

"I will," she promised.

Rob was silent as she turned the Deux Chevaux and drove back to the main road. Had Nick's oblique words been a warning? If so, a warning against what? Nick seemed on excellent terms with Analise, and Joubert hadn't been mentioned.

They were within sight of the iron gates of the estate before he even came close to sorting out his thoughts. And then, once again, they focused on the mysterious woman at his side.

"Who are you, Analise?"

DIANA DREW IN HER BREATH, but made no reply. What had Nick said to Rob? He would never betray her, she knew, but something had set the wheels turning inside Rob's astute journalist's brain. Leaning over, she pressed the remote control resting on the dash. The gates opened with stately deliberation. She drove between the tall stone pillars, her knuckles white as she gripped the steering wheel. "What does it matter?" she said tightly. "You'll be gone in a few days. In a month you'll have forgotten I exist."

"Let me be the judge of that," Rob said, his voice equally tense. "You're not a forgettable woman."

The irony of his remark was laughable. He'd been married to her, and now he didn't even know her.

Rob spoke again. "Your friend Nick comes from Makrino. Did you know that?"

She kept her face carefully blank as she glanced at him. "Yes, I knew that."

"Don't you think it's an odd coincidence that I was there, and then I meet someone who comes from the place?"

Diana shrugged, braking in front of the garage. Gravel crunched under the tires. She killed the engine, but made no move to get out of the car. The silence was broken only by the tick of cooling metal. "Everyone comes from somewhere," she said at last.

"But it's so far out of the way. I think the woman arranged to meet me there for that very reason."

"You don't know that she approached you. You might have contacted her."

"Except that I'd never heard of Makrino until the doctor mentioned it and I recalled the note at the banquet, telling me to go there. I remember everything before, coming to Corfu, exploring the old town for a couple of days, attending the awards banquet. But whatever happened in the village is a blank."

Heat was building up inside the little car. Sweat trickled from Diana's temple to her neck. Even so, she felt suddenly cold. Nick had known she was going to Makrino, had in fact suggested it as a meeting place.

She banged a lid on her suspicions. This case was getting to her, making her paranoid. No, Nick wouldn't have let anything slip, however innocently. He had been an agent once, too. He was careful, and she trusted him.

She pushed the door open and got out of the car. Rob slammed his own door and came around the back of the car to help her with the bags of produce. "I think the blond woman has a connection to this island, maybe even to Joubert," he said. "When did you say Joubert decided to give me the interview? After the story of the awards banquet?"

Diana frowned, shaking her head. "It was after he saw the newspaper headlines about your accident."

"Oh?" Rob's brows climbed. "That's odd, wouldn't you say? And that's what I don't like about this setup. Joubert has always been antagonistic toward the media, and suddenly he invites me here. I think he had something to do with the car crash, and wants me here to keep an eye on me, to see if I remember anything?"

Something along that line had occurred to her days ago. "Then why did you agree to come?"

Rob's grin lit up his whole face, and Diana felt a curious melting sensation in her midsection. He hadn't lost a bit of the charm that had enthralled her once; if anything, it had increased in voltage. "Because I've tried before to get an interview with Paul Joubert. I'd have been a fool to pass up this chance, and I try never to be a fool.''

"You've tried before?'' she said in surprise. "You mean before you phoned Paul's Swiss office and left your number?''

"Yes. I called when I first knew this trip was coming up. About a month ago.''

"A month ago.'' She thought for a moment. "Did anyone get back to you?''

"Not that I know of. I left my agent's number. Sean O'Hara is his name.''

Wheels were spinning in Diana's head. "So by the time you left for Corfu, you hadn't received a reply from Paul's Swiss office?''

"No, but I didn't make it a priority. I spent a couple of weeks' holiday in Paris and Nice before coming to Corfu.'' Rob frowned. "Sean didn't mention it, but is it possible that Joubert could have tried to contact me earlier, without your knowledge?''

Diana set down the bags. Closing the trunk, she reached into the back seat for her purse and the mail she'd picked up. "With Paul, anything is possible. And a month ago I was in Paris myself, on business for him. The paintings he's donating to the museum were stored there. I went to arrange shipping.''

Rob gestured to indicate the mail she held. "Didn't I see a phone bill with that stuff? There would be a record of the call, if he made one.''

Wondering what new complications she was entertaining, Diana riffled through the envelopes. "Yes, here it is.'' Sliding her fingertip under the flap, she ripped the envelope open. The list was short. "Paul faxes most of his communications. That comes on a separate bill. What's your agent's number?''

Rob told her. She nodded. "It's here. Let me see— Yes, that was while I was away. Wouldn't your agent have contacted you?"

"Depends. Joubert might not have left his name. People call all the time with hot stories, often with outrageous demands for secrecy." He picked up the bags and carried them toward the house. "Back to the blond woman. Did Joubert have any visitors around that time?"

Diana shook her head. "He seldom has visitors, other than occasional business associates. I was away for a week, but no one mentioned guests. Maria, the housekeeper, usually brings me up to date on what goes on. After I got back, the director of a gallery in Italy where Paul sells some of his paintings was here, checking out Paul's latest work. Then I had go to back to Paris for a couple of days, because there was a problem with the impressionist paintings. When I returned here, Kurtz was gone."

"Kurtz? Is that his name?" Rob shifted the heavy bags to a more comfortable position. "I'd like to know more about him. And I'd better call Sean as soon as possible."

Diana opened the kitchen door and stepped inside. The room was tidy and empty, Maria having gone home for the afternoon. "Use the phone in the office. Paul left orders that you should make yourself at home."

Setting the bags on the counter, Rob shook his head. "It can wait. I'll go to Corfu to make the call. I'd rather play this my way, for now."

Diana glanced sharply at him. She might just make a call, too, to clear Rob with her agency. It wouldn't hurt to have another ally who could be counted on. She didn't want to ask for Nick's help unless it was absolutely necessary. "You're taking this seriously, aren't you?"

"I think it's time I did."

"Be careful, Rob. Paul could be a dangerous enemy if he thinks you're stepping on his toes."

"That's why I'm going to be careful of his toes. What's this art dealer's full name, and where's his gallery?"

"Mohammed Kurtz. He operates out of Milan."

"Operates?"

Diana busied herself putting apricots into the fridge. "Poor choice of words. But Kurtz has several galleries. The others are in Hamburg and Marseilles."

Rob scribbled the information into a small notebook. "Unusual name."

"He's of German and Turkish extraction."

Turkish. Art treasures. Again the nebulous feeling that he was on the verge of something big pricked at him. He tucked away his notebook. Was it last year that he'd read something about art smuggling with a Turkish connection? Not that there weren't strict laws against removing archaeological treasures from the country, but with thousands of miles of rugged coast, Greece was impossible to patrol adequately. In smuggling, as in any crime, the simplest methods were the most effective. A deal with an archaeologist or laborer at a site, night transport to the coast in a truck loaded innocuously with grain or straw, and a quick pickup by boat from an isolated cove. Easily done, with the right connections. And money.

He'd thought about doing a story on it back then, but completing contracted proposals and his latest novel had taken up his time, and he'd put the idea aside.

Seeing Joubert's collection had triggered it again. He gnawed his lip in frustration. "Art smuggling," he said aloud.

Diana, her head in the fridge, stiffened. "What about art smuggling?"

"Is Joubert smuggling art?"

Straightening slowly, she folded the empty bag, giving herself time to consider her reply. She decided to remain on the safer side, at least for now. "What makes you think he's into anything illegal?"

"Rumors, for one. Rumors usually come from somewhere."

"And they're often exaggerated," Diana pointed out.

"Joubert's interest in art gives him a perfect cover. There are shipments of his own work, at random times. And he has the right connections. I don't recognize this Mohammed Kurtz's name as a major dealer, which could mean he keeps a low profile."

"That doesn't make him dishonest," Diana said, playing the devil's advocate. "Besides, Paul has a lot of other interests, too, if you're looking for something, some of which the law might take a dim view of. He has a munitions factory, for instance, and the Middle East isn't far away. Of course, there's nothing intrinsically illegal about owning a munitions factory."

Rob laughed. "Ever thought about being a lawyer, Analise? You argue a case most convincingly."

She hoped that she'd at least muddied the waters. Rob was sharp. If he stayed much longer, she was going to have to tell him something. But not until she'd cleared it with her superior.

Oddly, for just an instant, she felt a delicious anticipation at the thought of working with Rob, an exhilaration that she knew should have dismayed her.

Chapter Seven

Rob took an apricot from the second bag of fruit and bit into its succulent flesh. "Does Maria live in?"

"No. She lives in the village. But at this time of year her family stays at their beach hut. She goes there during her time off. It's only a twenty-minute walk. Several of their friends are staying there, as well."

"We did that one summer," Rob said. "Went down the east coast of Greece, near Vólos, and camped in reed huts for a month. It was great."

His happy childhood. Against her will, Diana felt that pang of longing. Not jealousy, just a sense of loss. He'd had so much; they might be two people from different planets.

Briskly she stowed the rest of the fruit and vegetables in the fridge, closing the door with a little thud. "I guess I'll lie down for a while. Feel free to use the computer in Paul's study if you want to work."

"What if I'm a hacker and ferret out all his secrets?"

A muscle in Diana's stomach tightened. "Go ahead," she said, her tone as careless as his. "I think Paul would consider you welcome to anything you uncover." She headed for her room.

It had been Paul's own suggestion that Rob use his study when Paul didn't need it. Which meant there was nothing incriminating to be found, as Diana already knew.

Neither Paul's study nor the personal computer contained information that couldn't have been discovered from any number of sources in libraries or in his companies' year-end reports. The computer had never even refused her access to a file. After months of searching memory banks, she'd concluded that Paul's business computer was the means by which he contacted his widespread enterprises. Joubert had kept it securely locked, using its information and communications only when Diana was not around. As time passed, its squat presence had seemed to taunt her.

Then, surprisingly, four months ago, Joubert had given her the key, along with a substantial raise in pay. And the access codes to many of his business files. He'd finally decided to trust her, she'd guessed. She'd seized the opportunity, devoting most of her spare time to snooping in the computer's intricate memory.

She'd had a friend in university who was quite an expert at breaking codes, and he'd taught Diana a few tricks that were useful, if not strictly legal. But even with the tricks, for weeks she hadn't been able to locate any secret files.

Then, a month ago, she'd made a breakthrough, into a file that either hadn't existed before or had previously been inaccessible. She had just begun to compile what looked to be useful data when Joubert sent her to Paris. When she'd returned from her second trip there, the main computer had been inoperative. And it still was.

She couldn't work on the information until the computer was once more on-line. And then only if the file was still accessed by the same code. She wouldn't put it past Paul to change the codes regularly.

Kurtz's presence on the island at the time the computer failed bothered her. He'd clearly never trusted her, although his manner had never been less than impeccable. If he'd managed to arouse Paul's suspicions...

She shivered suddenly. Come to think of it, all the events that were blockading her now had started about a month ago: her discovery of the secret files, Paul's unexpectedly sending her to Paris, Kurtz's visit, her second trip to Paris to unsnarl a foul-up in the shipping schedule, which had turned out to be only a minor clerical error—and Rob's call to Joubert's Swiss office. Was Joubert on to her, and craftily biding his time?

She shook herself. No use looking for trouble before it came to find her. A cool head cleared of all but the proven facts had served her best in the past. She'd be wise to remember that before letting her increasing uneasiness give her away.

Stripping off her clothes, she lay down on her bed, listening to the peacocks' plaintive cries.

MARIA HADN'T ARRIVED YET to make dinner, although she was due soon. Diana opened the kitchen shutters to let in the light now that the sun had moved to the other side of the house. An empty glass stood in the sink—probably Rob's. Was he working? She stepped briskly down the hall, her bare feet silent on the glossy marble tiles. The door of the study stood open, but the room was empty. Running her hand over the top of the monitor on the desk, she felt its coolness. The computer hadn't been used.

Her brows drew together. She left the study and was halfway down the hall toward his room before she realized what she was doing. Lifting her hand to her forehead, she rubbed the bridge of her nose. This was crazy. If Rob had a headache, he would know what to do. He didn't need her to mother him.

She swung around, scolding herself. Better if she concentrated on her own job.

Back in the kitchen, she picked up an apricot from the bowl she'd left on the counter. The golden-pink skin was warm, with the delicate texture of the softest velvet, and she unconsciously caressed it. Rob's skin felt like that....

A rainy afternoon in Paris, perfect for exploring each other in the warm feather bed. Every sensation had been new, as if they were the only people in the world who had discovered love.

Heat pooled deep in her belly, and she couldn't stop the sigh that parted her lips. Robby. When her eyes dropped closed, she brought herself up short. She must be insane, standing there dreaming about a man like a besotted schoolgirl, reliving a memory ten years old.

Thrusting her hands under the stream of cold water, she firmly shut off her thoughts.

ROB DIDN'T put in an appearance until dinner was almost ready. He came into the kitchen dressed in ancient cutoff jeans and a loose white cotton shirt. Only one button was fastened, exposing almost all of his chest, with its mat of silky dark hair. Remembering the tenor of her thoughts earlier, Diana, after one startled look at him, reached up to the door of the wall oven and pretended a consuming interest in its contents. If her face was red, at least she could blame it on the heat.

"You cook, too?" Rob asked, going over to the sink and running himself a glass of water.

"Not usually, although I enjoy it. I made the dessert— apricot cream." She slammed the oven door and turned off the broiler. "Maria stepped out to the garden for a moment and asked me to keep an eye on the chicken."

"Is Joubert back?" Rob filled a second glass, leaning back against the counter as he drank it.

"He phoned and said not to expect him for dinner after all. Excuse me." Still avoiding his eyes, she reached around him and picked up a fork. He didn't move except to settle his hips more comfortably and cross his legs at the ankles.

The sound of a car horn sent them to the window that overlooked the garage courtyard. Tamara, a wide-brimmed hat in her hand, was getting out of a battered little Skoda that looked as if it were held together by rust and baling wire. Laughter drifted across the patio as she skipped around the car and leaned into the open window. Rob and Diana couldn't make out her words, but a long, muscular arm reached out of the car and pulled her close, obviously for a kiss.

Tamara, still laughing, straightened, watching as the car turned to go. It had almost reached the corner of the house when she waved her arm and ran after it. The driver braked sharply, and they caught a glimpse of a handsome young man. Tamara bent down and kissed him once more, her fingers ruffling his black hair.

She was smiling as she ran lightly to the door that led into her wing of the house.

Diana let out a long breath. "Well, that's a surprise."

"So that's the attraction in the village."

Diana frowned. "It would seem that way. I wonder if Paul knows." Still, Tamara wasn't her problem, and the girl was certainly old enough to know what she was doing.

At the table, ten minutes later, Tamara wore the same reserved, almost sullen expression as the evening before, saying nothing during the meal unless she was addressed. Even then she replied in monosyllables. Rob and Diana exchanged glances, their expressions conveying mutual bewilderment.

Rob followed Diana into the kitchen with their plates when she went to fetch the dessert she'd made. "Do you suppose she's twins, and that was the other one we saw?"

Diana broke into giggles, then ducked her head in embarrassment. Giggles! "If she is, one of them must be invisible when the other is around."

Maria glanced questioningly at them, and they burst into further laughter. Clicking her tongue, she turned and resumed rinsing dishes in the sink.

"I wonder who the kid with the Skoda is. Do you know him?"

Shaking her head, Diana mounded the apricot cream onto plates and topped the dessert with a swirl of whipped cream. "It shouldn't be too hard to find out. Maria, who drives a Skoda? He's young with black hair."

Maria frowned thoughtfully. "A Skoda. Very old?"

Diana nodded. "Ancient."

"That must be the oldest Chellis boy. Yes, he would be home now, for the summer. He goes to the university in Athens."

"Doesn't look as if she cared who saw them together," Rob said. "What if Joubert had been here? She may just be his model but he seems a little possessive."

"Maybe she knew he wasn't."

"There was us, and Maria could have been here. Any of us could tell him."

"She probably doesn't care."

"Or she's playing a game."

"Well, we're not her parents," Diana said firmly.

"For which I'm deeply grateful," Rob replied, with a heartfelt sincerity that set off Diana's laughter again.

"Stop," she gasped when she could take a breath. "Let's get the dessert in there before she decides we're not coming back."

"And starts speculating about us?" Rob asked slyly.

Diana paused in the act of picking up the tray. "We both know there's nothing to speculate about, don't we?"

"Isn't there?" Winking at Maria, he stepped in front of Diana, trapping her against the marble counter. Before she could marshal her defenses, he kissed her, lightly, but with unmistakable promise. "A deposit on account," he said, and moved back, grinning at the hot color that washed up her face.

ROB JERKED UPRIGHT IN BED, a scream echoing in his head. Adrenaline surged through him, and his pulse hammered painfully at his temples. He shook his head to clear it.

Around him the room was dark and quiet, the white lace curtains swaying gently at the open window. Bright moonlight painted the floor with silver. A breeze carried the fragrance of stocks and jasmine into the room, drifting over his bare shoulders with a cool breath that raised goose bumps.

Had the scream been real, or only the residue of a halfremembered nightmare? Maybe he'd heard one of the peacocks, the self-appointed watchbirds.

Scowling, Rob got up and pulled on his jeans. From the window he saw the garden, deserted and eerily silent. The breeze he'd felt had died; not a leaf rustled. Even the crickets, which started their nightly concert at twilight, had gone to bed early. The junglelike tangle of plants lay in luminous anonymity in the moonlight. The moon's position told him he hadn't slept long, perhaps a couple of hours.

A shriek fractured the silence—this time unmistakably one of the peacocks. As if released from a spell, a dog barked on the hill outside the gates, and the wind sighed in the pines that guarded the cliffs above the sea.

Rob was about to go back to bed when a flash of white caught his eye.

Someone was down there, a figure barely visible above the hedge that bordered a garden path. As he watched, it stopped, a white blur, paler than the silver moonlight. The peacock cried out again, and the figure began to run, streaking down the complex system of paths as if familiar with them.

A security light, probably triggered by the motion, flashed on. Rob had a clear view of someone wearing a hooded white garment. As the runner reached the tall trees at the edge of the garden, the hood fell back, revealing long hair that lifted in the breeze. He had no more than a glimpse of it before the trees blocked his view.

The peacock screamed once more, as if angry at the intrusion.

Without bothering to put on more clothes, Rob ran to the door of his room. A woman, he thought as he sped down the hall. But who?

Not Tamara, whose hair was short and dark. Not Analise, and not one of the village women who worked in the house. The intruder's hair had been as blond as a palomino's mane. Like that of the woman who'd met him in Makrino.

Fumbling with the deadbolt lock on the terrace door delayed him for a moment. He gave a grunt of satisfaction when it opened. The gravel on the path bit into his bare feet as he took a shortcut to the wild portion of the garden. Thanks to the walks he'd taken this afternoon and evening, he knew the layout.

He knew also that there was no escape from the garden in that direction, unless one had rappeling gear for a descent down the cliff to the sea, which wasn't an easy escape, either, because of currents and vicious riptides. There was no beach, only a tumble of boulders, slick with age and lichens.

He reached the trees, pausing to get his bearings. And to listen. The path was narrow, hard to find in the dense undergrowth. He heard nothing, no sound of someone crashing through the brush. There was no sound at all, except the muffled roar of the waves, and the plaintive whistle of a night bird.

DIANA WAS LYING IN BED reading when she heard the faint squeak of hinges. Rob's door. Why would he be leaving his room at this time of night? He was in a hurry, too, judging by the thump as the door struck the adjacent wall.

Tossing down her book, she flung a robe over her night-dress and thrust her feet into thongs. The hall was empty, but when she reached the dining room she saw that the door was ajar and heard the receding crunch of feet on the gravel path.

Rob must have seen or heard something in the garden. His windows faced in a different direction from hers; their rooms were at right angles to each other, with bathrooms between them. She hadn't heard anything, except the pea-cocks once or twice.

She moved a little way down the path, stopping to listen. There were any number of directions he could have gone. She had reached the sundial when she heard his voice. He was swearing—a barely audible expression of disgust—and a moment later he came limping into view. He wore noth-ing but a pair of jeans, his chest bare above the narrow waistband. His feet were also bare, which explained why he was limping.

He froze when he saw her. Then he exhaled and came nearer. "Analise. For a moment I thought—" He laughed—it sounded forced and humorless—his eyes glittering with suppressed frustration, or perhaps anger.

"You thought what?" she asked. "What are you doing out here, stumbling around in the dark?"

"Following a ghost," he said flatly, sinking down on the bench and examining one foot. He cursed again as he picked bits of gravel from between his toes.

"A ghost?" She reached under the platform that held the sundial and flipped a switch. The silver-blue moonlight faded in the glare of a floodlight. Sitting down next to him, she looked at his foot. "You should have put on shoes."

"Yeah, Miss Practicality, I should have. Next time I'll tell the ghost to wait while I lace my sneakers."

She ignored his sarcasm. "What do you mean, a ghost?"

"Someone dressed in white who disappeared into thin air near the top of the cliffs." He brushed grit off one foot, then lifted the other and did the same. Fortunately, none of the stones had cut the skin. "You didn't happen to hear a scream, say about ten minutes ago?"

Diana shook her head. "Only the peacocks."

His mouth turned down. "The watchbirds. I heard them, too, but what woke me sounded different from the peacocks."

"You'd been sleeping," Diana pointed out. She'd heard him take a shower, much earlier, while she was reading the latest issue of *Art News*. The story of yet another museum robbery, in northern Greece, had held particular interest for her. "Maybe you dreamed it."

"Could be," he said. "But I wasn't dreaming when I saw someone in the garden."

A vague anxiety stirred in the pit of her stomach. She frowned, turning over the possibilities in her mind. Rigged with an elaborate alarm system, the estate was secure at night. Nick saw to it when he left. Or Petro did. The walls could be climbed, but why would anyone do that? Certainly none of the islanders would stoop to theft. They had too much natural pride, and too deep a sense of loyalty to Joubert.

Rob must have imagined whatever he'd seen or heard. He wasn't long out of the hospital after a concussion. He'd admitted to nightmares since the accident, and Diana's inclination was to dismiss this as another. Except he sounded so sure.

"Man or woman?" she asked. Some of the islanders did think the estate was haunted. It had once been the site of a battle between two rival groups of pirates. One group had slaughtered the other, leaving the bodies, including those of several women who had been captives, unburied on a beach when they set sail.

"Woman. She had long blond hair." He hesitated, as though he suddenly doubted his memory. "Like the woman who met me in Makrino."

"Unlike Corfu, this is a small island," Diana said gently. "If a woman of that description showed up here, we'd know about it." Could he have been hallucinating? Trauma did that sometimes.

He stood up, thrusting his hands deep into his back pockets. "Yeah, I know." He hunched his shoulders, welcoming the soothing dampness of the mentha plants against his bruised feet. Here there was no gravel, only worn flagstones that held a residual warmth from the day's sunshine.

His gaze sharpened when he noticed Analise's attire. A long white robe of shimmering satin. It might have been her he'd seen. Except for the hair.

The same thought must have crossed her mind. Her smile was thin and laced with irony. "You're sure the hair you saw was blond? You're sure you didn't see me haunting the garden like a restless soul?"

He gave her a reluctant answering smile. "Are you making fun of me, or deliberately clouding the issue?"

"Me? I wouldn't make fun of you." She sobered. "You haven't been talking to Maria, have you?"

"About what?"

"The legend. There's a beach down there that the locals avoid. It's reputed to be haunted by the ghost of a woman murdered several hundred years ago. Moonlight is tricky, though. It might have been a dog you saw. There are a lot of strays on the island. The alarms are set so that small animals don't trigger them. We even found a goat wandering in here last month, although he did set off an alarm."

"It got all the way up to the house?" Rob asked in surprise. "Then how is it that we didn't set off any alarms? Or are they the silent kind? All I noticed were a couple of lights coming on. I figured there were motion detectors down here."

Diana reached down and turned off the floodlight. "Only the perimeter has audible alarms. Paul doesn't really expect an invasion." Her eyes dropped to his feet as they started toward the house. "Think you can manage the walk back, or shall I fetch you some shoes?"

"I'll make it." He suddenly turned, grasping her by the shoulders. "Is there something going on here that you haven't told me? You don't seem to be taking this at all seriously, when there might well be an intruder on the grounds."

She could feel the warmth of his hands through the glossy fabric, and the familiar tingle danced along her nerves. "There's just no evidence that anyone was here. Rob, I don't doubt that you think you saw something, but we're not going to find out what it is scrambling around in the dark. And I can assure you that it wasn't me. I was in bed reading."

"Your windows don't face the same way as mine, do they?"

"Only partially. Besides, yours is a corner room. You've got a very wide view." She moved gently away from him, fighting the temptation to smooth away the frown that carved vertical creases above his nose. His hair, tousled from sleep, looked soft and touchable. Her palms prickled as she remembered their kiss earlier, too quick, too soon ended.

Gritting her teeth against the urge to repeat the experiment here in the fragrant moonlight, she stepped briskly up the path. She told herself it was wiser to put some distance between them. Maybe he had indeed seen someone, perhaps a woman Paul had secretly brought home. That woman might still be watching, and Diana had no desire to put herself on public display.

"WONDER WHAT'S GOING ON?" Rob said as he and Diana emerged from the dim, smoky interior of the village church the next morning. The diminishing chant of the priest and the sweet scent of beeswax candles followed them into the glaring sunlight.

Virtually all the villagers who hadn't been in the church were clustered on the stone jetty. A little way out, in deep water, a large yacht swayed at anchor, its sails tidily furled.

"Fifty-footer, I'd say," Rob observed, eyes narrowed against the sun.

Diana put on her sunglasses. "I wonder what it's doing here. This island is, in effect, private property. Paul didn't say anything about visitors."

"Looks like he got them anyway," Rob said dryly.

Ten or twelve people of assorted ages and sexes clambered out of a Zodiac and onto the jetty, enthusiastically assisted by the villagers. One of the strangers, a thirtyish man wearing a black wool fisherman's cap, seemed to be in charge. He raised his voice, addressing the group. "Kyrios Paul has promised transportation to the house. By the time your luggage is off the boat, it should be here."

"Do you suppose they could be long-lost relatives of Paul's come to spend the summer?" Rob whispered to Diana.

She didn't know what to think. Transportation? To the house? It sounded as if these people were expected. If they were, she didn't know about it. Paul was presumably still in Corfu, unless he'd returned during the night. The crowd on the waterfront blocked her view of the slip where he moored his boats.

Surely he didn't expect to accommodate this many people at his house. Large as it was, there just weren't that many bedrooms.

Before she could voice her concern, one of the village children came running out of a side street. "Kyrios Paul! Kyrios Paul!"

"He must be back," Rob commented moments before Paul drove up in the white Mercedes convertible he used on the island.

He was smiling as he got out of his car, and his smile broadened when his gaze fell on Diana and Rob.

"Good morning, Analise, Rob. Beautiful day, isn't it? *Très beau.*" He strode past them. "By the way, Analise," he added over his shoulder, "would you tell Maria there will be three extra for dinner?"

"What about lunch?" she called after him.

"All taken care of," he replied, barely pausing. "We'll eat in the village."

The crowd parted to let him through, as if he were royalty. To Diana's surprise, Paul greeted the man in the fisherman's cap with every sign of affability.

"Obviously they know each other," Rob observed.

"Obviously."

Rob glanced at her sharply. "Is he always this high-handed? I thought Maria had Sundays off."

"Usually she does, but she's willing to work if it's an emergency." She rummaged in her purse for her car keys. "I'm surprised, that's all. He's never had this many guests before." The Zodiac had returned from its second trip. A crew of young men in jeans and T-shirts was unloading crates and what appeared to be filmmaking equipment.

"Do you suppose they're here to make a movie?" Rob said. "Whatever's in the crates must be valuable. Those two guys are wearing guns, and they look as if they know how to use them."

The men who stood near the crates were dressed casually, like their companions, but wore shoulder holsters over their T-shirts. One was tall and muscular, the other shorter, wiry, and nervously puffing a cigarette. The only features they had in common were the hard, calculating look in their eyes and their watchful stance as they surveyed the village and the crowd, which was dispersing as the novelty of the visitors wore off.

"I suppose we'll find out soon enough," Diana said, flipping her keys back and forth between her fingers. "Do you want to go back with me, or stay here? I'm sure someone can give you a lift later."

"I'll go back with you."

She glanced at him over the top of her sunglasses, her tense muscles relaxing under his warm regard. Paul, with his summary orders, might be a chauvinistic dictator, but here at least was one man who wasn't.

Chapter Eight

Diana didn't see Rob again until just before dinner. She was standing near the windows, away from the guests, who were nibbling on hot appetizers, when he sauntered into the living room. He looked handsome and debonair in a white shirt and a navy sports jacket that sat on his broad shoulders as if made exclusively for him. As it probably had, she mused. With the money his thrillers made, he could afford a custom-tailored wardrobe.

It still surprised her, the elemental way he could make her respond to him, without even trying. She had always thought she preferred men who played the game of advance and retreat with a subtle sophistication. Rob had the sophistication, when he chose to use it, but with her he had been refreshingly—and disconcertingly—direct.

As he entered the room, his eyes went straight to her. She nodded a greeting, polite but reserved.

Paul and his three guests stood by the fireplace, holding drinks and plates of hors d'oeuvres. The painting over the mantel seemed to be the subject of a lively discussion, punctuated by much laughter. Rob glanced at the group but his gaze returned at once to Diana.

He winked at her, as if he knew a secret that he shared only with her. Heat curled in her stomach, and she felt again that mysterious bond that tugged her toward him. She hoped it didn't show on her face as he came over, picking up a miniature quiche on the way, which he quickly demolished.

"Can you meet me in the garden later?" he whispered, with another sly wink.

"I—I don't know." She swallowed to moisten her throat. "It might be late, and—"

She broke off as Paul strode up and slapped Rob jovially on the back. "Robert, you're here. Can I get you a drink?"

Rob noted that the guests, two men and a woman, were down to ice clinking in near-empty glasses. He was late, and dinner must be ready. He shook his head. "Thanks, but not right now."

"As you wish." Taking Rob's elbow, Paul led him across the room. "Come and meet my guests. Unless, of course, you've met before?"

"I don't believe I've had the pleasure," Rob said smoothly. "Should I have?"

"My dear fellow, in your line of work, you must get around."

Playing the gracious host to the hilt, Rob thought wryly. The guests must be important. Or was it possible that Joubert was using them as a distraction or another excuse to delay his interview? It was Rob's third day on the island, and he still hadn't seen Joubert alone.

"You might even get a story out of them," Joubert added.

"I'm here to do a story on you." He couldn't resist saying it, although he kept his tone mild.

Paul's smile broadened, his white teeth flashing. "All in good time, my dear fellow, all in good time. Robert Minardos, I'd like you to meet Katerina Stanos, and her costar, Dino Papanikas."

Katerina smiled and shook his hand. "I'm very happy to meet you." She was thin, with the dark beauty of a gypsy in her highly colored complexion and sultry eyes. Masses of deep brown hair curled over her richly tanned shoulders. She gave the impression of constant motion and barely contained energy. High-spirited animation lit her eyes and bubbled in her frequent laughter. Fascinating in small doses, Rob thought, but he guessed the charm of that restlessness would quickly wear thin.

In contrast, Dino Papanikas, as handsome as Apollo, with his perfect features and dark blond hair, had a languid air and the lazy grace of a cat lying in the sun. He merely nodded to acknowledge the introduction.

"They're going to play the leads in the film," Paul added.

"Film?"

"Yes. It's a docudrama about the fur business, both here and abroad. Haven't you noticed how many of the leading furriers all over the world are Greek?"

"Now that you mention it," Rob said slowly, "yes, I have." Immediately, questions spun in Rob's head. This island was a strange place to make a film about furs. At least he knew why the crates from the boat had been so closely guarded. Quality fur easily ran into the five figures.

Paul introduced the last man, the man Rob had seen this morning wearing a fisherman's hat and directing the crew on the jetty.

George Leonides.

Rob couldn't keep surprise and recognition from showing on his face as he shook the man's hand. Leonides was a maker of documentary films who had later branched out into avant-garde drama. "I've admired your work."

"And I yours," Leonides said with a grin.

"Didn't you do a remake of *Romeo and Juliet* with a nontragic ending some years ago?"

Leonides made a good-natured grimace. "You mean you saw that? You must be the only one. It bombed at the box office, as they say."

Apparently the "bomb" had thrown a serious kink into Leonides's career. If Rob's memory served him, the man hadn't made a film since. Or had he?

"You did a film on art after that, didn't you? Exploring the rationale behind paintings suddenly being sold for multimillions?"

Leonides frowned. "That was completed before *Romeo and Juliet,* although it was released later."

"I seem to remember it caused a lot of controversy."

"Yes, well..." Leonides shifted his feet and swallowed the last of his drink. "I took a few years off, licking my wounds, so to speak. But then I was offered a chance to do this fur thing, as part of a debate between furriers and animal activists, so I came out of retirement." He laughed. "Naturally, money also came into the picture. It was an offer too good to refuse. And Paul kindly invited us to use his home for the glamour shots."

"That was generous of him."

Leonides's eyes narrowed shrewdly. "Yes, wasn't it? And interesting that you should be here at the same time."

Very interesting, Rob thought. But what significance it had, he couldn't even guess.

ACROSS THE ROOM, Diana caught the look on Rob's face when Paul introduced George Leonides. Recognition, followed by pleasure mixed with speculation. She, too, had heard of Leonides, the boy-wonder film-maker whose career had taken off like a rocket, only to fizzle out when his work strayed too far from what his audience expected. He hadn't made a movie or a documentary in five years. Rumor had it that no one would take the financial risk of backing him.

She wondered who was paying for this endeavor. Some furriers' association, probably, but she was willing to bet that Paul had contributed, as well. She might be able to check it through the main computer, once the damn thing was working again. The feeling she'd had that something big was brewing intensified.

Maria's daughter, Penny, announced that dinner was ready. Paul let his guests precede him into the dining room. "By the way, Analise," he said, as she and Rob moved past him, "do you know what's become of Tamara? She hasn't been around all day."

"I haven't seen her," Diana said. "Rob, have you? Maybe this afternoon?"

He shook his head. "No, can't say that I have."

Joubert scowled. "She knew we were having guests. I wanted her to meet George. She'd be perfect to model the white fox."

Katerina, seating herself as George politely held her chair, overheard this remark. "So would I, darling, but let someone else do it. Unless we're doing it in here, where it's cool. I've always been grateful that I moved from modeling to acting."

George patted her shoulder. "So are we, Katerina." He turned to Diana. "You wouldn't be interested in modeling, would you?"

Smiling, she shook her head. "I'll stick to what I know, thank you."

He pursed his lips. "Shame. You've got the face and figure for it."

"She's clever, too," Paul put in. "I don't know how I'd manage my business without Analise."

"You're not married, are you, Analise?" George asked.

"No, I'm not."

"Then I think I'll marry you. I need someone to keep my financial affairs in order."

Katerina burst into peals of laughter. "You'd bring her back to live in your apartment? George, the sun has affected your brain. Analise, his apartment is one room and a bath. His office is a desk and a filing cabinet. And the traffic never stops. It's like the Grand Prix just outside his window."

"Don't listen to her, Analise," George said. "I'm back in business now. In a few months I'll be able to buy a house. Maybe not as grand as this, but with enough room."

"I'm afraid I would still have to say no," Diana said with a smile. "I've got a job here that I don't want to leave."

"Even if I would let her go." Paul's smile didn't quite negate the hard note in his voice.

George laid a hand dramatically on his heart. "I'm wounded. But never mind—maybe one day I'll catch Katerina in a weak moment and she'll say yes."

"In your dreams, George," Katerina retorted good-naturedly.

They lingered at the table after dinner as Penny cleared away the dishes and Paul handed out cigars. Only George took one, although Katerina lit a dark French cigarette. The topic turned to art and Paul suggested that his guests might like to see more of his paintings. "You've seen my collection in Paris, some of which are soon to find a home in New York."

"It's your own work I'm interested in, Paul," Katerina said. "If that fascinating canvas in the living room is an example, I'd love to see more."

Dino pushed back his chair. "Count me out. George, can I borrow the Land Rover to drive to town?"

"How do you expect us to get back to the house?" The chief participants in the film were staying in a house Paul owned a couple of kilometers from the estate. The camera crew was billeted in the village inn. Paul had lent his second vehicle, a Land Rover, to George for the duration of the filming.

"Never mind, then." Dino's mouth twisted sulkily. "I'll call a taxi."

"I'll drive you back in the Mercedes, George," Paul said.

"Okay, Dino. Take the Land Rover." George tossed him the keys, which he deftly caught. "But don't be late. We're filming tomorrow, and I don't want you looking hung over."

Dino gave a surly grunt and jogged out of the room.

"He has enough temperament to make up for my good nature," Katerina said, to no one in particular.

George got up and kissed her lightly. "You said it, darling. If it wasn't for his pretty face—and the fact that he's cheap because everyone else is sick of his moods—I wouldn't work with him, either."

"Shall we go?" Gesturing with his cigar, Paul extended his arm to Diana. "Won't you join us, my dear?"

Looking at Paul's paintings was the last thing Diana wanted to do. A hot shower and a quiet evening on the tiny balcony outside her window beckoned much more strongly. "Thank you, but I hope you'll excuse me. I have a lot of work to do tomorrow. I'd rather rest."

"As you wish." Paul stuck the cigar between his teeth and led the way out of the room.

Rob brought up the rear, head bent, hands in his pockets. At the door he paused, looking back at Diana with a question in his eyes. She shook her head emphatically. No, she didn't want him to stay, not only because Paul might question it, but mostly because she really wanted to be alone.

TWO HOURS LATER, she sat on her balcony, letting her hair dry in the faint breeze drifting over the garden. The moon sailed toward its zenith, casting a luminance almost bright enough to read by. She stared down into the shadows below her, wondering if Rob's mysterious running woman of last night had been real. If so, would she reappear?

A short time ago Paul had driven off with his guests, taking them to their own quarters. She was glad they weren't staying in Paul's house. A houseful of people would disrupt her work. As soon as possible, she needed to check out the guests, especially Leonides. First thing tomorrow she would send another fax, urgently worded, to the computer repair service.

A knock sounded on her door. She turned her head, debating whether to answer. It wasn't likely to be Paul. She hadn't heard the car come back, and besides, he wouldn't come to her room. If he needed her, he summoned her to the living room or to his study.

It could only be Rob. Against her will, her heart began to pound heavily against her ribs. Disgusted with herself, she exhaled. Her reaction to him was becoming far too predictable and unsettling, although perhaps understandable. She'd been alone too long. And there were always the memories.

The knock sounded again, a little sharper, more insistent. She pushed herself to her feet. She would go to the door, see what he wanted, then tell him she was tired and that they would talk tomorrow. That was what she told herself.

It didn't work.

He stepped into the room as soon as she opened the door, pushing it closed behind him. For a long moment, they stared at one another. He had discarded the jacket and the red tie he'd worn at dinner. The collar of his white shirt was unbuttoned, and his hair tumbled over his forehead in untidy waves.

"I've got to talk to you, Analise," he said, his voice hoarse, strangely breathless, as he took in her appearance. She wore the same satin robe as last night, and her hair was still faintly damp from her bath. It smelled of honeysuckle, or was that the vine that climbed the house outside her windows?

He shook his head, a dull heat fogging his thoughts. An enigma, that was what she was, and he didn't know what to do about it. He did know that he wanted to kiss her again, to hold her until she became part of his own body, and protect her. Take her away from here before she was caught in the cross fire of the war that he sensed was coming, although he couldn't have explained why.

There had been undercurrents in the talk at the dinner table, names mentioned that by themselves meant nothing, but taken collectively added up to trouble. George Leonides's comeback, for instance. He had been heavily into the European art scene five years ago, until audience disenchantment with his films had sent him out of the public eye. Where had he been during that time? And where had he gotten the money for this venture?

But first, Analise.

"Would you mind telling me what's going on here?" he demanded, keeping his voice low but nonetheless forceful.

"What do you mean?"

"It's obvious that you're unhappy about something. And it involves Joubert. I don't like his attitude. The way he talked at dinner."

"Don't concern yourself with me. I'm not in trouble."

"If you aren't, you soon will be, unless I miss my guess. How about sharing it with me?" He clawed his fingers through his hair. "If you were anyone else, I'd be tempted to think you're hoping he'll marry you. You'd be set for life."

Her face turned pale. An icy rage made it difficult for her to breathe. "I think you'd better leave," she said, in a frigid voice that was barely above a whisper. "I didn't ask for you to judge me."

Rob sucked in a hard breath. "That's exactly the point. I'm not judging you. I said, if you were anyone else. You're not, and I'm convinced you hate Joubert. So why do you stay?"

"Because I have a job to do," she stated simply.

"I'll help you find a better one." He stretched his hand toward her, wanting to touch her, but fearing her reaction. He was handling this badly. He wanted to shake her into talking to him, but this wasn't the way to do it. "Look, Analise, if Joubert has some hold on you, blackmail or something, I can get you a lawyer. You can't go on like this."

To his astonishment, she began to laugh. "You couldn't be more wrong. He's not blackmailing me. I'm here because I have to be. Just accept that."

"I can't, but we'll let it go for now. There's something else. Tell me everything you know about Mohammed Kurtz."

"Why?"

"George Leonides was talking about him when we were on the grand tour of Joubert's studio. I think Kurtz is involved in art smuggling up to his eyeballs. And I think Joubert knows it."

Chapter Nine

If Rob hadn't been watching her closely, he would have missed her reaction. As it was, she covered it well. But her pupils had dilated, and he had seen her sharp intake of breath. So he was on the right track.

Then she shattered his conviction by laughing again. "What makes you think that? This isn't a plot for one of your novels, you know."

"In Paul's studio there was an old copy of a collector's magazine. Katerina commented on the cover, which showed a well-preserved marble bust thought to be that of Alexander the Great. George said he'd seen one like it on sale in Kurtz's Marseilles gallery. And I happen to know that that piece disappeared years ago, part of a shipment lost en route to the United States. Its whereabouts has never been traced, and it's suspected of having been stolen. So what's it doing in a gallery?"

"It could be a reproduction." She didn't sound convinced.

"It could be, but I'm betting it isn't. These pieces have a habit of resurfacing after enough time has elapsed."

Diana turned away from him and closed her eyes for a moment. That day in Makrino, she had told him only who she was, not what she was doing. He had promised to hold off until she gave him the word, trusting that her reasons for asking for his cooperation were valid ones.

But now that he was in the middle of this mess, it wasn't fair to keep him in the dark, and it could prove dangerous for him, as well. But she couldn't tell him the truth without clearing it with her superior at the EFAC. And that meant a phone call, from a secure phone.

"How would you like to go to Corfu tomorrow?" she asked.

Rob looked startled. "I'd like to. I want to contact my agent. I need more information on a number of people. But I thought you had a lot of work to catch up on."

"It'll have to wait. The main computer is still down, anyway, and Paul will be busy with the film people."

"Yeah. He doesn't appear exactly anxious to give me my interview, so I guess a couple of days won't matter."

Diana rubbed her cold hands over her arms as she paced around the room. "We should go early. Can you be ready at seven?"

"Sure," he replied easily, his hand on the doorknob.

Diana, at the window, paused suddenly. "Rob!" she whispered roughly. "Come here! Quick!"

He reached her in three strides. "There, down in the garden. Is that the person you saw last night?"

He could see a blur of white, between two rows of stately cypresses. "I'm not sure." He grabbed her hand. "Let's go. Maybe between the two of us we can catch her."

They ran out through the still-unlocked dining room door, each of them taking one of the paths that converged near the sundial. Diana felt stones biting through the thin soles of her slippers, and she had a fresh appreciation of what Rob's bare feet must have suffered last evening. Motion-activated lights went on and off as she passed them.

She had reached the last intersecting path before the sundial when she heard Rob hiss her name. "Analise, this way."

The path he followed ended on the edge of a high embankment overlooking the estate's private beach. On the crescent of sand, they could see a figure running. It disappeared around a tumble of boulders that marked the end of the beach, and the edge of Paul's property. Moments later, the low putting sound of a motorboat drifted up from the sea.

"Well, she's gone," Rob said disgustedly.

"You were right." Diana frowned. Were there more strangers on the island than those they'd seen? She didn't like it. Joubert was becoming too unpredictable, and that could spell disaster for her, maybe even Rob.

"What about whoever models for his paintings?" Rob asked. "One of them has a blonde in it."

"These days, Tamara usually models for him. But she's been out all evening, so she can't be your ghost." She shivered, wrapping her arms around her waist. "Let's go in. I'm hardly dressed for traipsing around the garden."

Rob's eyes toured lazily over her satin robe, which gleamed softly in the moonlight. "Unless you're a Gothic heroine."

Casting him an exasperated look, she started back toward the house.

They were entering the dining room door when a car, the battered Skoda of yesterday afternoon, drew up in front of the garage. Tamara got out, saying a quiet goodbye to her companion, who immediately drove off. She hummed tunelessly to herself as she came across the patio with her elegant model's walk.

"Late, aren't you, Tamara?" At the sound of Paul's voice Tamara stopped humming. He stepped out of the shadows near the garage. "Who was that?"

Rob and Diana stood just inside the dining room, watching as Paul grabbed Tamara's arm. "One of the village boys,

I suppose. What did I tell you about getting too cozy with the natives?''

She twisted to free herself, and Diana heard her cry out in pain as Paul tightened his grip. Beside her, Rob muttered something, then stepped forward. "Joubert, were the alarms set during the time you were gone?"

With an angry exclamation, Paul dropped Tamara's arm. "Robert. I thought you'd gone to bed."

"Obviously," Rob drawled.

Tamara swept past Diana and ran down the hall to her room. The slamming of the door echoed through the house.

"And you're up, too, Analise," Paul said in a cold tone as he stepped into the room. He turned to Rob after securing the lock. "To answer your question, no, the alarms weren't set while I was out. Why do you ask?"

"We saw someone in the garden. A woman."

Paul threw back his head and laughed. "A woman in the garden," he said sardonically. "Are you sure it wasn't our resident ghost?"

Rob didn't bother to hide his irritation. "I don't believe in ghosts. In any case, they don't use motorboats."

Paul clapped him on the shoulder. "I wouldn't worry about it, Robert. The alarms are set now. I'll have Petro come and patrol the garden at night. But I'm betting we won't see your ghost again." With another laugh, he headed for his room.

"So Paul told you the island legend," Diana said as she and Rob went in the opposite direction.

"Yeah. In gory detail."

Diana frowned. "He would. Rob, I wouldn't underestimate Paul. He may appear to live on a different plane from the rest of us, but he's sharp and intelligent, and an expert at manipulating people. Be careful how you talk to him." She wanted to warn Rob that they might both be in danger if Paul suspected what she was up to, but she didn't think she could parry any of the questions that would inevitably raise tonight.

Apparently Rob had given up, for the moment. He only asked, "Joubert doesn't mistreat Tamara, does he?"

"You mean physically?"

"Physically or emotionally."

Pausing at her bedroom door, Diana gripped the cool brass doorknob. "I don't think so. He's a bit overprotective, but she seems to come and go as she pleases."

"Does she ever leave the island?"

Did she? Diana tried to remember. "If she does, it's not often."

A thought struck Rob. "Would it have been possible for Tamara to get from that beach to a place where her friend's car could pick her up in that time?"

Diana frowned, thinking of the terrain. She hadn't been paying attention to how long they'd spent in the garden. "I'm not sure. How long were we out there?"

Rob glanced at his watch. "Fifteen, maybe twenty minutes. Maybe ten or twelve since we heard the boat."

"It is possible," Diana said slowly. "It would take about five minutes to get to the public beach by boat, especially since the sea is calm. Then another five to get by car from there to the house. She could have done it. But why?"

Rob shrugged. "Good question." He pushed open the door of his room. "You didn't tell Joubert we're going to Corfu tomorrow."

"I'll tell him now. He won't be asleep yet."

Rob recalled the angry look on Joubert's face as Tamara had made her escape. He wouldn't put it past the man to go after her again. "Want me to come with you?"

Analise's brows lifted. "What for?"

Reluctant to spell out his fears, Rob hedged. "I wouldn't want you to get into an ugly situation."

"Don't worry, Rob. Whatever comes up, I can handle it."

She strode down the hall, the leather soles of her slippers whispering on the tile floor. Passing the deserted study, she topped at Paul's door and knocked.

He opened it almost immediately, his expression going from startled to speculative in an instant. He wore a paisley-patterned silk dressing gown and held the ever-present cigar between his thumb and forefinger. "Analise. To what do I owe this honor?"

"Rob wants to go to Corfu tomorrow. I'd like to go with him, if you don't mind. Do you have any idea when the main computer will be operational again? I'm wasting my time when I can't use it."

"I'll see to it, my dear." He smiled. "Take tomorrow off, and the next day, too, if you want. By then the computer should be working."

"Thank you," she said stiffly. "Good night."

"Good night, Analise."

After he closed the door, she moved farther down the hall, to Tamara's room. She knocked softly, and waited. No sound came from the room but finally, after she had knocked a second time, the door opened.

Tamara stuck her head around the door frame. "Oh, it's you," she said ungraciously. "What do you want?" She spoke in French instead of struggling with her careful English, an indication of emotional upset, in spite of her belligerent tone.

Diana was beginning to feel foolish for having thought the girl might want someone to talk to. In two years she'd never once initiated a conversation with Diana. "I wanted to make sure you were all right," she said, also in French.

"That Paul wasn't beating me or raping me, to establish his possession? As you can see, I'm fine. I don't need you."

She started to close the door, but Diana put her foot in the opening. Suppressing her normal reluctance to get involved, she pushed her way into the room. She wasn't taking any chances on Paul coming out and witnessing the unusual event of her talking to his reclusive protégée.

Tamara backed up. As the light fell on the young woman's face, Diana saw that she was far from fine. Her hair was damp and matted at the temples, and her eyes were red and swollen. Ugly black smears of mascara marked her cheeks.

"You've been crying," Diana said unnecessarily.

"So? I can handle it."

Diana gripped the edge of the door as a wave of sympathy swept over her. Although she was only seven years the girl's senior, she suddenly felt like her mother. *I can handle it.* How many times in the past had she used that phrase to establish her own independence, especially in situations where she did not feel at all confident? And just this evening she'd used it to keep Rob at bay.

"I'm sure you can. But if you need help, come to me. There's no excuse for Paul to browbeat you."

"You don't understand, do you? Paul has given me a home. He takes care of me."

"I understand more than you think. Why did you give up your career? You don't have to be dependent on Paul. You could leave here, go back to your real life. Won't he let you go? Or are you afraid to go back? Why do you stay here?"

"Why do you?" Tamara countered, showing more perceptiveness than Diana had given her credit for.

"I have a job. I'll move on when I'm ready to."

"And so will I," the girl retorted. "Now will you please leave?"

Diana laid her hand gently on Tamara's arm. "Just remember. I'm here if you need someone to talk to."

Jerking free, Tamara opened the door. "I won't. Good night."

ROB WAS STILL STANDING in the hall between their two rooms when Analise returned. She'd been gone so long he'd almost started after her, but he'd restrained himself by telling himself she would only resent his interference. He was going to have to cool it. Pushing her into a corner only increased her resistance, made her emotional walls stronger and thicker.

"It's okay," she said, her tone cool and remote. "I'll see you at seven. If the small motorboat isn't available, we'll get one of the village fishermen to take us over. Good night, Rob."

She was in her room, behind the closed door, before he could respond.

He started to grind his teeth in frustration, but then a slow smile came over his face. The coolness had been a little too pronounced. And she had been careful to keep her eyes somewhere around the third button of his shirt. She didn't trust herself, and she didn't want to trust him.

Well, it was only beginning. They would be together, alone among strangers, for the next two days. He would teach her to trust, and finally to love.

THE DOWN-AT-THE-HEELS charm of Corfu was a welcome sight to Diana as Rob steered the small boat into the harbor. He tied up at the public dock and helped her step ashore. Slinging their two bags over his shoulder, he took her hand in his and steered her across the road to a car-rental office.

"Why do we need a car, when we can do all our business here?" she asked.

"Because I want to try an experiment to see if I can jog my memory. We're going to drive up to Makrino. Maybe that'll bring it all back."

Chapter Ten

Rob had been to Corfu many times, but its pastel colors, contrasting with green foliage under the passionate spill of the Mediterranean sun always struck him anew. Citrus leaves bowed under the weight of heat, and trumpet flowers glowed a phosphorescent orange in the intense light.

It was only midmorning, but the inside of the car was like an oven. He glanced at Analise. She was adjusting her sunglasses for the tenth time in as many minutes. Perspiration beaded her face, and the plastic frames kept slipping down her nose.

Rob drove the little Renault he'd rented with quick efficiency up the twisting mountain byway. The roar of the engine echoed back from the dry rock wall bordering the road, making normal conversation difficult. He'd recognized the muffler's terminal illness as soon as he'd started the car, but since it was the only one available, he'd taken it.

They'd left Pagoni shortly after dawn, taking Paul's small motorboat. Rob had called his agent from the telephone office in Corfu town, asking him to send information on the people who had turned up at Paul's estate, as well as those who had been mentioned as having connections with Paul. "And check out Mohammed Kurtz, the art dealer."

"How soon do you need it?" Sean had asked him.

"Yesterday," Rob had said. "But since that might be difficult, send as much as you can find quickly on the next plane, so I can pick it up at the Ionian tomorrow. Anything you discover after serious digging, give me a call at Pagoni when you send it off so I can come and pick it up."

"Will do." As Rob's agent, Sean was used to urgent requests that had to be transmitted to odd parts of the world. "Why don't I send it straight to Pagoni? It'd save time."

"No, the Ionian's safer."

The phone line had hummed as Sean digested that. "You're not in trouble, are you, Rob? What's going on there?"

"Nothing, at the moment," Rob had assured him. Through the window of the phone cubicle, he'd seen Analise sitting on the hard bench, a notepad in her hand, making a shopping list. He'd frowned. "But something's brewing. I can feel it."

Sean had laughed. "Your famous sixth sense. Just be careful."

"I will, thanks," Rob said, wishing he knew how to protect Analise, as well.

THE CLAMOR OF THE ENGINE assaulted their eardrums as the little car labored up the narrow road leading to Makrino. At the edge of the village, tall cypresses stood guard over a cemetery. Rob steered the Renault into their shade and twisted the ignition key. The engine died with a hoarse cough.

Silence. It came so abruptly that Diana's ears rang. A breeze blew across the heights, carrying the astringent smell of resin to her nostrils.

Rob turned in his seat, resting his arm on the steering wheel. "Analise, I'm sorry about last night."

She stared at him in bewilderment. "Last night?"

"Yes, the way I came barging into your room. The things I said. I had no right to judge you."

"Forget it, Rob. It's not as if it'll matter after you're gone."

"Damn it, I want it to matter. Don't push me away."

She closed her eyes briefly. "Can't you see? I have to."

"You don't have to. You can leave with me."

"No." Her reply was firm, irrevocable.

She pretended a consuming interest in the village architecture as he restarted the car, releasing the clutch with a jerk. Her knuckles pressed against her teeth until her jaw ached, but she welcomed the small pain. What was wrong with her? The more she rebuffed Rob, the sooner he would get the message that she didn't want them to be anything more than friends, that they had only been thrown together temporarily.

The power he had to stir her emotions frightened her. Yet she knew he would never deliberately hurt her, any more than he had wanted to hurt her at the time of their divorce.

Perhaps he had felt betrayed. She knew all about betrayal, something she hadn't understood then. Five years ago, a man she had trusted with her life had almost ended it. Worse, she had loved him. It was the only time she had ever given her heart. And she'd had to suffer the mixture of agony and guilt and grief as she watched him die violently on a desert airstrip.

She'd vowed never to trust again.

And she hadn't, until these past few days. Rob's caring touched her heart, no matter how she strove to deny it. But his love was a luxury she didn't want.

Rob looked over at Analise, seeing the troubled frown that marred the pure lines of her profile. He wished he knew what went on behind those deep blue eyes. He'd always thought blue eyes transparent, easy to read, but hers were as deep as volcanic lakes, giving only hints of darkness beneath their surface.

Pulling into the shade of a massive plane tree in front of a coffee shop, he braked more sharply than necessary. Analise blinked and reached over to unfasten her seat belt. Her face remained impassive. Briefly, insanely, he wondered what she would do if he kissed her, in broad daylight, under the avid gaze of the old men sipping their morning coffee.

He couldn't, of course. Even he had that much regard for social convention.

They got out of the car, stretching tight muscles. The metal of the hood ticked as it cooled, in counterpoint to the click of backgammon pieces as two men at the nearest table moved them across the board. The church bell ponderously tolled the hour.

The coffee shop was dim and cool, with a vague scent of licorice. The hum of voices faltered as the visitors were observed and analyzed, but resumed when Rob stepped up to the counter and placed the order for two iced coffees.

The man nodded, then reached into a cupboard behind him. "*Kyrie,* your books."

"Th-thank you," Rob said, stammering in his surprise. He took the two books, and a flash of light went off in his brain as he touched them. He grabbed the edge of the counter, shaking his head. Cold sweat broke out on his body.

"Rob, are you all right?" Analise's concerned voice seemed to come from a great distance.

It took him a moment to moisten his dry tongue. "I don't know. For a minute there—"

"You remembered something?"

"No. Not really. I don't know what happened."

Outside, the *tavli* players had packed up their game and left. Rob and Analise sat down at the table they'd vacated, pushing empty ouzo and water glasses to one side. He thumbed through the books, pulling several pages of handwritten notes out of one.

Analise watched as he read them over. She seemed nervous, but he dismissed the impression as a reflection of his own tension. "Well?" she asked as he frowned.

"I'm not sure if I remember writing this or not, but since it's my handwriting, I must have."

"What is it? Does it tell you how you came to be in Makrino?"

"It's just general impressions of the village and of the bus ride here." He laid the pages down, tapping his finger on the top one. "'Makrino, eight-o'clock bus. Who left the message?' it says here." He raked his fingers through his hair. "It doesn't tell us anything. The note the waiter gave me also said to catch the eight-o'clock bus to Makrino."

"Would you have gone to meet a stranger about a story without knowing why?"

Rob smiled, a little ruefully. "I'm afraid so. You know what they say about curiosity." His grin faded, and he made a sound of frustration. "We're no further ahead now than before."

He pushed the books aside as the owner of the shop came out with their iced coffee and glasses of water. The man unloaded his tray and reloaded it with the empty dishes from the table before going back inside.

A road-worn Mercedes drew up in the square. The man who got out appeared as dusty as his car. Or perhaps it was just the impression given by his sparse gray hair and his clothes, a beige shirt and faded jeans. He went into the coffee shop and returned moments later with a cold beer. Pulling a chair into the shade, he sat down. He took a long swig from his glass, then closed his eyes, tipping the chair back so that it balanced on two legs against the wall.

Rob sipped his sweet, foamy coffee. "I want to go and look at the accident site. I suppose someone can tell us how to get there."

"That's really why we came up here, isn't it?" Analise said.

He rolled his water glass between his palms. "Yeah, I guess it is. I know the police have closed the case, but I want to see for myself."

They finished their coffee, and Rob went inside to pay. When he came out, Analise was waiting in the car. The Mercedes was gone, and the empty beer bottle was standing next to the chair its driver had occupied.

Following the instructions he had been given in the coffee shop, Rob had no difficulty finding the road that he must have driven the night of the accident.

"Does any of this look familiar?" Analise asked as the little car struggled up the mountain.

He shook his head. "Not a thing."

"Everything looks different in daylight. What about the moon? Was it shining that night?"

"The moon wasn't full until a couple of days ago. There couldn't have been much available light," Rob said, navigating around a particularly large pothole. How had anyone driven up here at night without breaking an axle or puncturing a tire? It was a wonder there weren't more accidents. A little too much speed, a pothole in the wrong place, and a driver could easily lose control of a car.

But *had* it been an accident, or something far more sinister? The question nagged him. *If* the woman had had some connection to Joubert, and *if* she had told him something incriminating about the art collector, how could Joubert have found out so quickly?

And when had his suspicions started? He couldn't remember. Even now, they were nothing more than a gut feeling that something wasn't right.

"Do you suppose Joubert is ever going to give me that interview he promised?"

Diana felt her heart rate speed up. She'd never believed Joubert had extended his invitation to Rob without ulterior motives. "I really don't know," she said honestly. "But why else would he have asked you to come to the island?"

"That's what I've been wondering. I've got a theory, though. Maybe the woman who met me knew something about Joubert. She told me, and Joubert is waiting to see if I'll remember."

Diana swallowed. Now was the time to tell him about the rifleman the night of the car crash, even if she didn't mention her own role in it. But the strict code of ethics she'd sworn to uphold under all circumstances prevented her. She had to consult her superior, if only by phone, but that morning she hadn't had an opportunity. Rob, in his hurry to reach Makrino, had rushed through his own business, giving her no chance to go off by herself.

Now the need to call seemed more urgent than ever. The presence of strangers on Pagoni, out of character for Joubert, made her suspicious. And the stranger in Makrino was driving a Mercedes much like the one that had forced hers off the road that night. He hadn't seemed to be paying them any attention, but that meant nothing.

Or everything.

"Then where is the woman now?" she asked Rob, again playing the devil's advocate.

Rob shrugged fatalistically. "Maybe she's in hiding, scared to come out."

Diana considered, then took a chance. She had to warn him, however obliquely, and make him aware of possible danger. "If it is Joubert, why doesn't he get rid of you now?"

"Probably because if I've another accident the police won't write it off so easily. There would be a thorough investigation. He wouldn't want to risk that. And as long as I can't remember, I'm no danger to him. He wants me where he can keep an eye on me, until he finds out what I know." He took his eyes off the road long enough to fix her with an intent stare. "Am I right, Analise? Is that why he got you to invite me to the island?"

Although his tone revealed nothing deeper than curiosity, the tension of his hands on the steering wheel told her he would not let her dodge the question. "Are you accusing me of luring you under false pretenses?"

"No. I'm asking you."

Evasion wasn't going to work. On the other hand, a counterattack might. "I'm not his slave, but I didn't have a reason to refuse to do as he asked."

"But you had your misgivings, didn't you?"

"Yes." The word was wrung from her.

"That's why you seemed ambivalent. You were so composed, hiding your face, your eyes. You thought they would give you away."

"Does anything ever escape you?" She twisted her fingers in her lap, pleating the edge of her shorts as if she were unhappy with their design. *I didn't blindly obey*, she wanted to scream; *I just did it to protect you. And myself, and the job I have to do.*

"Not much," Rob said grimly. "And I know now that you're not the perfect employee doing her master's bidding. It's an act, isn't it, Analise? You hate Joubert, don't you, although you take pains to hide it from him? Why?"

"Why don't you get yourself out of this while you can, Rob?" she asked wearily. It was getting harder to fight him. She wasn't sure how much longer she could keep it up.

Once Rob knew, he would be throwing himself into the fray, digging into Joubert's life in a way the man would immediately be aware of. And Joubert could have Rob killed, and her, as well.

Rob had only the slightest inkling of the ruthless man Joubert was. "Leave," she repeated. "Forget the story. And leave me alone. I didn't ask for your involvement, and I don't want it."

He made a sound of frustration, and then he downshifted, concentrating on the road. The grinding of the engine in low gear filled the silence. Undefined emotions flitted through the dark corners of Diana's mind. Briefly she allowed herself the luxury of wondering what it would have been like to meet Rob again under normal conditions. She had rarely been aware of her loneliness before he had moved into the room next to hers. Rob, with his clear eyes and clearer mind. Rob, who reminded her she was a woman.

Her disturbing thoughts came to an abrupt halt when he braked at the edge of the road. A cloud of dust slowly settled around the car. "This looks like the place," he said. "That outcropping of rock with the single pine tree growing on it, the oleanders next to it."

Diana unsnapped her seat belt and pushed open the door, glad to be free of the confines of the small car.

Rob stood with his head up, listening. The breeze, sweeping off the scrub-covered hillside, sighed past them. On it rode the pungency of pine. Diana felt the deep loneliness of the place, the isolation. If someone wanted to commit homicide by automobile, this was the perfect spot.

"Analise," Rob said in a whisper. "Do you hear that?"

"What?" The dry leaves of the shrubs clashed faintly against each other. Near her feet, grass rustled as a small animal or lizard went about its business. The breeze died, then quickened. She heard a shrill whistle, and the faraway barking of a dog.

Rob took her arm in his as he started across the road. "Sheep bells. That's what I heard that night. That odd, flat clanking. Sheep bells. There must have been a shepherd nearby who might have seen something."

Trepidation dried her mouth. "Then all we have to do is find him."

Chapter Eleven

"We?" He looked sharply at her, the beginnings of a grin playing around the corners of his mouth.

Diana flushed under his gaze. "Yes, we. I'm as interested as you are in getting to the bottom of this. I want to know what happened here that night." Especially who sent the gunman, she thought.

"Why?" His expression was harsh. "Do you know something you're not telling me?"

"Of course not," she said, as offhandedly as she could.

He was starting to remember. The strange look on his face when he'd picked up his books, and his recollection of the sheep bells, made her sure of it.

She turned away, pretending a consuming interest in the dusty gravel at her feet, searching for tire tracks.

The road surface was pitted with holes, treacherous for walking, never mind driving. It climbed steeply to a tight hairpin curve, then climbed some more, clinging to the side of the pine-cloaked mountain.

Just short of the curve, Rob paused, crouching down to examine the dirt at the edge of the pavement. Although more than ten days had passed, the weather had been dry, and it was at least possible that some traces of the accident remained.

"What do you expect to find after all this time?" Diana asked.

"Broken bushes, scrapes of paint or grease, even tracks. I asked the coffee shop man what the weather was like that night, and he said it was cool, with heavy dew. The ground could have been damp enough to show tire marks."

Where the pavement ended, the ground sloped gradually for the first ten meters, covered in tufts of grass that had turned brown under the relentless heat of the sun. The stony soil felt as hard as cement under Diana's sandals.

The terrain grew more rugged past the grassy section. They followed a narrow goat path down a hillside covered with rock and rough scrub. Thorns caught at Diana's clothes as she scrambled after Rob. Absorbed in sticking to the path, she didn't notice when he stopped suddenly. She careened into him, catching herself by putting a hand on his shoulder.

"Down there." He pointed to a blackened area far below them, at the bottom of a slope so steep it was almost a cliff.

The wind caught at her hair, loosening strands from her braid as she raked her eyes over the area. "I don't see a car."

Taking her arm, Rob pulled her close to his side. "If you look straight past that prickly pear, you can see it."

Her stomach churned sickeningly as she recalled her helplessness that night, the car going off the road, her yelling at Rob to jump after the first impact, the car tumbling over the cliff, and her not knowing where Rob had fallen after she pushed him from the vehicle. Her knees shook.

Rob steadied her with a firm grip on her arm. "Are you all right?" he asked.

Drawing on long experience, she pulled herself together. "Yes, I'm okay." She peered down the mountainside. "Yes, I think I see it. Why didn't they haul it away?"

"Too difficult to tow up this slope. The police checked it over, but they decided to leave it." He let go of her arm, taking a step toward the edge of the bluff. "I'm going down for a closer look. Do you want to wait here?"

"I'll go with you."

Up close, the car was a blackened skeleton of twisted metal. Its doors hung open at crazy angles. Not a centimeter of glass remained in the windows. Fighting nausea, Diana stared at the wreckage in horror. It looked as if it had been destroyed by a bomb blast.

Eyes narrowed, Rob glanced up at the slope they'd just descended. "It exploded up there. You can see the burned shrubbery from here. The force of the explosion must have caused it to roll down here. Those are fresh scrapes on the exposed rocks."

"How did you get out?" Her voice was strangled. "Of course. You don't remember."

"No, damn it. But I must have managed to jump out or been thrown clear before it came to rest down here. The doctor said a passing driver picked me up on the main highway, just over the hill there. I had only superficial burns, probably from spot fires set by burning debris that flew away from the car."

Glass from the windows, shattered into tiny, diamond-faceted pieces, carpeted the ground around the vehicle. The steering wheel lay under a shrub, charred and bent. Drawing closer, they gazed inside. The interior was a hollow shell, covered in black soot, the seats virtually consumed by the conflagration.

Rob stepped back, his face set in grim lines. "It's completely gutted."

"Was it the gas tank?"

"I don't know." Rob frowned skeptically. "Probably. But, contrary to what you see in the movies, gas tanks rarely explode." He scrambled over a mound of rocks to the back of the vehicle. "Yeah, the gas tank exploded, all right, so I guess this was one of those rare occasions."

Diana shuddered, her skin chilled despite the blazing sun. "Isn't that what the police told you?"

"Yeah." He scowled, as if he weren't satisfied. "It's odd, though. The pattern of broken shrubbery up there seemed to indicate that the car came up against a pile of rocks at the edge of the cliff. Which brings up the question, what made it go over after it had come to a stop?"

A twig snapped under his foot, and his face suddenly turned white. He swayed on his feet. Stumbling away from the car, he sank down on a boulder outside the scorched area. Head down, he buried his fingers in his hair, clutching the top of his head.

Diana forgot her determination to remain aloof. Pushing her way through the clawing shrubbery, she sat down at his side. "What is it, Rob?" she whispered. "Did you remember something?"

He lifted his head. His eyes were bleak and empty. "No. No, I didn't. Just for a moment, I thought I did—I thought I heard an explosion. No, more than one." He shook his head. "I don't know."

"Rob..." Her heart lurched in her chest. She didn't know what to say. There *had* been more than one explosion, and she'd crouched in the bushes, not knowing if Rob was safe or not. She moved closer to him, clasping his hand tightly in hers, willing comfort to him. For the first time, she allowed herself to care about him.

He turned his hand so that he held hers. "Analise, I don't believe this was an accident." He closed his eyes briefly. His upper and lower lashes meshed, giving him a look of vulnerability that made her want to cradle his head against her breast.

When he opened his eyes, they were clear, hard, glittering with suppressed anger. "The car didn't go over this cliff by itself. I think someone deliberately ran me off the road."

Diana swallowed, a chill gripping her heart. "Joubert? It seems farfetched. He invited you to the island. He could have refused you the interview."

"Don't forget, he didn't invite me until after the accident. And you say he knew of the amnesia. No, I still think there's something to my theory that he's waiting to see if I remember anything."

Diana pinched the bridge of her nose, pushing her sunglasses high on the top of her head. That thought had occurred to her, too, along with the possibility that Rob had been the target in the accident. It could be Rob who had been followed to Makrino. Riding on the bus, unsuspecting, he wouldn't have noticed a car keeping pace. "I'm not sure it's wise for you to go back to Pagoni," she said slowly. Not that she was at all sure he was safe anywhere else.

His mouth thinned to a grim line. "Are you going back?"

"Of course. I have no choice."

"Then I'm going with you." His expression softened as he got up and held his hand out to her. "Analise, don't say you have no choice. There's always a choice."

In silence they returned to the boxy little Renault waiting on the road. Rob started the engine and turned the car, heading back to the village. His knuckles were white as he held the steering wheel, and his body was tense. "If only I could remember. I thought seeing the place where it happened..."

Diana heard the frustration in his voice. She wished she could help, but what could she say? Turning her head, she studied the valley they were leaving behind. On a barren ridge to their right, light flashed on some shiny object. A broken bottle, probably. People threw them out of cars all the time, creating fire hazards when the sun reflected through the bottles' magnifying bottoms.

Or binoculars. Her mind flashed back to the man in the Mercedes who had stopped in the village. Well, if he'd been watching them, he would have nothing to report. No dramatic revelations had occurred, no miraculous restoration of Rob's lost day.

"Do you suppose it would help if you saw it at night?" she asked hesitantly. "After all, it was dark when the accident happened."

"Maybe." He scowled blackly. "You don't mind if we stay?"

She shrugged. "Of course not. If there's a room we can rent." Even as she said the words, an indefinable emotion shivered through her. There was a room over the coffee shop, sometimes rented to visitors. One room. They would have to share.

Last time she'd stayed with a relative of Nick's. He was away at the moment. Fortunately. It would never do for Rob to find out she knew anyone in the village.

A harsh roar enveloped them as a gray Mercedes rushed by, overtaking them on the last hill before the village. Rob glared at its taillights, which flashed only briefly as it crested the hill. "Damn idiot."

"Wasn't that the car that stopped while we were drinking coffee?" Diana asked, her smile evaporating as a knot clenched in her stomach.

"Sure looks like it," Rob said. "Has he been following us?"

"I wouldn't be surprised. In fact, down at the crash site, I think he was watching us with binoculars." She'd considered keeping that suspicion to herself, but she'd decided it was better if Rob knew and was on his guard.

He stared at her in angry disbelief. "Why didn't you tell me sooner? Is he Joubert's man?"

"I don't know. I've never seen him before." She chewed her lower lip. "I don't like this. First Petro appears out of nowhere, and now this. But I don't understand. If Paul wanted to keep an eye on you, or on both of us, why wouldn't he just keep us on the island? He could have found some reason for us not to leave—a disabled boat, or too much work for me. But he didn't even blink when I said we were going."

"There's a saying that if you give someone enough rope, they'll hang themselves. Maybe he's just waiting to see what we find out and figures we'll come back no matter what because I won't give up the chance to interview him."

This case was taking turns Diana had not expected. Dread formed a hollow where her stomach had been. "Playing a game," she whispered. "That would give him pleasure." She schooled her expression, willing herself to appear unmoved.

"What did you say?" Rob said sharply. But at that moment the car hit a pothole in the road, and its strained exhaust system backfired, the loud report sounding like a rifle shot. Rob cursed and tightened his hands on the steering wheel as he cruised down to the village square.

There was no sign of the Mercedes, only the usual collection of small, dusty sedans and Japanese pickups. Rob parked the Renault near the plane tree in front of the coffee shop, getting out and banging the door shut. "First some lunch," he said as Diana got out the other side. "And then we're going to look for a shepherd. Somebody must have seen the accident, and I'm going to find out who."

HIS QUESTIONS in the coffee shop as they waited for their lunch of eggs and salad to be prepared were met with blank looks and shrugs. Yes, several of the villagers had flocks. They would have been in the hills overnight. No one remembered who had been in that part of the countryside that particular night.

"They're protecting somebody. I know it." Rob slammed his fist against the unyielding concrete-block wall of the room they had been given over the coffee shop. Disgruntled and out of sorts, he sat down on one of the twin beds that comprised the major furnishings of the cramped room. The air was stifling, the heat unrelieved by even a suggestion of a breeze from the open window.

Diana lay down on her own bed. She had taken a shower in the primitive bathroom, and wore only an oversize cotton T-shirt that covered her from neck to midthigh.

Any awkwardness that might have come up between them over sharing a room had died a quick death. Rob, angry at his lack of progress in either recovering his memory or eliciting information from the villagers, had shown no interest in her, except as a sounding board.

Somewhere over the mountains, thunder rumbled. She turned her head, staring at the blue patch of sky visible from the window. There were no clouds as yet, but they were coming. She lifted her arm to cover her eyes, letting Rob's angry tirade wash over her. It would be better if he got it out of his system.

Her limbs felt heavy and languid in the heat. Her eyelids drooped as sleep began to overcome her.

"Are you listening, Analise?" He was suddenly standing over her. "Or are you asleep?"

She struggled up from the soft haze enveloping her. "I'm asleep."

"You haven't heard a word I said."

"Mmm . . . Does it matter?"

"No." He laughed shortly. "No. Go to sleep."

His voice faded.

She dreamed of men fighting, guns firing in sharp, staccato bursts, fires and bursting shells. She woke, shaking, wet with the sweat of terror. The Middle East. Antonio's betrayal and violent death.

The nightmare was one she'd had before, although rarely in daytime. The oppressive heat and weariness were responsible, no doubt. Focusing on the ordinariness of the shabby room, she pushed it to the back of her mind and willed her racing heart to slow.

The slant of the light told her it was late afternoon. Rob slept on the other bed, his chest naked above the white sheet around his waist. His face wore a troubled frown, as if his dreams, too, were unpleasant. She gazed across at him, a peculiar ache blossoming in her chest. She should be more forceful in her warnings, tell him to run, forget Joubert, forget her. But she knew he wouldn't listen, not unless she ran with him.

For a startling instant, she was tempted. Give up her job, make some excuse to get out. They would understand her reluctance to involve Rob, the strain on her because of their previous association.

She sighed. She couldn't quit now. But as soon as they got back to Corfu town, she had to make the phone call, get clearance to enlighten Rob, give him the chance to protect himself in case she couldn't keep him safe.

Chapter Twelve

The vicious snarl of thunder woke Rob. Lightning forked across the sky, turning the room a lurid blue. Thunder erupted once more, with a bang like an exploding mortar shell. He burrowed his head under the pillow. The room was still hot, close and airless. His body clung to the sheets, sticky with sweat.

Rain began to drum on the tin roof of a storage shed next to the building, and the dark room was soon filled with the fragrance of parched earth drinking in moisture. As if dampened by the downpour, the lightning flashed dimly, followed by a more distant rumble of thunder.

Another sound entered Rob's consciousness, barely audible above the sluicing of water from the roof. He sat up, listening. It came again, a low whimpering, definitely in the room.

Analise. Having a bad dream? In the flare of dying lightning he could see her, hunched in a fetal position under the sheet. She cried out again, and curled in on herself more tightly.

Rob crossed the room in two strides, dropping down to kneel beside the bed. "Analise." His hand hovered over her shoulder. He hesitated to touch her, for fear of frightening her further. "Analise, wake up. It's only a dream."

She jerked as if scalded. "No, don't!" In a single movement, she flung herself away from him. She huddled in the corner against the wall, one arm wrapped around her raised knees, the other extended as if to ward off a blow.

"Analise, it's Rob. I won't hurt you." He took hold of the outthrust hand, startled to find that it was icy. Sitting on the edge of the bed, he gently drew her nearer.

At first she resisted, but then, all at once, she threw herself into his arms. "Oh, Rob, they were trying to kill me."

Her body lay against his, warm and pliant. The astringency of sweat was barely noticeable under the scent of gardenia that emanated from her skin. Desire slammed through him. He wanted to lie down beside her, hold her, love her. He wanted to protect her from the demons that terrified her.

"It's all right now. I'm here." He kept his voice low and even, soothing her as he would comfort a child. Only she didn't feel like a child in his arms.

He stroked his hand up and down her back. The T-shirt she wore was soft and thin. He could feel the individual bones of her spine through the cloth, and the shivers she tried to suppress.

"It's so dark." Her voice was low, a bare thread of sound.

"I can put on the light," he said.

"No, no—in my dream. It's so dark and so cold, and I can hear feet, heavy footsteps. They're looking for me, and I'm hiding."

"Do they find you?" Rob asked, instinct telling him the best way to defuse a nightmare was to discuss it.

"I don't think so. I always wake up."

"You've had it before, then?"

"Many times. All my life." She sighed, her breath warm on his skin.

A nebulous memory stirred in him, as if he'd lived this scene before. Diana. Yes, that was it. The first night he'd spent with Diana, she'd awakened from a nightmare, one she refused to discuss. Instead, she had kissed him, and under her spell, he'd made love to her. In the morning, the episode had been forgotten.

Why did he recall it now? "Did you ever talk to anyone about it?"

She stiffened, as if she were about to pull away. "Who would I talk to? And what good would it do? It's all in the past. It doesn't matter anymore."

"Doesn't it?" Rob said, holding her firmly enough that she couldn't put a distance between them, yet not so tightly as to be threatening. "I think it matters a great deal. If it doesn't allow you to trust. Or to be happy."

Her hand clenched into a fist. All her muscles tensed.

"Easy, Analise," he murmured. "Be easy. I won't hurt you."

"Then don't criticize the way I live. It suits me."

"Because you think there's no other way. I can show you how much your life would change, how rich it would become, if you'll let me."

This time she succeeded in freeing herself, her eyes flashing in the light of the waning moon, which had emerged from behind the clouds. She sat back against the wall, as far from him as she could get. "That's what all men say. Until they get what they want."

"What do they want?" Rob wasn't sure whether to be amused or hurt by her scornful tone.

"Someone to wait for them. To be there whenever they decide to return home from their adventures."

He allowed himself a grin, not sure if she could see him in the dark. When he spoke again, his amusement was evident in his voice. "Did that happen to you? Tell me his name, and I'll have a talk with him about how to treat a woman."

Instead of laughing, she winced. To his horror, her eyes shimmered with sudden tears. One rolled down her cheek, glistening in the dimness. "Forget it, Rob. It's over and done with."

"Are you sure?" Slowly extending his hand, he wiped the tear away with his fingertip, then laid his palm gently on her cheek. "Analise, I wouldn't leave you, not if I gave you my word."

"I would have to leave you," she said sadly. "Rob, can't you see? There's no future for us. You don't even know who I am."

She sounded so forlorn and lost that Rob felt his own eyes prickling. "Analise, I can see *what* you are—a determined, independent woman. It doesn't matter *who* you are."

"I don't want to talk about it anymore. What time is it?"

A ploy to get him off her bed? Shrugging, Rob crossed to his own bed and checked his watch, which he'd laid on the chair that also held his clothes. "Just after midnight. There's still time to sleep before we leave. Or, if you want, I'll go by myself. I can pick you up later."

"No. I want to go with you." She settled back on the thin mattress, putting the sheet up around her shoulders. "Good night."

"Good night, Analise."

On his own bed again, he lay awake, mulling over their conversation and her unsatisfactory answers to his questions. *Analise, I would cherish you,* he thought, *I would love you.*

He fell eventually into a troubled sleep, painfully aware of her, so near to him in body, yet so far in spirit. Her essential loneliness seemed to permeate the space between them.

The shrill beeping of his watch alarm broke into a dream in which he and Analise were sitting on a tropical beach with improbably bright flowers around them. Groaning, he rolled over and punched it into silence, then strapped the watch to his wrist.

He walked over to Analise and touched her shoulder. "Analise, it's time to go."

She was instantly alert, as if she, too, hadn't been deeply asleep. Her hair was tangled from her restless night, and her face was a pale blur in the predawn darkness. "I'm awake." Her voice was husky, a little tremulous.

He wanted to hold her against him, to reassure her that nothing in her past, known or unknown, would shock him or make him turn away from her. But now was hardly the time. Instead, he said, "I'm going to take a quick shower. Would you pack our things?"

He turned toward the bathroom, quickly removing himself from temptation.

While he dressed, she showered. When she came out of the bathroom, she was in the same shorts as yesterday but wearing a fresh, if wrinkled, shirt. He picked up their bags, and they left the room.

ROB WAS SILENT as they drove out of the village. Glancing at his shuttered face, Diana wondered what he was thinking. Most likely cursing her for being neurotic and keeping him awake.

She cleared her throat. "Rob, I'm sorry I disturbed your sleep," she said stiffly.

"What's to be sorry for? You couldn't help it."

No, she couldn't. That didn't lessen her embarrassment, or her feeling of vulnerability. Once again she had revealed to him a part of herself that no one knew about.

"What are you afraid of—that you spoiled your image of self-sufficiency?" Rob added, cutting straight to the bone. "Don't worry. I won't use it against you."

Although his tone was brusque, it served to restore the balance between them.

"Thank you," she whispered. Only a niggling feeling of unease remained. What if he was right about her, that she hugged her loneliness like a security blanket?

"Are we coming back this way?" she asked, trying to shut off her thoughts.

Beyond the reach of the headlights, the road was dark, dawn not yet a glimmer on the horizon. The crescent moon, frequently obscured by scudding clouds, cast little light. "I don't think so," Rob said at last. "Nobody in town seems to know anything."

"Is it possible they're afraid?" Diana asked, chewing fretfully on her lower lip. The night of the crash might have been blocked out of Rob's memory, but it was all too clear in hers. The sudden, piercing beams of light, and the first shocking bump of the other car against the Peugeot. She had valiantly fought to keep it on the road, but once her wheels hit the gravel she'd lost control, and all her evasive-driving training couldn't save them. She'd yelled at Rob to jump. She'd abandoned the lurching car only when she'd seen that he was clear.

"If they're frightened," she said, "that must mean someone saw something that night." She glanced back nervously, as she had half a dozen times since they'd left the village. No lights appeared behind them.

"It doesn't matter why we think they're not talking," Rob said gloomily. "This has been a waste of time."

"Unless your memory comes back now."

"Yeah."

Silhouettes of the mountains were becoming visible against the sky by the time they reached the crash site. Rob got out of the car, gesturing for Diana to wait for him. She leaned across and rolled down the window on the driver's side. "You'll be careful, won't you?"

"I'm not clambering down to the wreck, if that's what you're worried about."

He moved around the car, out of her line of vision. It was still too dark for her to chart his progress. Diana kept her eyes on the formidable bulk of the mountain ahead, counting the minutes ticking away. The pungent scent of thyme drifted into the car, another detail she remembered from that night, when she'd found herself entangled in a thorny shrub, disoriented and with a lump on her head. By the time she'd extricated herself, the shepherd had picked up Rob and was carrying him up an ill-defined path to the highway.

She felt tired and dispirited. Nightmares aside, she hadn't slept soundly at all. Seeing the burned-out car had brought back memories of other horrors she had seen or lived through. With them came a chill of foreboding, a premonition of danger both for herself and for Rob, who wouldn't be involved in this if not for her.

The sky lightened, turning pearl gray. A bank of clouds sat on the eastern horizon, the tattered edges trimmed with gold as the sun rose behind them.

She was thinking of going to see what was keeping Rob when a voice spoke next to the open window. "Is there a problem, miss? Trouble with your car?"

The man, stocky and gray-haired, held a shepherd's staff with an intricately carved crook at its end. His black dog eyed her curiously, its pink tongue lolling. Apparently deciding she was harmless, it flopped down and settled its nose on its paws.

"Are you all right?" the shepherd asked, a note of anxiety entering his deep voice.

"I'm fine," she said, forcing a smile. "I'm waiting for someone."

"A bad car crash took place here not long ago. Perhaps it isn't safe."

Before Diana could form a response to that, the dog jumped up and barked. "Your friend is coming," the shepherd said. "I must get back to the flock." He touched his temple in a kind of salute. "Go with God."

Diana turned in the seat and saw Rob coming up behind the car. He paused and spoke with the shepherd. To her frustration, they were slightly too far away for her to hear the conversation. She was about to get out of the car when the shepherd again raised his stick in farewell and turned toward his sheep, shouting at a stray that had wandered onto the road.

Rob looked oddly triumphant as he got in behind the wheel. Setting the car into motion, he tipped his head in the direction of the flock, which was scrambling down to more verdant pastures as the shepherd whistled and shouted to guide them. "That shepherd gave me a lead. There was someone else here that night."

Diana's heart lurched in her chest. Here it comes, she thought. He knows.

But when he spoke again, it wasn't what she expected. "He told me the name of a shepherd who was here that night. Apparently he picked me up and carried me to the road."

She dared to breathe again. "Oh?"

Rob shot her an odd look, evidently wondering at her tepid response. "Yes. His name is Thomas. I want to thank him, but apparently he's taken a flock up into the mountains."

Disaster averted, Diana thought with a surreptitious sigh of relief. Her secret was still intact, and likely to remain so for a while longer.

"However," Rob continued, his eyes on the road, "his brother, Elias, owns a nightclub in Corfu town. He should know where I can get hold of Thomas."

Rob DIDN'T REALIZE what he was getting into, Diana thought for the tenth time as they tramped around Corfu late that evening. If only he would leave it alone. But no, that stubborn streak of his was out in full force. He wouldn't give up until he'd tracked down this Elias and spoken to him in person.

Diana could only gamble that Thomas hadn't talked. She couldn't think of any plausible way to divert Rob from his quest. In the meantime, she was going to stick with him every minute, and try to keep him out of trouble.

"San Rocco Square," she muttered, to distract herself. "I wonder who Saint Rocco was."

"Italian, probably," Rob said. "Plenty of Italian influence in the architecture too."

The main street of the district where the nightclubs were located was tree-lined. More modern than the old town, the shops displayed goods of a cosmopolitan flavor, with little evidence of gimcrack tourist junk.

The desk clerk at the Ionian had given Rob only a vague idea of where to find Elias. "Ask around the district," he'd said. "Someone will direct you." So far, those directions had petered out in dead ends, like so many of the streets they wandered down. Finally, they came up against the bulk of Lofos Avrami, a sizable rocky hill that seemed to have been dropped in the center of the town.

Diana stepped under a streetlight, squinting at the map she carried. "I think it's the next one over."

The nightclub was dimly lit, with strident rock music and cigarette smoke rolling out of the open door. On the step a young man gave a running commentary of the attractions inside. "Food. Drinks. Belly dancers. Music."

"The probability of deafness," Rob said, his mouth against Diana's ear.

She laughed.

Rob addressed the young man in a firm voice, cutting his advertising patter off in midstream. "We'd like to see Elias."

"He's not here tonight. He's over at his other club, on the coast."

Rob swore softly. "When will he be back?"

The man shrugged. "Who knows? When the weather's hot like this, he usually stays for a while. It's not far, about an hour out of town." He glanced at his watch. "The place will just be coming to life by the time you get there."

"Thanks."

"Are we going?" Diana asked fatalistically. Knowing Rob, they were.

"We're going," Rob said shortly, unable to hide his frustration. He paused in front of a souvlaki booth that was spewing blue smoke into the street. "Are you hungry? We can get something to eat here."

They continued down the street toward the hotel, eating fresh bread and chunks of meat on bamboo skewers as they walked. A passenger jet roared off into the night sky overhead. "Noisy place to live," Rob commented. "It's right on the flight path from the airport."

Wing lights blinked as another plane descended in preparation for landing. A man jostled Diana, and she stumbled, almost losing her footing. She stared at him as he rushed by. "I wonder why he's in such a hurry. Everyone else is just strolling along."

Rob followed the man's progress until he turned the corner at the end of the block. "Business or pleasure—could be either." Suddenly he stiffened, senses alert. Leaning close to Diana, he murmured, "When we start walking again, look back without being obvious about it. I think I just saw that fellow who was in Makrino yesterday."

The souvlaki skewer snapped between Diana's fingers. Working at controlling her tension, she dropped it into a waste bin, making a production of extracting a tissue from her purse and cleaning her hands. Yes, that was the man, nondescript in a black shirt and black pants, staring into a shop window. She almost laughed when she read the sign installed at right angles to the door. Helena's Boutique. It specialized in silk lingerie.

Her amusement disappeared as anger took over. "Do you think he's been following us?"

"Probably," Rob said. "Let's give it a test, shall we?"

They weaved through the streets in an apparently aimless path. The man stayed behind them, mimicking every turn they made.

"Let's ditch him."

On the slopes of the hill, they ducked through an open garden gate. A convenient break in a chain-link fence brought them to a path leading across a vacant lot. Several tourists were coming down from the lookout point near the top, and they joined them, emerging on the harbor side. From there it was only a short walk back to the Ionian.

Before going to the parking lot, Rob ran inside to find out if the package he was waiting for had arrived from his agent. "Not yet. Probably tomorrow morning," the desk clerk informed him.

THE SEASIDE VILLAGE teemed with people, mainly young British vacationers. Its atmospherc was lively and prosperous. It could have held its own against any of the popular Mediterranean sun spots.

Rob had kept an eye on the rearview mirror during the drive, purposely keeping his speed low. Although his caution had earned him rude gestures and ruder comments from the motorists who overtook him, he was sure they hadn't been followed.

After parking the car, he locked it and pocketed the keys. He tucked Analise's hand in the crook of his elbow, keeping her close to his side as they pushed their way through the noisy, laughing crowd. "There it is," Rob said suddenly. "The Pink Elephant Pub."

Inside, the smoke was as thick as fog, and the noise level was stentorian. A small band played wild bouzouki music. The crowd, which appeared to be about twice the size the room was meant to hold, danced and sang along, gyrating madly as the tempo reached a crescendo.

Elbowing a path to the bar, Rob shouted to be heard. "I'm here to see Elias."

The bartender flicked his thumb at a man standing in the shadows behind him. The man, dressed in a wrinkled white linen suit, plucked a cigar out of his mouth and came forward, dangling it between his thumb and forefinger. "Can I help you?"

"Maybe," Rob said laconically, "if you're Elias."

"I am. And who might you be?"

"Robert Minardos."

Elias's eyes narrowed above his beefy cheeks. He put the cigar between his teeth and drew deeply on it, blowing a vile-smelling smoke that swirled upward to add to the thick air in the room. "The journalist. I trust you've recovered from your accident?" His tone conveyed supreme indifference.

"I'm looking for your brother. Thomas is his name, I think."

Elias laughed. "What do you want with him? All he understands is looking after sheep."

In Makrino, Rob had been honest and up-front about wanting to know more details of the accident. But confronted with Elias, he decided a little deviousness might be in order. "I'd like to talk to him, to get some local color for an article I'm working on."

"About sheep and goats? Who would be interested in that?"

"A travel magazine," Rob said, undaunted. "Back-to-nature is in style, haven't you heard?"

The man laughed again. "Not here. Here we all want to get away from nature and into the city. I'm afraid I can't tell you where Thomas is, not within fifty square kilometers, at any rate. He took a flock into the high hills, as he does every summer. Won't be back for weeks.''

Rob fought to hide his disappointment. He knew looking for one shepherd in acres of unfamiliar mountains would be hopeless. ''I guess I'll have to talk to someone else,'' he said, going on with the fiction of an interview.

''Good idea,'' Elias said, puffing on the cigar. ''You won't get much from Thomas anyway. He's—what do you call it?—simpleminded.'' He gestured with his arm. ''Stay and have a drink. On the house.''

''No thanks,'' Rob said. ''I'm driving.''

He and Diana forced their way out again, gulping in great breaths of fresh air once they reached the street.

''Well, that's that, I guess,'' Rob said, in a discouraged tone.

Diana tucked her hand through his elbow. ''At least we tried.'' And she was still safe, her identity still secure.

THE ROAD BACK to Corfu town wound through olive groves. In places the gnarled trunks grew almost on the roadbed, making each curve an adventure, especially since oncoming cars were invisible until one was virtually on top of them. Flashes of headlights through the trees were of little help, since the network of roadway was as convoluted as yarn tangled by a cat's paws.

Fortunately, the traffic was light. Those going to the outlying villages and resorts were already there, and few of the revelers in the local night spots left until the small hours of the morning.

''We're not in sync with the rest of the population,'' Rob said wryly as a young man in a passing car waved an open bottle of wine out the window, offering to share it.

He was downshifting to negotiate a particularly tight curve when a loud bang came from under the car. ''There goes the exhaust system.'' Diana hunched down in her seat and covered her ears with her hands.

A second bang reverberated off the hillside next to the road. The car swerved sharply to the left, and she realized it wasn't the muffler. Rob fought to keep the little vehicle on the road, at the same time applying gentle pressure to the brake.

Despite his efforts, the car lurched to the right, skidding in loose sand at the edge of the pavement. ''Cover your face!'' Rob yelled, desperately swinging the wheel around. With a sickening crunch, the car came to a stop, the fender crushed against the massive trunk of an olive tree.

Chapter Thirteen

Agony shot through Rob's head, and it took him a moment to realize that he hadn't thumped it against the windshield. He closed his eyes, willing the pain to subside. Whirling stars spun in his mind, heat seared his lungs, and then he had the sensation of being carried. An odor, musty and strong, filled his nostrils, and he could feel the roughness of wool under his cheek.

The impression began to fade. "No!" he cried. "Come back."

Darkness. Dense and soundless. He must have blacked out for an instant. The next thing he knew, Analise was tugging at his shoulder. "Rob, are you all right?"

"Damn it. It was so close, almost real, just for a moment."

"You remembered!" she exclaimed incredulously.

He grimaced. "Not enough." He looked at Analise in the red glow from the dash. "Are you hurt?"

"No, I'm okay, thanks to the seat belt. What happened? Did we have a puncture?"

"Felt like it. Let's see if this thing will go." He turned the ignition key to restart the stalled car. It cranked over smoothly, the engine beginning to purr without any sign of temperament. Hearing it, Rob scowled. "Those bangs certainly weren't the exhaust system. Must've been a tire blowing.''

Shifting into reverse, he backed the car up, steering it into a clear place between the trees, well off the road. ''Tire's flat, all right,'' he muttered. ''I wonder what the spare looks like. Or even if there is one.''

As he had expected, the spare was bald, but, fortunately, it *was* filled with air. He changed tires in short order, slinging the flat into the trunk.

ROB HAD TO RING THE BELL several times to arouse the night clerk at the Ionian. The man stumbled out of the back room, buttoning his shirt with one hand and rubbing his eyes with the other. ''I don't know if we have anything available. Tourist season, you know.'' His voice was husky with sleep.

Turning his head, Rob met Analise's eyes. Her face was pale and drawn and he saw that she was beginning to tremble. He raised one brow. She nodded.

''One room will do,'' he said to the desk clerk.

The room, obviously intended for a family with a child, contained a double bed and a cot.

''I'll take the cot,'' Analise said. ''You'd never fit.''

We'd both fit in the bed. Like heat lightning, the thought flared through Rob's mind.

We'd both fit in the bed, Diana thought, trying vainly to dredge up concrete reasons why she shouldn't make love with him. She lifted her eyes to his, and saw the tenderness in his face. He held out his hand. Hesitantly she placed hers in it.

''We were lucky we weren't hurt when the car went off the road,'' she said, buying time. Her voice was strangely breathless. ''And lucky the spare was in the car.''

Rob put his forefinger against her lips. ''Please, Analise. Nothing will happen unless you want it. I'm not taking your agreeing to share a room as an invitation to your bed. But I do want you. I can't think of any reason why I should deny that."

He held her against him, and she parted her lips for his kiss. At the first touch of his mouth on hers, she knew that, at least for her, the past was gone. This was not the sometimes hesitant young man who had loved her gently and stoically accepted her request for a divorce.

This new Rob was dynamic, powerfully male, tender yet sure of himself as he unbuttoned her shirt. She shivered as he molded one hand around her naked breast, lowering his head to suckle the nipple. A liquid fire danced through her, pooling in her abdomen, and she moaned softly.

"Yes, Analise... Yes..." he murmured. He pulled off her shorts and laid her gently back on the bed, his mouth warm and soft on her skin.

When she lay quivering and boneless beneath him, he stripped off his own clothes. She watched him, looking for changes, finding that he had become more muscular in his chest and shoulders but his stomach was still hard and lean. When he reached into the pocket of the jeans he had tossed on the floor, she grasped his hand. "That won't be necessary, Rob. I won't get pregnant."

In her line of work, she couldn't take the chance that her cover might be blown and that the object of an investigation might exact the most elemental revenge. She always took precautions.

The haze of desire cleared momentarily from Rob's eyes as he glanced at her sharply, but then she touched him, and he came down beside her, joining his body to hers.

DIANA WOKE from a light doze to find him standing at the window. He hadn't dressed, and tension was evident in the hard lines of his body, outlined by the illuminated hotel sign just outside their room. He lifted a hand to rub the back of his neck, and turned, switching on the bedside lamp.

His eyes were troubled as they fell on her. "Have we met before, Analise?" he asked.

Her mouth felt as if she'd swallowed cotton wool. "No," she whispered. "Why?"

He shook his head as he lay down beside her. "I just had the oddest feeling—that this wasn't the first time we made love." He shrugged, and bent his head to cover her mouth with his. "Must be this memory loss, mixing me up."

A chill of dread chased over her skin. When he found out the truth—

Shutting out the thought, she submerged herself in the sensations he was arousing in her. The past and the future faded to nothing in the face of the overwhelming present.

SUNLIGHT STREAMED into the room. Diana buried her head under the pillow, closing her eyes against the glare. She groaned as she felt twinges of discomfort in various parts of her body.

Abruptly she sat up. Memory of the night before flooded back. Rob? He was gone, as were his clothes. The bed sheets next to her were cold.

She groped for her watch among her own scattered clothes, gasping as she read the time. He'd probably gone to have the tire repaired before returning the car to the rental agency. And he could be back at any moment. She hadn't much time to make the call to her Paris office.

She was halfway through her breakfast when Rob joined her in the hotel garden. He banged his tray, loaded with juice, fruit and bread, down on the table. With a sinking feeling, she saw his anger and knew she was the object of it.

"I think it's time you leveled with me," he said tightly, bread crumbling as he plastered it with cold butter.

She was glad she'd finished her own food. As it was, it sat like a hard, indigestible lump in her stomach. "What do you mean?"

"You know something. And I want you to tell me."

She compressed her lips, stirring sugar grimly into her coffee before adding hot milk from a pitcher. She had official sanction to tell him the bare details of her case. But when he was in this volatile mood, there was no telling how he would react. "What brought on this interrogation? I don't like it."

He glared at her. "I took the tire in for repair. It was punctured, all right. By a bullet."

Diana felt the blood drain out of her face. This she hadn't expected, not even after the accident with her own car. Especially after that. She hadn't thought they would risk a police investigation. Whoever *they* were. "A bullet?"

"Yes. Those bangs we heard—they were shots. Someone wanted to scare us. At the very least." He paused. "I want to know what's going on. Did Joubert make a deal with you to be my watchdog?"

Diana took a deep breath. "All right, I'll tell you. I'm investigating Paul Joubert for art smuggling."

Stunned, Rob stared at her. Clearly this was not what he'd thought she would say. He swallowed audibly, shaking his head. "Lady, you have got to be out of your mind. You could get killed."

She tilted her chin up. "Your opinion."

Rob pushed his plate to the middle of the table, his appetite gone. "Do you realize what Joubert is, what he can do to you?"

"Naturally I do. But I'm not alone. I work for an organization called the European Fine Arts Commission. All I have to do is make a phone call and Joubert would be under arrest. But it would be only a minor charge, such as possession of a protected art object. We want to catch him in the act of smuggling. And we're so close now that I can't let you jeopardize the work I've done. So you have a choice. You can leave now, or you can come back to the island and get the story of your life. I'd rather you left, but—" she shrugged fatalistically "—I've a feeling you won't listen to me. All I ask is that you don't stir things up, and that you stay out of my way."

Rob clenched his fist on the table. His knuckles were white. "Generous of you." A nerve ticked at the corner of his eye. "Did I stumble into this, or was it planned?"

For a long moment, she was silent, considering whether she should tell him everything, including her own identity. No, it was too risky. It would be too easy for him to make a slip. Not to mention that protective urge of his. He would be watching over her every moment, getting in the way. She couldn't work like that. "I suppose one could say you're the wild card. And I did try to warn you."

"Yeah," he said wearily. "You did. But to take on someone like Joubert . . ."

"I do this for a living, remember. Somebody has to. It's time he was stopped." Her voice rose as her anger hardened into determination. "Sitting there on his island, like a toad in a pond. Surrounded by luxury and the art treasures that belong to the world."

Rob took her hand in his. "Analise," he said gently, "it's okay. I understand."

She smiled, a little sheepishly. "I'm sorry."

He squeezed her fingers. "But I still say you're crazy."

"Maybe I am."

He let go of her hand and drummed his fingers on the table. Sunlight filtering through the grapevines overhead cast a dappled pattern of shadows on the table. Birds chattered and cooed in the high surrounding hedge. A scene of tranquillity, completely at odds with the danger that Analise's plans promised.

It didn't even cross Rob's mind to let her go back to Pagoni alone. Whether it was some long-buried chivalrous instinct, or just his own taste for adventure and the lure of the story, he wasn't sure. But abandoning her now was unthinkable. "I'm going with you."

Abruptly he got up, went to the buffet table and poured himself another coffee. He sat down again, added sugar and drank deeply. The caffeine hit his empty stomach with a jolt he felt through his whole body.

He suddenly realized Analise hadn't moved or said a word. "Well?" he said brusquely, wondering if her insanity was contagious. "Nothing to say? Not even 'Thank you. I'm so glad there's another person in the world who is reckless enough to take on Joubert?'"

"You don't understand, do you? I'm a trained professional. You're not."

He scrubbed his hand across his chin. "And you enjoy getting shot at and crashing up cars? It's enough to scare off most men."

"Are you implying that I shouldn't be in this business because I'm a woman?" she said, exasperated. She'd been right to follow her instincts and continue to conceal her identity. Endearing as his chivalrousness was, it could get both of them killed. "I've been shot at only a couple of times in eight years. I don't even carry a gun. And women are good at this kind of work, probably because most criminals are men and they tend to think of us in the usual stereotypes."

Rob put up his hand. "Wait a minute. I wasn't trying to put you down."

"Maybe not," she said crisply. "But I can't have you interfering. You'll have to do as I tell you. If you have a problem with that, you can still back out. Just go back to England, or wherever. I'll tell Joubert you changed your mind about the interview."

"I'll stay." He stared at her for a long moment. "Yes, definitely. I'll stay." He set his cup down with a clatter and pulled his plate back in front of him, resuming the butchering of his bread with the butter knife. "I guess I'd better eat after all." He chewed and swallowed, then fixed his eyes on her pale face. "Suppose you tell me how far you've gotten, and what you know about Joubert."

Sighing, she leaned back in her chair. "I've worked for him for two years. Until about a month ago, I hadn't seen anything that I could use to indict him. He's very secretive about certain aspects of his business. Then I found something in the main computer, shipping dates that followed a pattern and coincided with the movement of artifacts destined for museums and galleries in Europe and the United States. What it showed was that the list of goods shipped didn't match what arrived. And some of the destinations were warehouses, not galleries."

"Where is that list?"

"Part of it, what I found initially, is with my superiors in Paris. I haven't been able to work on finding the rest because the main computer's been down. The only thing I'm sure of is that another big shipment is about to take place. And I suspect some of the goods might be in those crates unloaded from the film crew's yacht. They looked much too heavy to be only furs."

"How did you manage to get yourself hired by Joubert? He doesn't strike me as the type to advertise for an assistant in the employment ads."

She held up her hand, a faint smile softening the tension on her face. "Trade secret. I know a lot about art, and I'm proficient in several languages. When Joubert's last assistant left his employ, I applied for the job."

"His last assistant left? Convenient, wasn't it?"

She tossed him a spontaneous grin. "Yes. He received an offer he couldn't refuse. My résumé was flawless, thanks to the information he gave us. So I got the job."

Rob found himself thinking of her determination. To work for such a man on an isolated island, where she would have no immediate help should she get into trouble, took a great deal of courage. "And stuck to it even when Joubert was being obnoxious."

"In my business, one learns patience," she said calmly. "I was prepared to wait until he made a mistake." It had been disheartening at times, but now her work was about to pay off. And when it did, she would take a long vacation. She'd earned it.

"And now he has," she added with an iron certainty.

Rob's brows lifted. "Oh?"

"What I found in the computer."

"Can you retrieve it?"

"I will. And soon, before Joubert gets more suspicious. He must suspect something, if he's having us followed." She fixed Rob with a questioning stare. "Unless you've got enemies that you haven't told me about. Maybe we're completely on the wrong track here."

"I can't think of anyone. Unless it's in the part of my memory I've lost."

"Then we'd better keep our guard up."

Rob drained his coffee cup. "My thoughts, exactly. Partner."

"I'm in charge. Don't forget it." She softened the words with a smile, adding earnestly, "Until we know if Joubert suspects that I may be other than what he thinks, we have to be very careful. I don't know if he's having us followed, but we'd be wise to assume he is and take evasive measures if necessary. In the meantime, don't do or say anything that will arouse his suspicions. I want to get him. I can't let all my work go to waste now."

"I understand." But he was frowning as he pushed back his chair. "My package from London should be in by now. The clerk said the shuttle from the airport gets in at half past eight. And then we'll get back to the island."

"So I can't talk you out of it."

Rob tipped her face up and dropped a light kiss on her mouth. "My dear lady, I wouldn't miss it for the world."

"Just remember what I said about Joubert. Act normal, and don't antagonize him."

"You got it."

THE PACKAGE was thick and bulky, a reinforced envelope marked with Rob's name in an assertive scrawl. Rob weighed it in one hand as he met Diana's eyes. "Quick work," she said. "Let's hope it has some useful information."

By noon they were tying up at the jetty on Pagoni. Diana's car stood in the parking lot where she'd left it. Some aspiring comedian had written Wash Me in the dust on the flat trunk cover. Their laughter at the words lifted some of the uneasiness they felt at returning to Paul Joubert's private domain.

"I wonder how the filmmakers are doing," Diana said idly as she wheeled the car onto the road.

Rob frowned. "Is it possible they figure in whatever scheme Joubert is cooking up? George Leonides made no secret of the fact that he needs money."

"I don't know. Let's wait and see if they're still here before we start speculating." She gave an uncertain laugh. "A person could become paranoid, suspecting everyone."

"Better paranoid than dead," Rob said grimly. "I wouldn't trust Joubert an inch."

Maria greeted them as soon as they entered the house. "Oh, I'm so glad you're back, Miss Analise. Everyone is upset. The news is all over the island. We had to leave our camp. People say a ghost has been walking the beach at night, and no one wants to stay there."

"Do you believe it's a ghost?" Rob asked.

Maria shrugged and crossed herself. "I saw it myself a couple of nights ago, a figure in white. I don't know. But boats have been coming and going at all hours along the coast. There's no peace anymore. And Miss Analise, we have more visitors."

"More visitors?" Diana echoed, a cold feeling settling into her stomach.

Maria rolled her eyes. "Yes. That dreadful Kyrios Kurtz. And an associate of his. I don't remember his name. Kyrios Paul is most unhappy, especially since you weren't back yesterday. The main computer is working again, and he had work for you."

Diana gave the woman a quick hug. "Don't worry, Maria. I'm here now."

Anticipation raised her spirits, chasing away the slight unease she felt at knowing the odious Kurtz was here. No matter. If she could find the information she'd been looking for, which should be available now, she could make her plans. Joubert would walk right into the trap.

"Anything I can do?" Rob asked.

She shook her head and thanked him absently, her whole mind concentrated on the work she had to get through before evening.

CARRYING HIS PACKAGE, Rob walked down the hall, shaking his head. He would never figure out her ability to compartmentalize parts of her mind.

Four hours later he was wishing he had acquired the same knack. The clippings and photocopies he'd spent the afternoon reading were thorough, detailed and disturbing. At least one of them involved Kurtz, a bit of information he wondered if Analise had. Kurtz had been arrested once for art smuggling, but not convicted. The circumstances of the dropped charges were suspicious. Shortly after the case was dismissed, Kurtz had opened his gallery, apparently with funds from one of Joubert's companies.

Did Analise know how closely they were connected? He would have to ask her. Perhaps she would find she didn't need the information in the computer after all.

Chapter Fourteen

Absorbed in her work, Diana hadn't gone to her room to change for dinner until she heard Joubert come in with several of the film people. As a result, she was late for the cocktail hour.

Pausing in the doorway, she swept her eyes over the guests assembled in the living room. George and Rob were deep in conversation, the filmmaker gesturing with his hands as he made some point. Tamara leaned languidly against the wall near a group composed of Katerina, Joubert, Kurtz and another man.

Diana's blood congealed in her veins. For a wild instant, she wondered if she could run back to her room, pleading bubonic plague, or the onset of rabies. It was an agent's worst nightmare—coming face-to-face with someone she'd met when not on a job and therefore using her real name.

Too late. Joubert had spotted her.

"Ah, Analise. So nice of you to join us. Come and meet our newest guest."

Cedric Blackwell.

A slender, scholarly-looking man wearing horn-rimmed glasses, he affected a vague air that hid a sharp brain. Diana had met him in Paris three years ago, at a party with several hundred people in attendance. She could only pray he didn't remember the occasion.

She shook his hand, hoping he didn't notice the perspiration that made her palms wet and slippery.

"Miss Dubois," he said, with an expansive smile. Bending his head, he kissed the back of her hand. She had to stop herself from snatching it away.

Her eyes flicked to Rob, who had looked up from his conversation with George Leonides. He frowned in concern. She should have guessed she couldn't hide her emotions from him. With a faint shake of her head, she warned him off, drawing on her training to keep her voice neutral as she turned and greeted Mohammed Kurtz.

He responded with his usual oily smile and clammy handshake. He was a short man whose fondness for the good things of life showed in his portly stomach and his double chin. "My dear Analise, you look more beautiful than ever."

"A pleasant surprise to find such beauty out here," Blackwell said in an uppercrust British accent, another affectation. Diana knew he'd emerged from the gutters of Liverpool some twenty years ago. "No wonder Paul never takes you to civilization."

"I go where I want, Mr. Blackwell," Diana said crisply. She glanced around to find that Katerina had wandered off to get another drink. "Excuse me. I must speak with Katerina."

Diana ate almost nothing at dinner, leaving the table before dessert was served, with the excuse that she had work to finish.

She went into the office and leaned against the closed door for a moment, letting out a long breath. Voices came to her from the hall, and she quickly locked the door.

A close call, one of those moments that could blow a case wide open. Still, since her specialty was the art world, and Cedric Blackwell was in the business, it wasn't entirely surprising. And if Cedric Blackwell had been just another dealer or wealthy buyer, she might not have been so thrown by his appearance.

In fact, the situation couldn't have been worse. He was a man her agency had investigated a number of times over the years, a man who dealt in art on a free-lance basis, acting as a go-between for major dealers. They'd had strong suspicions for years that he wasn't fussy about the provenance of the works he handled, but there had never been any proof.

Fortunately, he seemed not to have recognized her. During the meal, he'd tried to engage her in conversation a couple of times, using the smooth lines of the experienced womanizer. When she'd responded in monosyllables, he'd turned his attention to Katerina, who had treated him with a superficial aloofness.

Diana was safe. For the moment.

Sitting down at the keyboard, she turned on the main computer. As yet, she hadn't had a chance to look for the shipping lists. Paul had left her enough work to occupy the entire afternoon.

But now she was on her own time. She hit a key. A series of numbers and messages materialized on the screen. Holding her breath, she typed in a code.

Data unavailable. She tried another code. Nothing. Swearing, she called up the main directory and scrolled through it.

Nothing.

With a sinking heart, she realized that the passwords had been changed. That would ordinarily not present an insurmountable problem, but it appeared that the files were missing, too. Or hiding in a remote corner of the machine's memory.

She needed time. Much more time.

A KNOCK on her bedroom door roused Diana from a restless doze. Ever since she'd gone to bed, around midnight, the peacocks had been shrieking, not constantly, but often enough to keep her from a deep sleep.

Shrugging on a robe, she padded to the door. "Who is it?"

"Analise, it's Rob. Can I come in?"

Frowning, she opened the door. Still fully dressed, Rob strode past her to the window.

"Thanks." He looked out, standing to the side so that he wouldn't be seen from outside. "You don't have any binoculars, do you?"

Diana shook her head. "No. Why? What's wrong?"

"I thought I saw lights out at sea."

"Maybe some fisherman," she suggested.

"I don't think so. Not bright enough."

"Want to go check it out?"

He grinned. "You guessed it. If there's a boat, I want to see who's in it. Could be our mystery woman."

Diana yanked a pair of jeans and a sweatshirt out of the closet, turning her back as she discarded the robe and put them on. Pulling the sweatshirt down over her hips, she faced Rob. "It's nearly two in the morning. You're still dressed."

"I couldn't sleep. Those damn peacocks."

She clicked her tongue in sympathy. "I thought I was the only insomniac. Other than the peacocks, of course."

OUTSIDE, the night was dark and humid. Clouds hid most of the stars. The garden was heavily fragrant with jasmine and honeysuckle.

"We'll have to be careful," Rob whispered. "I don't think I want to advertise this little excursion."

"No one seemed to notice we were out the other nights. The motion-detector lights are designed to light the paths, and most of them can't be seen by anyone in the house. I'll try to steer us away from them, though."

The paths Analise took were confusing to Rob, and virtually invisible in the shrubbery. He would never have found them on his own in the dark. Only once did they set off a security light, and it was covered so completely by honeysuckle vines that it was highly unlikely anyone would notice it.

He recognized the place where he'd lost the mysterious figure in white. A sheer cliff lay beyond it, he remembered. With unerring confidence Analise proceeded, taking his hand to guide him through shadows so thick they were almost tangible.

Spiderwebs clung stickily to his face, and he brushed them away with his free hand. "At least we know no one else has been along here," he murmured.

"Not necessarily," Diana whispered back. "Those webs can be respun in minutes."

A low growl of thunder mingled with the sibilant mutter of the sea as they picked their way down a steep, rocky trail. "No alarms?" Rob asked.

"Not here. Down on the beach there's a motion sensor, but it doesn't light up. It triggers a buzzer in the house. Careful here. You'll have to jump. And make sure you land exactly where I do."

She let go of his hand and climbed onto a tumble of boulders slick with lichen and sea spray. "Over here. On this side."

He landed hard on dry sand that quickly sifted into his shoes. Diana was already removing hers. "Okay," she said softly. "There's a sea cave. Actually, not a cave, more like a cleft between two rocks. It gives access to another beach, much like this one."

"How many beaches are there within the estate boundaries?"

"Several. But it's a difficult climb down to them."

The second beach was almost completely cut off from the sea by a circle of stony ridges. The sand, and the tiny natural harbor, were deserted.

"Well, the boat didn't put in here," Diana said quietly. She climbed up on a little ridge of tumbled stone, her eyes scanning the calm, flat sea. There was no sign of a boat, or lights.

"Visibility's not great," Rob said beside her. "A boat could be a hundred meters offshore and we wouldn't see it." He dropped to the sand and held out his hand to help her down. "Guess we'd better get back."

At the top of the cliff, Diana looked back out over the sea. Dark and empty. Small ripples whispered faintly against the sand far below. The growl of thunder vibrated across the dark sky.

She led the way back to the house by a circuitous route that brought them through the garden on the side opposite where they'd started from. The roof of the garden shed, with its rooster weathervane, had just come into sight above the trees when Diana froze. "Wait." Her voice was the merest breath of sound.

Laying her hand on Rob's chest, she pushed him off the path into the shadow of a high yew hedge. She could hear shoes crunching on the path that led toward the house. Running feet. A shimmer of white appeared around the curve of the path. A moment later, a figure covered from head to foot in a long garment glided past them and disappeared.

A peacock, perched on the roof of the shed, cried out with a harsh shriek. Diana jumped, grabbing a handful of Rob's shirt. He placed his finger across her lips. "Who was that?"

"Our ghost?" Diana swallowed down her heart, which felt as if it had leaped into her throat. "I'd guess it was Tamara."

"Coming in from an assignation?" Rob asked sardonically. "Or haunting the garden?"

"Let's find out."

The side door of the house was locked, and there was no indication that anyone had used it in the past few minutes. Rather than fumble with her keys, Diana slid open the glass door of the dining room, which she'd left unlocked earlier. Leaving their shoes by the entrance, she and Rob crept down the hall, acutely aware of Joubert sleeping in one of the rooms they passed.

At Tamara's door, Diana paused. "What if she's asleep? What if it wasn't Tamara?"

Rob's mouth tightened. He reached around her and knocked on the door.

A minute ticked by. In the study, a clock sounded the hour melodiously. Rob knocked again, a little louder. Another minute crawled into infinity, feeling like an hour.

Diana was about to try the handle when the door opened. Tamara poked her head around the jamb. "*Qu'est-ce que c'est?* What is it?" She rubbed at her eyes, then lowered her hand to tug down the hem of her short, ruffled nightdress.

Diana hesitated, wondering again if she was wrong. Tamara gave every appearance of having been asleep. Should she apologize and leave?

The decision was taken from her when Rob pressed the small of her back with his hand. She stepped into the room, Rob close behind her.

The floor felt cool against Diana's bare feet.

Too cool. She felt the slickness of moisture on the marble tiles. Groping beside the door frame, she flipped the switch on the wall, lighting up the room. A line of clearly delineated running-shoe tracks led to the closet.

Rob strode across the room while Diana closed the door and faced Tamara. Without makeup, the girl's face was young and vulnerable. The biggest surprise in her appearance was her hair—her own hair—which Diana realized she'd never seen. It was dark, like many of the wigs she wore, cut short in a feathery cap.

The girl looked pale under the bright ceiling light, and her eyes were skittering nervously left and right.

Rob emerged from the closet, holding a pair of sneakers. The canvas toes were wet, and pine needles clung to the trim around the soles. In his other hand he held a white robe and a blond wig.

"I only did it once." Tamara spoke in her accented English, her voice wavering. "He told me to. I did not mean any harm."

"What do you mean, only once?" Rob demanded. "We've seen you three times."

Tamara shrank back. "That was not me. Only tonight, and once before. But the first time was an accident. Tonight he told me to go down to the large beach, where Maria and her family camp, walk along it past the summer huts, and then across the top of the hill and back through the garden. I had to make enough noise that someone would come out and see me."

"Did anyone?" Diana asked.

"I'm not sure. I thought I saw a curtain move at one of the doors. The sea was very quiet, and rocks slipped down when I climbed back up the hill."

"Who told you to do this, Tamara?" Rob's voice was quiet but firm. "Joubert?"

She shook her head in an agitated manner. "Yes. No."

"What do you mean? Yes, or no?"

"The first time, I had been in the studio with Paul. It was warm and I went out to the garden when we finished. I didn't realize until later that Rob had seen me."

Diana frowned. Her explanation sounded innocent enough. But maybe not.

"And tonight?" Rob prompted.

Tamara twisted her hands together. "It was Dino. He'd heard the ghost story and thought it would be a good joke if the ghost appeared."

"Then you didn't go out in a boat three nights ago?"

"A boat? I don't know how to run a boat."

"She doesn't," Diana confirmed. "She's never gone out in any of Paul's boats since she's been here."

"I do not like the small boats," Tamara said, color returning to her cheeks. She pressed a hand to her stomach. "In a small boat, I feel sick."

"So Joubert doesn't know you've been out there in this getup," Rob said.

Tamara's eyes widened, and a spasm, almost of fear, crossed her face. "Paul would be angry. He likes me to stay here at night."

"What about the boy from the village?" Diana asked. "Does Paul know about him?"

"He must not know," she whispered, her eyes darting to the door as if she expected Paul to charge in like a protective father. "He must not. He will send me away."

"And why don't you want to go away? You can't waste your whole life here on this island." Diana lowered her voice, made it gentle and persuasive. "Why did you leave your career?"

Tamara bit her lip. Running across the room, she threw herself onto the bed, pulling the sheet up to her chin. The hands that gripped the edge of it were tense with strain, the tendons standing out like cords.

Diana approached her slowly and knelt beside the bed. Tamara lay on her side, her face half buried in a mound of pillows. Her eyes were open, and dark with emotion.

Diana felt her heart turn over as she recognized the signs. A woman exploited by a man, or men. And running.

She laid her hand on Tamara's cropped head. "Who are you hiding from, Tamara? It's all right. You're safe here."

Diana was aware of Rob standing by the door, silent, waiting. She thought of suggesting that he leave, but was afraid that if she spoke to him Tamara would retreat deeper into her protective shell.

"Tamara, who was it? He can't hurt you here." The short curls beneath her fingers were damp, reminding her of Tamara's excursion into the garden. "Was it Dino? Did you know him before?"

Tamara sniffed, her breath catching as if she'd been crying. Her eyes remained dry. The sight of them tore at Diana's soul. She'd read about Tamara's career, its success, and wondered what price this girl and others in her position had had to pay for that success.

"No, it was not Dino." Her voice was muffled by the pillow. "Dino is a child. It was the man I worked for. He was married, but he wanted me to be his mistress."

The old-fashioned term didn't seem strange coming from Tamara. Anger surged through Diana, and she had to fight to keep her hand steady as she stroked Tamara's hair. "And I suppose he threatened you."

"He said he would see that I didn't work again. I pretended I was ill for a couple of days. Then Paul—I knew him from when I did art modeling a few years ago—suggested I come here for a vacation. He said he'd help me find work later, that he would take care of me." Her gaze swung toward the closed door. "It won't be much longer," she whispered.

"What won't be much longer?" Diana asked, keeping her tone level, her voice low and soothing, even though adrenaline was racing through her.

To her disappointment, Tamara twisted her head away. "Nothing. Please, I'm very tired. I want to sleep."

She turned her back and pulled the sheet over her head.

Diana stood up, her heart troubled as she stared down at the tense figure on the bed. Then she shrugged. Perhaps sleep was the best remedy. And she could always try to corner the girl in the morning and ask her a pointed question or two.

Rob held the door open for her, and together they left the room.

"You heard?" Diana asked when they reached their wing of the house.

"Yeah, I heard. Poor kid. I was looking through some of the magazines in the study the other day. Seems her mother pushed her into modeling when she was only twelve. The mother remarried when she was sixteen, and Tamara left home, went out to work on her own. Mustn't have liked the new husband."

Diana gaped at him. "You've really been busy, haven't you?"

"Just doing my job. I wonder what's between her and Joubert."

"I don't know. It's puzzling. Most of the time he ignores her. But there's no question that she gives in to his wishes."

"Except maybe with that boy from the village?" Rob guessed. "I wonder if he knows she was a famous model."

"Maybe it wouldn't matter to him if he did. But I don't like this business with Dino."

"I figured he was a troublemaker from the first day. But, as she said, he's a child. He probably means no harm." Rob bent his head and dropped a kiss on Diana's cheek. "Time we were in bed, too. By the way, what was that all about just before dinner? You looked like you'd seen a ghost."

"I had. Cedric Blackwell. I've met him before."

Rob let out a long whistle. "Can he blow your cover?"

"If he remembers, he'll wonder why I'm using a different name. He doesn't know what I do, of course. Although the EFAC has tried to get something on him more than once, I wasn't involved. Still, if he gets suspicious, it could blow the case I'm developing on Joubert. Paul's distrustful at best, and he might fire me rather than take a risk. Would you mind if I looked through those papers of yours?''

"What? Now? It's almost three in the morning."

"I couldn't sleep anyway."

He pulled her into his arms, cursing himself for taking advantage of her vulnerability. "You slept fine last night. Would it help if I held you again?"

"Rob, I—" She swallowed. Her body was growing warm, just from the memory of last night. "Rob, it's better if we don't. Last night was a dream. Now we're back in real life."

For some reason, her resigned tone irritated Rob. Reaching behind her, he pushed open the door to her room and propelled her inside. Then, holding her against the closed door, he kissed her.

She moaned—in protest, he thought at first. But then he looked down into her face. She had closed her eyes, and her mouth was parted in a half smile. "One more night. Then I'll be able to forget you."

"Oh, yeah? I'll have to make damn sure you don't."

Chapter Fifteen

Rob found Analise in the study the next morning, a frown etching her brow as she typed commands into the computer. Although it was only six-thirty, he'd been awake since she extricated herself from his embrace and stole into her bathroom for a shower. The image of her naked under running water had tempted him, but he had remained in her bed, pretending sleep when she came out. He'd made a little progress last night; he wasn't about to jeopardize it by pushing.

She would need to put some distance between them now. For a little while.

His assessment of her state of mind was confirmed when she quietly said, "Good morning. Coffee's ready in the kitchen." She didn't meet his eyes, concentrating instead on the screen.

Gently Rob tilted her face upward. "Analise, it's only me. You don't have to hide."

"I'm not hiding," she said tartly. The heat faded from her voice, and she gave him a hesitant half smile. "I am hiding."

He smiled back, kissing her lightly. "Good. You're being honest. That's another step."

"Toward what?"

"Trust. Love. And speaking of trust, if I ask a favor of your friend Nick, will he keep it to himself?"

She hesitated, and he could almost see the wheels turning around in her head. "I'd trust him with my life," she said at last.

Restless, Rob went out into the garden and found Nick trimming the roses. They exchanged pleasantries, Nick grumbling about the lack of rain, unusual for the Ionian Islands, which were normally well watered.

"You didn't have the storm we had at Makrino, then?" Rob asked.

Nick gestured with his pruning clippers. "It often storms in the mountains while it's dry on the coast, even in a small area like Corfu." He shook his head. "I don't like it. The brush is as dry as kindling. And with that film crew running all over, someone's bound to drop a cigarette butt or a match and set a fire."

"And burn this jungle?" Rob waved his arm over the lush greenery surrounding them. As if to punctuate his words, a peacock screamed.

"This jungle, Kyrie Rob, is in the middle of dry scrub. Once a fire starts, it generates its own momentum."

Rob hunched down to examine a particularly beautiful miniature rose. The blossoms were as dainty as fairy flowers. "Nick, you wouldn't happen to be going up to Corfu in the next few days, would you?" he asked casually.

Nick clipped a dead rose and dropped it into his wheelbarrow. "I might. Why?"

"The Ionian Hotel will have a package for me. I need someone to pick it up."

Nick's teeth flashed under his thick mustache. "Without Kyrios Paul's knowledge."

"Yes, I'd prefer it that way. Incidentally, you haven't seen lights on the water at night, have you?"

Pursing his lips, Nick frowned. He hitched up his pants, tilting his head to stare at a tall Queen Elizabeth rose covered with pink blossoms. "I should have pruned it more in the winter," he muttered. "Now it's so tall I can hardly reach the top." He turned back to Rob, who lay sprawled on the manicured lawn, looking as if he hadn't a worry in the world. "I will go and get your package."

Rob nodded. "Just be careful. Don't wait for me when you deliver it. Just leave it by the gate. I wouldn't want to jeopardize your job here."

Snipping off another dead rose, Nick threw Rob a fleeting smile. "Don't worry. I'll make sure no one sees me. As for the trip to Corfu, no one will question it. I need to pick up fertilizer and a couple of shrubs a nursery is holding for me."

"Good." Rob stuck a blade of grass between his lips and chewed thoughtfully. "You wouldn't know where I could find a shepherd named Thomas, would you? Brother of Elias?"

Nick's eyes sharpened. "They say Thomas is a little—" he tapped his temple "—simpleminded? I wonder, though. He knows more about sheep and goats than any of us want to. If a man knows his work and is happy in it, that's more than one can ask of life. Isn't that so, Kyrie Rob?"

"I agree." Rob waited, impatient with Nick's evasions but hiding it as best he could.

"Fishing is in a decline in these waters," Nick went on, apparently at random. "Too many fishermen. Too many years when they used dynamite to kill the fish. Some of them might be on the lookout for another way to make a living."

Rob sat up, his senses alert. "Smuggling?"

Nick shrugged. "I wouldn't like to say, but there's always the possibility. Young Adoni isn't driving that pathetic Skoda anymore. Yesterday the ferry delivered a little

Alfa Romeo sports car for him. I ask you, where would he
get the money?''

Rob's mind leaped ahead. Adoni with the Skoda had to
be the boy who had brought Tamara home. Where indeed
would he get money to buy a new car? Unless Tamara had
given it to him. Living on the island, where there were few
stores, restaurants or other amenities, she would have little
opportunity to spend what he suspected might be a consid-
erable fortune. During her working days, she had been at the
top of her field, commanding fees that would have left her
rich.

Maybe that was why she stayed. Maybe she'd simply tired
of the frenetic, cutthroat world of modeling and retired to
live off her investments. Perhaps he and Analise were looking for sinister reasons where there were none.

"Did he work with the film crew?'' Rob asked.

"He did. They filmed on several beaches accessible only
by sea. He ferried them back and forth. But that wouldn't
pay for a car.'' Nick pulled out a gnarled briar pipe and began to pack it with tobacco. "He's also been going out at
night. And he didn't take fishing gear on the boat.''

Now they were getting somewhere. "Where does he go?''

Taking his time lighting his pipe, Nick shrugged. "Who
knows? Perhaps to the mainland. I'm not a detective, Kyrie
Rob. I only know what they're saying in the village.''
Reaching up, he clipped a magnificent truss of newly opened
blossoms from the Queen Elizabeth. Moving down the rec-
tangular bed, he cut a couple of deep crimson Chrysler Im-
perials. "For perfume. And for a contrasting color,'' he
said, thrusting the roses into Rob's hands. "Here, take them
to Miss Analise. And tell her about Adoni. She'll know what
to do.''

Rob carefully kept his expression neutral although his
pulse sped up. "What to do?''

Nick moved down the rose bed. Over his shoulder, he said, so softly that Rob almost missed the words, "Take care of her. She's inclined to be reckless when a case is heating up."

DIANA SENSED Rob's presence as soon as he entered the study. Or perhaps it was the sumptuous perfume of the roses he carried. "Nick wants you to have these," he said.

She looked at them; the delicate petals, still beaded with dew, were so perfect they didn't look quite real. "I should have thought of it myself," Rob added. "But you're a practical woman, aren't you? Not one who expects flowers."

She couldn't read his face, or his even tone, yet she sensed an undercurrent of tension. "Thank you. They're lovely," she said, taking refuge behind social niceties. "I'll remember to thank Nick, as well. Could you ask Maria to get you a vase? She should be in the kitchen."

"In a minute." He went back and locked the door. "There's something I have to tell you." In a low voice, he related what Nick had told him. "And were you aware that Joubert financed Kurtz's galleries, and that Kurtz was once charged with smuggling, although the charges were dropped for lack of evidence?"

Her eyes were blue and direct as she looked at him. "Yes, I knew that. And there was more in the computer on the business and art connections between them." She clenched her fist around the computer mouse, her knuckles white. "If only I could find that file."

"Still no luck, then?"

"Not a thing." She renewed her efforts at the keyboard.

He was at the door, on the way to the kitchen, when he spoke again. "Analise, does Nick know who you are, and why you're here? More to the point, does he know you've told me about the case?"

She hesitated for a moment, then decided it would b
useful, and safer, for Rob to know who their allies were. I
anything happened to her, he would know who to trust
"Yes, he knows everything. He and I worked together on
case when I first started with the EFAC. He retired right af
ter that. It was he who suggested the best time to make th
move to get into Joubert's organization."

"Good. I'm glad you're not alone."

She glanced back at him, not sure whether she shoul
appreciate or resent his attitude. "Thanks. But I'm used t
working alone."

When he was gone, she let out a long breath. Her life wa
falling apart. This morning she'd had to force her way ou
of Rob's arms, even though she wanted nothing more tha
to stay and cling to him. Forever. Pulling away and going i
to shower, she had felt as if she were amputating part of he
soul.

Irrational need had stolen over her, an emotion com
pletely different from what she'd felt ten years ago. Like
child who had to touch the stove once to see if it was reall
hot, she had to experience sex with Rob again to find out i
it lived up to the promise in his glances and kisses. It had
And then she'd had to try again, to make sure she hadn'
dreamed the first time.

Weak. That was what she was. Overactive hormones an
her self-imposed celibacy had undermined her inner forti
fications. It was only sex, she kept telling herself, an aber
ration of the moment.

But Rob called it love. And when she was in his arms, sh
could almost believe it.

"Good morning, Miss Dubois. Paul said I might use th
telephone in here."

Cedric Blackwell's voice brought her thoughts to a skic
ding stop. She hit the key that blanked out the screen
"Good morning, Mr. Blackwell," she said politely, forcin

a smile when her strongest instinct was to run from the room. "Would you like me to leave while you make your call?"

"That won't be necessary. Just checking my answering service."

He dialed a series of numbers while she restored the screen and began checking the household accounts. With half an ear she heard Blackwell speak into the receiver, listen for a moment and then hang up.

"Nothing critical." He stood behind her, so close she could smell his after-shave. Lime. "How do you stand it?"

"Stand what?" she asked, keeping her face averted while she made a notation on a pad next to the keyboard.

"The isolation. The feeling of being cut off from society. The silence—especially the silence. I couldn't sleep last night."

"You get used to it," Diana said. "And you're lucky you're down at the guest house, outside the grounds. Otherwise the peacocks would have kept you awake."

Blackwell, apparently bored with the routine figures she was arranging on the screen, stepped around the desk, facing her. "They are rather noisy birds, aren't they? Miss Dubois—Analise—would you have lunch with me?"

To avoid looking at him, she pulled open a drawer at her side and pretended to rummage through it. "Aren't you watching the filming?"

"If not lunch, then dinner," he went on, as if she hadn't spoken. "I trust there's a decent restaurant in the village?"

"Of course there is. But I'm sorry, Mr. Blackwell. I need to get caught up on my work. I won't have time for lunch or dinner."

Blackwell frowned. "You have to eat."

"Here you are, Analise." To Diana's relief, Rob came into the room, carrying the roses arranged in a crystal vase. He set them on the corner of the desk. "Maria says breakfast is ready." The last words were spoken with a pointed look at Blackwell.

"I'll be there in a moment," Diana said, letting out a breath she hadn't been aware of holding. Having Blackwell here made things sticky. How long could she fool him?

Blackwell left with Rob. By the time Diana joined them in the dining room, Joubert, Blackwell, Kurtz and, surprisingly, Tamara, had already started to eat.

Diana helped herself to bacon from a chafing dish, and to the fresh toast that Maria brought in. Maria offered the toast to Tamara, but she shook her head.

On close inspection, the girl looked tired. Diana kept that observation to herself. Paul, however, had no such compunctions.

Laying down his fork, he added cream to his coffee, fixing Tamara with a hard stare. "Were you late again last night, Tamara? No, don't bother to deny it. You've used that paste under your eyes. I can't imagine why they call it cover-up."

"I had trouble sleeping," Tamara said in a small voice.

"I heard your door close long after midnight," Joubert said. "You knew you had to film today."

Film? Diana's eyes met Rob's, her brow creasing in perplexity. Joubert intercepted the look. "Tamara has consented to model some of the coats. We needed a blonde to set off the color of the darker furs."

Tamara pushed her food around on her plate with her fork, eating very little of it. "Katerina can wear a wig. I'll even lend her one."

"Katerina is ill this morning. And we can't afford delays." He didn't bother to hide his irritation. "I want you to do it. I want the job completed by Monday."

"All right." Tamara gulped the last of her coffee. "Excuse me. I must get ready." She got up and ran from the room.

"Silly child," Joubert said, applying himself to his meal as if the scene hadn't happened. He glanced up, his cold eyes flicking from Diana to Rob and back again. "Why don't you come with me and watch the filming? You'd find it interesting."

"What about my work?" Diana asked. "You know how far behind I am because of the computer being down." She paused, then plunged boldly ahead. Nothing ventured... "I noticed that some of the passwords have been changed. Do you have the new ones? I need to check the shipping dates against the invoices that came in."

She held her breath, her mouth dry, as Joubert looked at her. His eyes had a crafty look that she didn't trust. Her heartbeat sped up, becoming a painful pounding in her chest, as she waited for a question or an accusation. But he merely said, "I'm sorry. I should have told you. I changed them. Security, you know. I'll give them to you after breakfast. But I still suggest you might take the day off and join us."

Maybe it would be wiser to go along with him this time, she thought, weak with relief. Besides, observing Leonides and Dino might prove useful. She wondered suddenly about Katerina's illness. Tamara had denied being in the garden the second time they'd seen the woman in white. Had it been Katerina? "All right," she said to Joubert. "But let me have the passwords so I can work later."

"A ROYAL COMMAND?" Rob quipped an hour later as they sweated in the hot sun while George strode around a rocky headland, grumbling about the light being too intense. Tamara must have been boiling in the red fox coat she wore, blond hair flowing over the collar. Dino had been absent all morning.

"What are we doing here, anyway?" Rob added.

"We can leave," Diana said, plucking her shirt loose from her back and trying to find a comfortable position on a rough boulder.

Eyes narrowed, she watched as Paul consulted with a cameraman before going over to speak to Tamara. His words were inaudible, but the set of his body told her he was displeased about something. Tamara's head was bent, and her shoulders were slumped. Even from a distance Diana could see the pallor that left her face fragile and translucent.

Diana felt her skin crawling, and shivered. Seeing the involuntary tightening of her muscles, Rob frowned. "Why doesn't that girl leave? She's obviously unhappy."

"It's getting worse," Diana said worriedly. "Paul used to treat her like a doll or a pet, but lately he's started browbeating her. I don't like it."

"But what can you do? She didn't want your help last night."

"No, and she probably won't want it now." Diana got up from the rock, dusting off her shorts. "I'll see if I can get a chance to talk to her later."

Rob stood up to face her and took her hand, smiling gently. "Why does it upset you so much? Does it remind you of something in your past?"

She tensed. "I never let any man treat me as a slave."

"Analise, I didn't think you did. But did someone try?"

She crossed her arms, clasping her elbows with her hands. "It doesn't matter," she muttered.

Rob said nothing, merely keeping his eyes on her with that all-knowing look that she had no defenses against. "Oh, all right," she said crossly. He wouldn't give up until he had all the answers, anyway.

Walking to the shade of a scruffy pine, she threw herself down on the dry grass, startling a grasshopper. It sailed away with a distinctly annoyed click of its wings. She frowned, trying to organize a hundred milling thoughts. Above them, cicadas sawed monotonously, drowsily.

Rob lay down on his side, propping his head on his palm. With his other hand, he plucked a blade of timothy and chewed on the end, his gaze intent on the full-bodied seed plume. "Analise, were you abused as a child?"

"I moved around as a child, but I wasn't abused. Nor was I later." Sinister shadows encroached on her consciousness, threatening the bright sunlight of the day. With the force of long habit, she pushed them away, shutting them back into an unused corner of her mind. "Five years ago, someone I trusted betrayed me. He was killed, and I was a prisoner in a Middle Eastern jail for three months. I learned firsthand about the psychological abuse a man can inflict on a woman."

Rob looked startled. "It didn't make you resign from the agency."

She shrugged. "No. I survived, so I continued. It's what I've been trained to do. But I won't be taking any more assignments in that part of the world." Antonio's betrayal had gotten her into that mess; her own ingenuity had gotten her out, wounded in body and in spirit, but alive. And in possession of a lesson she had vowed never to forget: She would never depend on anyone but herself again.

She was relieved when Rob stood up, apparently satisfied. "Would Paul object if we left?" he asked.

Diana stared at the film crew, and at Paul, who was pacing importantly among them. Exhaling, she forced her tense body to relax. "He probably won't even notice."

"Let's go, then. I want to phone my agent."

Diana had brought her own car, which took them back to the house in short order. Maria was dusting the living room when they came in the door, humming along with a softly playing radio. Diana stopped to talk with her while Rob continued down the hall to the study.

He was out again in less than ten minutes. "Did you get through?" Diana asked.

He grinned. "Right away. He's sending me more stuff. Should be there tonight." He turned to Maria. "Is Nick still in the garden?"

"Down by the shed, I think."

Nick agreed readily to take his own boat to Corfu. He would meet Rob at midnight at the gate to the estate with the package.

"Did you enjoy your stay on Corfu with Rob?" Nick asked Diana when the arrangements had been made.

"Very much," Diana replied, hoping her face didn't look as warm as it felt.

Nick nodded. "It's good to get away sometimes. On Corfu one can breathe freely." He set his foot on his shovel, resuming his task of digging a new perennial border. "I'll see you later this evening, Kyrie Rob. Take care of Analise."

"He's full of obscure observations, isn't he?" Rob commented as they left Nick to his work. "Or are they warnings?"

Chapter Sixteen

At two the next morning, Rob sat by his window, staring down at the document in his hand. Exhaling a long breath, he let the paper flutter to the floor. He leaned forward and dug the heels of his hands into his aching eyes.

He'd spent an hour and a half reading faded newspaper clippings, bad photocopies, and a couple of police reports that made him wonder what semilegal means Sean had used to obtain them. Taken separately, they meant little, but together, they added up to a very interesting portrait of Paul Joubert.

What had surprised him most was the intertwining of several people no one would have guessed were connected. Dino of the sullen demeanor and engaging baby face had worked for Joubert in the past. He was no innocent, although he seemed to have escaped a prison term. Rather than being in his early twenties, as a casual observer would estimate, he was actually thirty. His acting and modeling jobs were few and far between but he managed to own a Lamborghini and a classy apartment in Athens.

Sean had also sent a number of catalogs from fine-arts galleries scattered throughout Europe. Mohammed Kurtz's name came up on several lists of boards of directors. Joubert was also on one of them, as a director of Kurtz's Milan gallery. And Cedric Blackwell served on the board of Kurtz's Paris gallery.

An article on Kurtz's galleries expressed admiration for the man's ability to come up with virtually any item requested by buyers. And at reasonable prices.

Rob straightened in his chair, rubbing a kink out of his neck.

A press release from the Paris gallery, dated two months ago, announced the acquisition of a Greek bronze long thought to have been lost. No details were given, but any ancient bronze was rare enough to create interest among collectors. Too many of them had been melted down to be reshaped into armor or guns and cannons during the many wars that had torn the Mediterranean world apart at regular intervals.

Reaching for the file folder on the table beside him, Rob sorted through the news clippings until he found the one he wanted. It was a brief paid advertisement dated ten days later than the original announcement, saying the bronze would not be offered by Kurtz Galleries after all. Apologies were offered for any inconvenience to the gallery's clients. No explanation was given.

Too hot? Rob wondered cynically.

He scowled at the clippings. He had to talk to Analise about all of this. Probably most of it would be stale news for her but the connection to Dino might not be.

Going out into the hall, he knocked on her door. It was a moment before she opened it, her robe half off her shoulder, her hair tangled from sleep. She raked it away from her face with her fingers. "Couldn't it wait until morning? I just fell asleep."

"At least the peacocks were quiet tonight," he said with a disarming smile. He thrust the sheaf of papers toward her and had the satisfaction of seeing her eyes lose their languor.

"Nick came through, did he?"

"I just hope no one saw him. You probably know most of this stuff, but the item about Dino is interesting."

Analise scanned the pages, her face thoughtful. "Hmm . . . is it a coincidence that so many of them are here at this time?"

"I don't know, but maybe we can figure something out. Tomorrow. Good night, Analise. I'm sorry I disturbed you."

She seemed distracted as she handed the papers back to him. "It's all right. See you in the morning."

He couldn't help feeling a little piqued at her casual dismissal, but then, he had work to do. When he was back in his room, he didn't waste any time. Pulling a yellow legal pad toward him, he picked up a pen and began to write.

Dawn was graying the sky when he finished. He folded the sheets and tucked them, along with the packet of information, into a cleverly hidden pocket in the lining of his suitcase. He hoisted the case to its former place on the closet shelf.

Then he stripped off his clothes and flung himself onto the bed, falling at once into a deep sleep.

DIANA MASSAGED her throbbing temples, frustration gnawing at her. Even with the new passwords, she'd been unable to reconstruct the information she'd previously dredged from the computer. It had taken her about an hour to discover that the files had either been altered or drastically shifted. It looked as if she would have to do without them, and just wait until Joubert made his next move. That had to be soon.

She took a sip from a mug of coffee, grimacing at the cold bitterness. It was noon, but the house was quiet around her. Apparently no one was home for lunch. She wondered where Rob had gone. He hadn't come to talk to her, and at midmorning he'd driven off in her car.

She was about to shut off the computer and look for something to eat when Joubert himself stepped into the study, closing the door behind him.

"Have you found anything interesting, Analise?" he said softly as he walked around her and sat down at his own massive desk across the room.

Was it her imagination, or did his voice hold a sinister note? "I wanted to check some files, but they don't seem to be here." She kept her voice steady, her manner relaxed, as if the problem were only a minor annoyance. "Has someone been using the computer, perhaps when I was in Paris last?"

Joubert lounged back in his chair. She didn't like the smile that slid across his features as he linked his hands over his stomach. It had a cruel cast to it. If snakes could smile before they struck a defenseless rabbit, they would look like Joubert.

She wasn't a rabbit, she reminded herself, defenseless or otherwise. But when he spoke again, a chill raced over her skin.

"Yes, Paris. Who did you see while you were there, my dear Analise?"

"Why, the people in your business office, of course. And the museum and warehouse staff about the shipping of the paintings. Is something wrong?"

"You might say so, Mademoiselle Dubois—or is that your real name?"

Thanks to her training, she kept her face from changing although she must have paled. "What do you mean? You checked my references, didn't you?" She rose from her chair, pushing it back so hard it hit the wall with a thump. "Are you accusing me of something? If so, tell me now and we'll resolve it."

"Sit down, my dear."

"I'd rather stand, thanks."

He shrugged. "Suit yourself. No, I'm not accusing you of anything. For the moment. But I'm checking your references again."

"My work has always been satisfactory, hasn't it? Isn't that reference enough?"

"Perhaps. But I've been wondering why you need to get into files to check invoices when no new ones have come in."

A cautious relief rose in her. "I found discrepancies in some of the figures. I needed to do a double check. It concerns invoices I brought back from Paris with me," she went on, improvising quickly. "One of the shipping companies we deal with may be padding their bills."

Joubert scowled. "They'd better not be."

"Why did you change the codes? Between that and the computer being down since I returned from Paris, I've wasted a lot of time. Time you're paying for."

"It's given you a chance to get to know Robert Minardos." He picked up a pen and ran it slowly between his thumb and forefinger. "To know him very well indeed."

"You made it clear when you hired me that my spare time was my own."

"I've no problem with that, my dear. However, I may have been amiss in bringing Minardos here, after all. He's been a very busy fellow."

Her heartbeat nearly clogged her throat. "In what way?"

"Come, come, Analise. You've become so close, he must have confided in you."

She pretended to be baffled. "Confided in me? I don't understand what you mean."

"No matter." Joubert opened a humidor and took out a cigar, leisurely trimming the end and lighting it. His face wreathed in smoke, he laughed softly. "Minardos is a very thorough reporter, but he should have known he couldn't hide from me. I saw him go out last night and come back with a package. It was a simple matter to search his room after he left this morning."

Sweat trickled coldly down Diana's spine. He had found the papers. No doubt about it. She waited, sure there was more.

He tapped ash off the cigar, contemplating its glowing tip. "I don't suppose he's decided to desert us."

"How would I know?" she said, not bothering to keep the defensive note out of her voice. "He didn't tell me anything."

"No? And he didn't ask you questions about the household?"

"Only with reference to his article, background material."

"Are you sure he wasn't using you?"

The question jolted her. She knew Joubert was a master at manipulation. She had seen it often enough in the way he handled Tamara. He had to be lying about Rob's motives. Yet deep down inside her lived the seeds of insecurity, the knowledge, finely honed through her insecure childhood, that she was not good enough.

Suspicion surged out of the shadows of her mind, dark and menacing.

She beat it back resolutely, but when she spoke again, her voice sounded weak, even to her own ears. "Rob would never use me. He didn't have to."

"No, you went willingly to him, didn't you? Like a lamb extending its neck for the butcher's knife."

She closed her eyes, summoning up the strength to fight him. "I know nothing. Why are you questioning me?"

"Cedric Blackwell thinks you look familiar. He's mentioned it a number of times. Yet he's never heard your name. It bothers him, and therefore it bothers me."

"I don't know Mr. Blackwell," she said. "If you're dissatisfied with my work, just say so. I'll be out of here by tonight."

Joubert shook his head, his expression almost sad. "I'm afraid I can't let you go. Not until I'm ready. Not until I find out. Or Minardos, either." He tilted back his head and blew smoke rings at the ceiling. "However, look at the bright side. If you check out, you've nothing to worry about. You'll have your job, and a raise besides."

Getting up, he moved around the desk and held the door open for her. "Now, why don't you go and have some lunch?"

Head high, she walked toward her room, her steps neither fast nor slow. He was never going to see her defeated. And soon she would have the satisfaction of turning him over to the police.

She knew her references would stand up. Only Blackwell presented an immediate danger. If he remembered her real name, he would expose her as an impostor.

Reaching the end of the hall, she looked back. Joubert had closed his study door; he was not in sight. She paused, then entered Rob's room.

To her surprise, the only sign of a search was Rob's suitcase lying on the floor, its lining ripped. There was nothing much she could do about it, and the information itself didn't point to her.

She heard an engine start. A moment later, through the open window, she glimpsed Joubert's car going down the driveway toward the gates. She left Rob's room and walked briskly back to the study. The door was unlocked, but when she turned on the computer, a red message flashed onto the screen: Access Denied.

A grim smile curved her lips. Joubert was no slouch with computer programs himself, and the thought struck her that he had clued in to her hacking by some built-in safeguard installed to detect unauthorized snooping in the files.

"Oh, you're here, Analise."

Damn! That was all she needed, another oh-so-polite sparring session with Cedric Blackwell. She hit the shutoff button on the computer.

"Yes, Mr. Blackwell?" She kept her voice even and courteous as she swiveled her chair to face him.

The man mopped his face with a linen handkerchief and sank down on a chair next to Joubert's desk. "I don't know why I let Mohammed talk me into coming here. The heat never agrees with me, but this extreme temperature has made me positively ill. Why don't you drive me to the village, where we can sit in a shaded taverna and get to know one another?"

She almost recoiled in horror at the thought. Standing up, she pressed her palm to her forehead. "I'm afraid I have the most dreadful headache. Besides, you'd find it cooler here in the house with the air-conditioning than anywhere in the village."

Blackwell groaned. "I agree, but the film crew is arriving at any moment to do interior shots. It's too hot to work outside, so they're moving the operation indoors."

As if to confirm his words, gravel crunched outside, followed by the slamming of car doors and the voice of George Leonides giving orders.

Diana threw Blackwell a harried look she didn't have to fake. "Excuse me."

In the living room, two of Leonides's muscular assistants were rearranging the furniture, under the direction of Joubert, who'd obviously come back with them. "Analise," he called when he spotted her. "When Robert returns, could you tell him I'd like to talk to him?"

"If I see him," she replied, making her escape down the hall.

With the door closed, her own room was quiet. She was tired after her disrupted night, and the hum of the air-conditioning and the torpor of the midday air soon made her drowsy. She lay down on the bed and slept.

Some time later, she woke, sure she'd heard a sound in the hall. Sitting up, she listened, but either the noise wasn't repeated or a sudden shriek by a peacock in the tree near her window drowned it out. She got up and went out on the little balcony. Heat haze shimmered over the garden, the leaves limp under a blinding sun. The air smelled of smoke. Overhead, the sky was the color of sulphur, the sun a copper disc.

A fire somewhere. Weeks had passed without rain. It had been bound to happen, a careless smoker tossing a match into the explosively dry brush, or a tourist failing to douse a campfire completely. Even broken glass could condense the sun's rays to a single point, igniting the grass on the rocky slopes.

She shivered, even though sweat beaded her upper lip and trickled down her temple. If there was a serious blaze, she wondered, how would that affect Joubert's plans?

She turned away from the window, feeling restless and wired, and more tired than before her brief nap. The headache she'd used as an excuse with Blackwell was fast becoming a reality.

A thud in the next room made the hairs stand up on her nape. Rob? Or someone else, probably up to no good?

Before she could reach her door, she saw the handle turn. The lock held. She heard Rob's low voice. "Analise, are you in there?"

She unlocked the door, pulling it open to let him in. The sounds of shouts and curses—"Damn it, Katerina, not like that!"—carried down the long hall from the living room, and she quickly closed it.

"Do you know what's happened?" Rob said without preamble.

"Yes. Joubert found the information your agent sent. He told me earlier."

Rob's expression grew more grim. "How did he react?"

"Let's say he's not too happy with you."

"And what about you, Analise?"

Diana closed her eyes, averting her face. The knowledge of her duplicity ached within her, but there was no purpose to be served by telling him the truth now. When this was all over...

"Analise?"

"Nothing. He's suspicious, but he knows nothing. Yet. But it's only a matter of time until Blackwell remembers. Is the whole crew in the house?"

"Looks like it. Even Kurtz and Blackwell are sitting on the patio, going through a pitcher of martinis."

Reaching a decision, Diana pulled a pair of jeans and a clean T-shirt from her closet. "Okay. Wait here while I change. We'll take a look at the house where they're staying—it's something we probably should have done long ago. Then we'll figure out what to do next."

Chapter Seventeen

They managed to get out of the house undetected. Diana gasped as she breathed in a lungful of the dense air pressing upon them like a smothering blanket. The garden shimmered in the heat, the green plants tinged eerily with copper in the smoke-filtered sunlight.

"It's getting worse," Rob said. "They're worried in the village. They say it's the most serious fire in twenty years." He glanced toward the garage, and the motley assortment of vehicles parked on the gravel apron in front of it. "Your car?"

"It's not far to walk," Diana said. "I'd rather they didn't notice we're gone."

"Too bad we can't take a shortcut," Rob muttered as they walked down the shady side of the driveway.

"The fence, remember?"

They had reached the gate, which stood open, when a shiny red sports car roared by, entering the estate.

"Who the hell was that?" Rob said, coughing as a cloud of dust enveloped them.

"I think it might have been Tamara's friend. You know, the kid with the Skoda."

"He's come up in the world, just like Nick said."

Diana frowned thoughtfully. "I wonder how he managed it. This way, Rob. Now we can take a shortcut."

The single-story guest house stood on a promontory with a commanding view of the sea, sheltered at the back by a stand of robust pines. Closed shutters gave it a deserted look. Diana tried the door, which opened readily.

"Good. No one's around."

Rob laid his hand on her arm. "Wait. I hear a car."

She tensed, listening. The low rumble carried up the hill, and then she saw it, far below in a loop of the road—the little red convertible, heading for the village. It was too far away to tell how many people sat in it.

"Tamara, no doubt," she said quietly.

The interior of the house was dim, filled with the scent of stale cigarette smoke. A quick search of the living area and the five bedrooms turned up nothing suspicious. In fact, nothing at all was evident beyond the ordinary accoutrements of a group of people living in temporary quarters. The bedrooms were small and sparsely furnished. The kitchen was Spartan and littered with coffee cups.

It didn't take long to look through the place. If any of the occupants were involved in smuggling, Diana doubted they'd be so foolish as to leave incriminating papers lying around. And with no cellar or attic, there was nowhere to hide anything as substantial as a half-dozen or more wooden crates.

"Very unlikely that they're all criminals," she mused aloud. "So whoever is, he or she would keep a low profile."

"That's right." Rob raked his fingers through his hair as he poured a glass of water at the kitchen sink. He offered it to Diana. "Want some?"

She took the glass and drank deeply, wiping her mouth with the back of her hand. "Thanks. Did you notice anything odd?"

"Yeah," he said. "There's nothing here, except the trunks for the furs. What did they do with those crates we saw them unloading the day they came?"

"They have to be somewhere. We would have known if they'd brought them to Joubert's house."

"Unless they moved them while we were on Corfu."

Diana shook her head. "Then why bring them here first? No, I'm betting they're around."

"Let's have a look outside."

The air had an acrid taste to it, and the sea was hidden under a murky brown haze. No birds sang in the trees. Diana's sneakers crunched on the sandy path as they moved around to the back of the house. A sparse lawn, drying out in the heat, ended in a row of thistles and low-growing squirting cucumbers.

The low stone wall surrounding an old, unused well stood guard at the edge of the lawn. Beyond it, the ground dropped sharply into a ravine. The slope was covered with thorny shrubs.

Diana gave a sharp exclamation. "I think we're on the right track. There's a path that looks as if it's been used a lot lately." She fingered the raw end of a bramble. "See, it's been cut, probably to widen the trail."

The descent proved surprisingly easy, the path zigzagging across the slope. At the bottom, the air was cleaner, and a musical murmur of running water came to their ears. The trail faded in a rocky clearing, with no indication of where it resumed.

"Now what, boss lady?" Rob asked with a mischievous grin.

She stooped and retied a shoelace. "We keep looking."

"And just what are we looking for?"

She threw him an answering grin. "We'll know when we find it, won't we?" Sobering, she picked up a stick and drew a pattern of lines in a patch of sand. "You remember I told you there are a lot of coves along the coast of this island that are only accessible by sea? Well, some of them can be reached by land, if you go underground. These hills are predominantly limestone, and they're riddled with caves.''

''You've been in them?''

Diana shook her head. ''Up until now, there's never been a reason to. No one goes in there. If anyone did, Nick would know about it. He's shown me the entrance of one of the caves, near his house, but I'm not sure how all of them connect. If there's one here, it could run out to the sea. I've seen them from a boat—holes in the rock cliffs like Swiss cheese.''

''You know, a cave with access to the sea would be a great way to ship out contraband. Haven't you thought of that?''

''Of course I have. But don't forget, the marine police regularly patrol the coastline. And in all the time I've been here, Joubert's never received anything that would need to be shipped out. Usually when there's movement of art anywhere in the world, legal or illegal, there are rumors first. It's been quiet for months now. The only major robbery was that museum in northern Greece, and no trace of the artifacts has shown up so far.''

She dropped the stick. ''Come on, we're wasting time. The film crew could be back anytime.''

''Water,'' Rob said. ''If we find the running water, we should find the cave. Limestone caves almost always have water.''

''NOT THIS WATER,'' Diana said five minutes later. She dipped her hand into a little pool bubbling out of a mossy bank. ''It's a spring.''

''But it could come from some source deeper underground,'' Rob stated stubbornly.

''Okay. Keep looking.''

After a half hour of poking the shrubbery, becoming hot and short-tempered, they found the cave, and water had nothing to do with it. Its mouth, a narrow opening between two massive slabs of stone, was hidden behind a camouflage net festooned with branches so recently cut that they'd barely begun to dry out.

"Someone must cut fresh cover every day," Rob mused aloud.

They ducked behind the heavy covering. Sweat soaked Diana's T-shirt as she entered the enclosed space against the rock face, where the heat had condensed during the long day.

Inside the cavern, the air was cool, making her skin clammy. Her breath hitched in her throat as she took in the darkness beyond the entrance. Memories of crouching in a dark cell while chaos reigned outside flooded into her mind.

"I can't do it," she muttered.

"Why don't we get a flashlight from the guest house and check this out," Rob suggested.

"No!" Her refusal was so abrupt and forceful that he spun around.

"Why not?" His voice was gentle, and she knew he sensed her fear.

"Not now."

"Analise, you don't have to be perfect." He wrapped his hand around hers, and she clung to it, absorbing the heat of his skin, shivering.

"I have no trouble facing a man with a gun or a knife, but I just can't get over this. I'm scared of dark, closed places."

"Your dream," he said.

"Not only my dream. When I was a prisoner, they kept me in the dark for days." Alternating with days of unrelenting light, which to her had been less harrowing. She shuddered, and Rob held her tighter.

Ashamed of giving in to the fear, she pulled free. "Let's get out of here. We'll have to talk to Nick. He grew up on the island, and he'll know where this cave leads. There has to be another way in."

She was about to step around the camouflage netting when she heard a stone rolling down the slope across the clearing. Goats? Perhaps, but it was better not to take a chance.

Crouching down, she parted the shrubbery. Cedric Blackwell stood at the top of the path, scanning the area with binoculars. Had he been following them, or was his presence just a coincidence?

She sank back into the cover, putting her hand on Rob's arm when he crept up beside her. "Wait. I don't think he's seen us."

An eternity ticked by. A wasp buzzed around them, settling for a moment on Diana's hand before flying off again. A mosquito bit her ankle. She had to restrain herself from slapping it. Rob's breath tickled her neck.

She let out a long breath of relief when Blackwell lowered the binoculars and disappeared from sight.

JOUBERT WAS WAITING when they stumbled into the house at sunset, hot and bedraggled from making a path through the dense underbrush at the estate's perimeter. The film crew was gone, the living room restored to order.

"Oh, you're back." His tone was mild enough, but the look he gave them was malevolent. "I wanted to talk to you, Minardos."

Rob lifted one brow. "The interview, you mean?"

"Indirectly. I've changed my mind. I'll hire a press agent to do the publicity."

"So you wouldn't mind if I took Analise away with me for a couple of days?" Behind her back, he squeezed her hand, signaling to her to play along.

Joubert pulled a cigar from his pocket and stuck it between his teeth. "You're taking this very calmly."

Rob shrugged. "You win some, you lose some."

"Clichés, Robert?"

"When they're apt. Can you spare Analise until Monday?"

Leisurely touching a lighter to the cigar, Joubert puffed on it, then exhaled blue smoke. "Actually, it's impossible for you to leave at the moment. The larger boat is being used for a film sequence tomorrow, and the smaller one has developed an engine problem. I'm very sorry, but I'm afraid you'll have to suffer my hospitality for a few days longer. And I'd advise you to stay close to the house. Brushfires can be dangerous." He turned toward the study. "Dinner will be in half an hour."

"We have to see Nick," Diana whispered as soon as Paul was gone. "Come on. He might still be in the greenhouse."

Rob inclined his head in the direction Joubert had gone. "Was he saying what I thought he was saying?"

Diana nodded soberly. "I think so. I think we can consider ourselves prisoners."

Their suspicions about their new status were confirmed as soon as they stepped outside. A tough-looking man with a scarred face stood on the patio, a bulge at his waistband testifying to the gun he wore. He followed them through the garden in a lackadaisical manner, keeping his distance. A peacock shrieked a complaint, and from the roof of the house another answered.

They came upon Nick in the potting shed. He nodded a greeting, his gaze going past them to their shadow. The man came as far as the doorway, pausing to light a cigarette.

"Hey," Nick said sharply. "I don't want you smoking in here. It's not good for the plants."

The man grunted something and moved farther out, sitting down on a bench, out of earshot. Under the guise of showing them an orchid he had repotted, Nick drew them into the glass-walled greenhouse adjacent to the shed.

Keeping an eye on the doorway, Diana spoke quickly. "Nick, I need that map of the caves. Do you have it?"

"In the truck. Why?"

She told him about the path and the camouflaged cave entrance. He let out a low whistle. "I should have thought to check out the guest house. Analise, you're not going into the caves, are you?" He knew of her paralyzing fear. Some weeks ago they'd discussed the caves. He'd gone through them one night, but had found no sign that anyone had been inside them in years.

"I may have to, Nick," she said grimly. "And if it comes to that, I will. Somehow."

Nick frowned as he placed his hand on her shoulder. "Let me, Analise. Tonight."

"Nick, no. It's not your job anymore. Think of Eleni and the children."

"They'll be all right. I sent them to Corfu yesterday because of the fire."

An unoiled hinge creaked as the greenhouse door opened. Joubert's thug stood there.

In a louder voice, Nick said, "Now, this orchid is very rare, and there's another one over on the far wall. Why don't you have a look, while I get the fertilizer from the truck?"

The guard followed him out, sitting down again to light a fresh cigarette.

Nick came back with a plastic sack of fertilizer on his shoulder and a couple of seed packets in his hand. He grunted as he put down the sack. In a tour-guide voice meant to carry to the man outside, he began to explain about temperatures and the feeding of exotic plants. He didn't even pause as he slipped Diana a folded sheet of paper, which she carefully put in her pocket.

"Get out of here now," he said, covering his words by dragging a heavy pot toward the water tap. "I'll be home all night. If you signal, I'll call Bouchard."

ROB STEERED DIANA into his room when they reached the house. Licking her lips nervously, she glanced at her watch. "We're going to be late for dinner by the time we get cleaned up."

"So? Why don't we make it later still?"

A million reasons why she shouldn't let him make love to her again clamored in Diana's brain. When he found out who she was, there would be hell to pay. But her misgivings faded obligingly into nothingness as he kissed her. It was a gentle kiss that quickly burgeoned into urgency.

Leading her into the bathroom, he pulled off her dusty clothes and then his own. He turned on the shower. Diana closed her eyes, feeling pampered and cherished. Who knew what might happen tonight or tomorrow? At least they had today. "Rob, I want you."

The note of desperation in her voice made him pause. But then he saw her smile and the pink flush of arousal on her skin and he knew that, whatever strange mood she was in, this wasn't the time to question her. He tested the water, making a slight adjustment to the temperature. Wrapping his arm around her waist, he positioned them under the spray, closing the curtain around them.

He lathered his hands, rubbing them over her body with long, slow strokes. Laughing, she took the soap and began to wash him. The sweet movements of her hands made him groan, and he couldn't hide his arousal.

Far from withdrawing, she concentrated her touches until all pretense of washing died away and there was only heat and passion. "Rob, please . . ." Her hands running over his body, she whispered words he would never have expected from her, words that drove him to the edge of reason.

His mouth against her shoulder, he made one last attempt to control the raging need within him. "Analise, are you sure this is what you want?"

"Yes, yes... Now..."

Somewhere in the distance he heard a warning bell, but the wet heat of Analise's mouth on his skin deafened him. If she was only using him as a path to a world where there was no pain, he didn't care. He would give her whatever she needed, always.

Her back against the tiles, she pulled him close, wrapping one leg around his hips. Tenderly he entered her, wanting it to last, wanting it to be good for her.

But Analise, at the first stroke of his body within hers, caught fire. She moved against him, hot, wet, abandoned, the towel falling from her head to drop in a sodden lump on the shower floor. The overhead spray enveloped them, and her hair clung to him as tenaciously as her hands.

He felt his control slipping and fought to get it back, but when Analise cried out and shuddered in completion, he lost it. Covering her mouth with his, he gave a final thrust, gasping when he felt the clenching of her inner muscles. His body convulsed, and he abandoned himself to pleasure.

Analise was the first to recover. Turning her head to one side, she let out a ragged sigh as her breathing settled down to normal. She reached around him and shut off the water. Avoiding his eyes, she flipped back the curtain and stepped out, wrapping a towel around her body and a second one around her hair.

"Analise—" Rob held out his hand to her as she went to the door. The eyes that looked back at him seemed to be drowning in sorrow. Then she moved away, closing the bathroom door behind her.

He dried himself quickly and haphazardly, listening for the sound of the outer door. It was only a couple of steps to her own room.

To his relief, he found her lying on his bed, on her side, her knees drawn up to her chest. Picking up a brush, he sat down behind her and drew her up until she was sitting, braced against his raised knee. He rubbed her hair with the towel, then began to brush it. In the heat of the room it dried quickly, the fine strands fanning out over her shoulders.

He removed the other towel and laid her down, gathering her into the curve of his body and covering them with a single sheet. Her breath was moist and warm in the hollow of his throat and he could feel the feather strokes of her lashes as she blinked.

"Analise, I love you." The words came from deep within him. He could no more help saying them than he could help breathing.

Analise recoiled. "No. You can't." She pushed at his chest, hard enough to make him grunt in discomfort. "I don't want you to."

He grinned into the darkness. "I'm afraid in this case it doesn't matter what you want. It's already happened."

"You don't even know who I am."

"It doesn't matter, Analise. We'll sort that out later. For now, it's enough that I love you."

"Please." She struggled against his embrace and, surprised, he slackened his arms just enough to allow her escape. She ran across the room, grabbed her clothes from the bathroom and dragged them on.

Rob sat up, the sheet pooling around his hips. "I do love you. Even if you go, you can't escape that. And I think you love me."

"No, I don't!" she cried vehemently. She gazed at him in despair, her eyes deep blue pools. "Rob, it won't work. It didn't work before, and it won't work now."

"You're afraid. Don't be. I won't let you down, I promise."

"But I'll let *you* down. Don't you see? And I can't put you through that again."

Rob stilled, a nebulous memory struggling to reach the surface. He felt as if his blood had chilled. "What do you mean, again?"

Her gaze flitted around the room, touching everything but him. "Nothing, nothing.... All I know is that I'm no good at relationships. And I don't want to hurt you."

"I'll take the chance," he said sturdily, his heart dying a little. He clenched his fist in the folds of cloth around him. Something about this . . . something he had to remember . . . "Anyone can learn to love, if someone is willing to teach them. Even if it takes forever."

"Rob, I can't."

"Why not?"

"Do you want me to lie? Promise what I can't deliver? Happily ever after? There is no happily ever after."

She whirled and ran out of the room. A second later he heard her door close with a thud.

DIANA WOKE UP COUGHING. She sat up in bed, surprised she had slept at all. The peacocks, somewhere close by, probably on the roof above her room, were crying out, their harsh squawks more than normally distressed.

She ran to the open window. The air was thick with smoke, the sky a murky tan through which the sun shone dimly, like a bloodshot eye. The fire was worse.

Stripping off the clothes that she hadn't removed last night after her flight from Rob's room, she showered and dressed in jeans and a long-sleeved shirt. The drone of a plane drew her back to the window. A water bomber flew low over the house, scaring a group of pigeons into flight. The peacocks voiced a raucous protest.

As she headed for the kitchen, she heard the clock in the hall strike twelve. So late—she'd slept away half the day.

Rob sat at the table, nursing a cup of coffee. Maria stood by the stove, holding a tea towel that she twisted over and over in her hands. "What is he trying to do?" she was saying. "Keep us prisoner? Armed guards all over the place..."

"He can do anything he wants," Diana said, walking into the room. "Don't you realize that by now?"

Rob's eyes lit up at the sight of her. She studiously avoided meeting his gaze, but that didn't stop a grin from spreading over his face. "What's the plan?" he asked as she poured herself a cup of coffee and sat down across the table from him.

Maria threw down the tea towel and headed for the door. "If anything happens to you, I promise he won't get away with it." She left, and a moment later they could hear the vacuum cleaner starting.

"It could be dangerous. I wish you'd left when I first suggested it," Diana said, her heart picking up in an unsteady rhythm. There was a faint mark on his cleanly shaven jaw where she had bitten him in the shower last night. She had never behaved so wantonly in her life, had never said the words she had whispered to him.

"It couldn't have been me," she muttered, clapping her hand over her mouth when she realized she'd spoken aloud.

His eyes twinkled. "No, it was your evil, abandoned twin. Analise, why did you run? You knew you couldn't get away."

She lifted her chin haughtily. "I said it last night. No promises. Once you're away from here, you'll forget me. It's only the circumstances that make you feel the way you do."

"Can't you trust me even a little?"

"I trust you."

"Yeah, with anything but your feelings. It's not real until you trust your feelings, and mine."

"It's not real at all," Diana insisted. "You don't know the half of it. It's only make-believe, a game."

"Oh, sweetheart, you are so wrong." He drank the last of his coffee and got up to put the cup in the sink. "Shall I make you some toast?"

"I can make my own toast," she said, getting up and rummaging in the bread box, taking out two slices and putting them into the toaster. "Have you seen Joubert this morning?"

"No, but we have acquired more guards. That's what upset Maria. She doesn't know what's going on, but she doesn't like all these strangers hanging around."

"How did they get here?"

"Probably in the helicopter I heard at six."

Diana shook her head as she retrieved the toasted bread and buttered it. "I must have slept more soundly than I thought. I didn't hear anything except the water bomber a little while ago."

"The helicopter didn't fly over the house. I wouldn't have noticed it except that I was out in the garden at the time, having a look around. Our friend Petro followed every step I took."

Tamara came into the kitchen, the wooden soles of her sandals loud on the tiled floor. Sparing them only a brief, disinterested glance, she went straight to the coffeepot. "Is there anything to eat?" she asked peevishly. "I missed dinner last night."

"You too?" Diana said ironically.

"Paul found out about Adoni. He saw the car and came to the village to bring me home. He was furious, especially since it took him some time to find me. We were at a friend's house outside the village. He says Adoni is beneath me." She gave a short laugh. "It's none of his business."

Diana rolled her eyes toward the ceiling, but Tamara took no notice. "Then why don't you leave? You're an adult. No one's holding you here."

"He's not letting you go, is he?" Tamara said, turning to put bread in the toaster.

"Did he tell you that?" Rob asked.

"He didn't have to. Maria did." She lowered her voice, her eyes flitting around the kitchen as if she expected Paul to materialize at any moment. "I know a way out of the house that isn't hooked up to the alarm system. Once you're out in the garden, it shouldn't be too difficult to get away from the guards and avoid the other alarms."

Rob and Diana looked at one another. They would never have expected help from the sullen Tamara.

"What about you, Tamara?" Diana said. "You're not happy here. I'm sure you could get work again. You don't have to live with Paul."

"What is he to you?" Rob asked. "Your father?"

The girl's eyes flew wide, and then her expression became wary. "Why would you think that? No, he's not my father. He's a family friend. I hadn't seen him in years, but when I had the trouble with my boss and needed a place to stay, he let me come."

"But can't you see? Paul is taking advantage of you, too." Diana's voice grew urgent. "He's—"

"He has never touched me," Tamara said, interrupting. "I'm safe here."

And she was a prisoner, even more than they were, Diana thought in despair. Tamara stayed by choice, acting as her own jailer.

They waited until she had eaten a couple of slices of toast. Restless, Diana washed out their cups and put away the toaster.

Tamara rose from her chair. "Come. I'll show you the way out."

She led them downstairs into the wine cellar. At the end of the damp, gloomy room, a wooden door was set into the stone wall. It appeared to have neither a latch nor a handle.

Tamara disappeared behind the wine racks, coming back a moment later with a key. Standing on tiptoe, she groped along the top of the door. There was a faint click, and it swung silently open.

Beyond the opening lay the garden, wilting in the thick heat. "They use it only for deliveries of wine, once every couple of years," Tamara explained.

"Why didn't I know this?" Diana asked.

"The last time wine was delivered, you were away on holiday. I watched them bring it in, and I saw where Paul put the key." She closed the door, relocked it, and thrust the key into Diana's hand, where it lay like a cool talisman to protect them from evil. "Don't worry about me. I can look after myself."

She turned toward the stairs, then looked back. "One more thing. The shipment is going out tonight. Adoni told me. From the sea cave."

Chapter Eighteen

The shipment is going out tonight. The words echoed in Diana's brain as she crept stealthily through the garden late that evening. Rob followed close behind her. Despite her warnings, he had insisted on going with her.

She held a damp handkerchief over her nose and mouth, but it was scant protection against the smoke. Overhead, the sky was a lurid orange, the superheated air thick and close. It felt as if every molecule of oxygen had been replaced by smoke and ash. During the day, the fire had moved inexorably closer, although nearly every able-bodied man on the island had turned out to fight it.

Except Paul, the film crew, and the guards. Joubert, who had put in a brief appearance that afternoon, seemed oblivious of danger, and of his civic duty. Not that a half-dozen more men would have made much difference without additional equipment.

Tomorrow would bring relief. Maria reported that army fire fighters were being sent to the island to battle the blaze. They would bring a second water bomber. With luck, they would contain the fire before it reached the valuable orchards and fields.

The fire was now only a couple of kilometers from the boundaries of the estate. Fortunately, it had reached an area of lush, green deciduous trees that were slowing its progress. Still, after nightfall, the flames had been visible from her window.

The night was perfectly calm, but the smoke and the heat filled Diana with a sense of foreboding. She felt as if the fire were a ravenous beast, breathing down their necks. The thought of going into the network of unlit caves was a nightmare she didn't dare think about. She hoped they wouldn't have to go farther than the sea cave, which was clearly marked on Nick's map. Its entrance was more easily accessible by boat than on foot, but there was a trail down the cliffs. As a precaution, she and Rob had spent the afternoon memorizing Nick's map. She could only pray that they wouldn't have to put the information to use.

Rob stopped and waited for her when they reached the top of the cliff. "Are you all right?"

She coughed, removing the handkerchief. It was useless by now, having dried out in the heat. "I'm okay. At least here it's easier to breathe."

The smoke was less oppressive near the sea, where a faint wind stirred the dense air. A muted rumbling sounded in the distance, and Diana tensed. A ship approaching, invisible in the haze? No, she thought as the noise faded, probably thunder. The breathless stillness that characterized this night often presaged a storm.

"Let's go," Rob whispered.

Apprehension churned in his gut. Would they be able to enter the cave where the goods were stored undetected? And then what? He had no doubts about Analise's abilities, but her claustrophobia was an unknown factor he didn't like to think about.

He moved slowly, picking his way in the dark, making sure they didn't stray from the precipitous path. He didn't dare keep the flashlight on for long, in case someone was watching. As long as they remained on the island, especially on the estate grounds, they were in danger, and he wasn't sure Joubert would bother to take them prisoner if he caught them. He might have his men shoot first and sort it all out later.

Analise touched his arm. "This way. The path forks here."

"So it's not the same beach where we were before?" he whispered.

"No. Remember when we heard the boat after the woman in white disappeared? I think this leads down there."

The beach appeared deserted, deep in shadow. They crossed it, clambering over loose boulders heaped at the foot of a cliff.

"Look." Rob pointed to the scattered rocks that formed a breakwater around the cove. A motorboat, its hull a pale outline against the sand, was drawn up on the beach.

"We could get away now," Rob said softly. "Call your contact—what did you say his name was, Bouchard?—and let him take care of it."

"No." Analise's voice was firm. "That's not how I work. I'm seeing it through to the end."

"The caves?"

She lifted her chin. "I'll handle it, if it comes to that. But first we have to find out if the goods are really here. That boat—"

"It would be gone if the job was done," Rob said.

DAMP EARTH squelched under their feet as they entered the cave. The cool air was pungent with the odor of decomposing seaweed. Diana's heart pounded heavily in her chest, and her breath came in labored, shallow gasps as the darkness closed around her.

Ashamed of her fear, she compensated by staying a little distance ahead of Rob, doggedly forcing herself to keep going. Not for anything would she let Rob see her weakness, her childish fear of the dark.

She nearly fainted in her relief when they came to a large cavern. The beam of Rob's large flashlight cast eerie, elongated shadows back and forth, emphasizing the high ceilings and distant walls. Free of the confining darkness of the passage, Diana could breathe again without feeling as if she were choking.

"Look over there." She kept her voice barely above a whisper but even so it echoed hollowly. *There, there, there.*

The crates they had last seen being unloaded from the yacht stood neatly stacked against one wall. Only one appeared to have been opened, its lid lying askew. Fine shreds of plastic packing material spilled over the edge of the crate.

Rob leaned down and groped among the shimmering strands. He let out a low whistle. "Will you look at this? You remember the museum robbery that was written up in *Art News?* This looks like one of the items reported missing."

He lifted a bronze sculpture partly out of the crate. It was a startling realistic statue of a child, approximately life-size, a little boy whose mischievous smile was frozen for eternity.

Diana pursed her lips. "It certainly does, and it's priceless. It's not often that bronze is found so perfectly preserved. I'll bet Paul meant to keep this one for his private collection."

"You are so right, my dear Analise." Paul Joubert's voice boomed through the chamber, spinning them around. His glittering dark eyes swung over them. He clicked his tongue in pretended dismay. "I should have kept a closer eye on you. But no matter, you didn't get far, and I'll take measures to see that it doesn't happen again."

He made a gesture with his arm. Two men stepped out of the shadows. Diana recognized the first as one of the guards from the yacht. He carried an automatic pistol with the ease of one who regarded it as an extension of his arm. The second man, who held a hunting rifle, was the one who had been guarding the house during the day.

"Good thing I stationed Bruno in the garden while Millar watched the house. They were both able to follow you at a discreet distance." Joubert glanced almost negligently at the crates of artifacts. "We were hoping to get the goods off the island by helicopter, but the fire and smoke have made visibility too poor. We'll be forced to use a boat instead."

He fixed a harsh stare on Diana. "After that, we'll take care of you. I'll be sorry to lose you, Analise. You were a great asset to my business, but you should have stuck to your end of it instead of meddling in mine."

"You won't get away with this, Paul," Diana said in a hard voice. "Wherever you try to land on the mainland, you'll be searched."

"Then we'll have to make sure they're busy with a diversion, won't we?" Joubert said silkily. "The two of you going away in a motorboat, a tragic explosion... Yes, that should do nicely, and serve a double purpose."

Rob cut in. "I've sent my story. This morning. If anything happens to me, it'll be on the front pages of every leading newspaper. You won't find a place on earth to hide."

Joubert's eyes narrowed, but his hands were steady as he lit a cigar. "Maybe I shouldn't have let you come here. Vanity is a dangerous thing." He blew out smoke, and it hung in the cool, humid air, reminding Diana sickeningly of the brushfire raging outside.

Rob's hands tightened on Diana's shoulders. She had been almost unaware of his movements toward her. His breath feathered over her ear as he whispered, "Be ready to run. Just follow me."

She realized that Rob's flashlight was the only real illumination in the cave. Joubert had been carrying a battery-powered lantern, but he'd put it down to light his cigar, and the beam was not pointing away from them. Rob suddenly turned off his light. At the same instant, he pushed Analise into the tunnel by which they'd entered the cavern. The harsh *spang* of a rifle bullet hitting a rock echoed through the cave, and he stumbled, falling to one knee.

"Stop shooting. You'll bring down the roof!" Joubert yelled, diving for his lantern.

"Robby!"

Rob heard the shrill cry, and the world tilted. The beam of Joubert's flashlight swept over him, and then strong arms pulled him upright.

"Robby, you fell! Did he hit you? Oh, it's my fault! I should never..." The words turned into a buzzing in his ears. He was going crazy, his head spinning, pressure squeezing his temples.

"Diana," he whispered hoarsely, pain exploding in his brain.

She grabbed his arm. He shook his head to clear it, willing his legs to move.

"That's far enough."

The harsh voice penetrated the fog, and he opened his eyes. Petro stood in front of them, pistol in hand. They had no choice but to precede him into the main cavern, Rob leaning heavily on Diana's arm.

"Ah, Petro," Joubert said, with a satisfied smile. "You've got them. Tie them up over there until we're finished."

Diana's mind raced. If Petro came a little closer, she could grab his gun. Of course, there were the other two thugs to deal with, although she saw that they'd put down their weapons as they prepared to transport the crates. All she needed was one slip, one chance.

Rob. Something was wrong. His breathing was harsh in her ear, and his weight was dragging at her.

"Move," Petro growled. "We don't have all night."

Diana glared at him. "I thought you were my friend. Turn in Joubert and I'll see that you get off lightly."

He sneered. "Why should I? With the money we'll get from this shipment, I can get off this forsaken island and live a good life somewhere else."

Rob slumped against her, and she caught his arm. His skin was cold, and beaded with sweat.

Petro gestured with his gun. "Into the corner. Move."

"Wait!" Diana cried. "Can't you see he's hurt?"

Petro took hold of Rob's other arm and propelled him into a niche formed by a small forest of stalagmites. "You can look after him here. I don't want you running off again."

Rob groaned, swearing, as he sank down onto the ground. "Damn it—I think I've been shot. My leg's gone numb."

Diana knelt beside him. "Which leg? Do you feel pain anywhere?"

He gave a strangled laugh. "Not yet. But my leg won't support me."

"Let me see."

"Get on with it," Petro said impatiently.

"Shut up." Her voice was cool, and her hands were steady and competent. She found the tear in his jeans, below the knee. The stickiness of blood clung to her fingers. He'd taken a bullet, all right, probably when the shot had ricocheted off the rock. She could feel the ragged edges of torn skin on his calf where the bullet had grazed him. "At least there's no bullet in there."

"Small consolation," he muttered, his teeth clenched. "How bad is it?"

"It's only a scrape, but deep enough to traumatize the muscle. Give me your handkerchief. I'll wrap your leg to stop the bleeding."

With quick efficiency, she secured the makeshift bandage. Petro stood over them, scowling. When she'd finished, he tied first her wrists and then Rob's tightly behind their backs. As an added precaution, he looped the ends of the cord around a convenient stalagmite. Lighting a cigarette, he moved away to sit on a crate on the far side of the cavern.

Diana flexed her arms, feeling the cord biting into her wrists. She'd tensed her muscles when he tied the knots, and now she found she had a fraction of slack in the bonds. Enough to allow her to extract the miniature blade she carried in her watchband. She and Rob sat at the edge of the circle of light; with luck, their captors wouldn't notice what she was up to. If she could get her hands free, she might have a chance to get away.

In the black tunnels, she could lose a pursuer and reach Nick to call for backup. It might not be too late. Resolutely turning off the vision of crawling through the caves without a light, she worked on freeing the blade.

"Diana," Rob whispered hoarsely.

Diana. He'd said her name. An odd heat, a mixture of dread and relief, washed through her. She waited, breath suspended, for the anger, the accusations, the rejection.

His eyes rested on her face, their expression unreadable. "Diana," he said. "It *is* you, then. And you were the woman in the car."

"You remember," she whispered in a strangled tone.

"Yes, I remember. You called me Robby just before the explosion. Only you ever used that nickname."

"You're not angry?"

"Angry?" He gave a short laugh. "Maybe later. You lied to me. You could have trusted me to keep your secret."

"I didn't dare take the chance. I trusted a man once before, and broke the rules. He died, and I nearly did—in that hell hole where Antonio's killer kept me prisoner."

She shifted slightly, earning a glare from Petro. "The floor's hard," she said, giving him a smile she hoped was tremulous rather than defiant. Slowly, carefully, she began to saw at the cords.

She glanced at Petro, who was lighting another cigarette. The other men, under Joubert's direction, were carrying the crates out of the cave—not a small task, considering the heavy statuary they contained. "How do you feel?" she murmured to Rob.

"Actually, like I've been hit by a truck. Never mind that, though. I want to know what happened to you after the car went over the cliff."

He shuddered, remembering the sickening thud, the wild lurching of the car across the small mountain meadow. Only Diana's skill had kept it from rolling. Luckily, they'd both been wearing their seat belts; they hadn't been knocked unconscious or thrown around inside the vehicle. Diana's scream to him to jump, and his subsequent landing in a prickly shrub, seemed like a blur of impressions. He must have blacked out for a second when his head hit a rock.

Half-stunned, he'd scrambled to his feet and run for the car through a thicket of head-high holly oaks. A violent explosion had shaken the ground. He'd fallen, then pushed himself to his feet. If Diana was trapped, he had to get her out.

He'd nearly reached the car when the second explosion lifted him and tossed him onto the ground some distance away. Burning debris had rained around him as the car rolled slowly over and landed, in flames, down the steep slope. The wind knocked out of him, he'd been unable to move. He thought he'd screamed Diana's name, the sound swallowed up by the roar of the fire. Then he must have passed out again.

"It was like a nightmare where you can't move. I thought you'd died in the explosion. That must be what caused my mind to block out the accident. Those were gunshots I heard, weren't they?"

"Yes." She squeezed her eyes shut. "Rob, I'm sorry."

"For what?"

"Getting you into this. And leaving you."

"You left me?" His level tone gave away nothing of what he was thinking.

"Yes," she said with brutal honesty. "I left you after I saw the shepherd pick you up."

Rob moved his shoulder against hers, in a gesture that was oddly comforting. "So you knew I was safe. You hardly left me to die."

She choked down the lump in her throat, feeling as if she were about to cry. "After the shooting, I didn't want to risk being seen with you, risk being recognized. And I still don't know who the gunman was. Not one of Joubert's men, I would guess, since we haven't seen him here." She stifled a gasp as the blade pricked her skin.

To cover the sound, she continued, in a low voice. "As soon as I saw you were safely out of the car, I jumped and rolled clear. I stayed down, waiting for the other car to leave. Then the shots came, and my car exploded. I waited until the fire died a little. I tried to find you, but I hid again when the shepherd came. I followed his shortcut through the scrub to the main road. A car stopped and took you to the clinic. I managed to hitch a ride right after you were picked up. I phoned the clinic later, when I got back to Corfu. They told me you weren't in any danger." She shrugged. "The rest you know. Since you'd lost your memory of that day, I thought it would be safer if you didn't know who I was."

"You took a chance," Rob said.

"I know, but that's my life—taking chances." The cords were loosening. Drops of blood from small cuts made her wrists slippery. Another moment and she would be free.

"What are you doing, squirming around like that?" Rob sounded stronger, more alert.

"Trying to get us out of here," she muttered, wincing as the blade nicked her skin again. She twisted her wrists, keeping her movements to a minimum. The cords gave way, sliding to the ground.

She glanced toward Petro. He was no longer sitting on the crate. Swinging her glance around the cave, she saw him near the tunnel, talking to one of Joubert's men in a low voice. He bent his head, lighting another cigarette, clearly confident that they couldn't escape.

Diana edged one hand behind Rob and deftly slicked through his bonds. His eyes widened, but he kept his expression neutral. "Resourceful, aren't you?"

"I'm going to try to get away, to call Bouchard. Once I'm gone, if you get a chance, run and hide. Wait for me. And whatever you see me do, don't react. Trust me."

Rob's leg ached dully, but his head was once more clear. He couldn't figure what kind of plan Diana—strange to think of her by that name, when she didn't look like the Diana he'd known—could come up with. He wasn't sure he could get up, much less run on his wounded leg.

To distract himself, he said, "In Makrino, you asked me to wait until you contacted me rather than try to talk Joubert into an interview at that time, didn't you? You knew what was coming down, didn't you?"

"I expected it, from what I'd found out."

"Would you have given me the story? Or was that just an excuse to keep me out of the way? I can understand that you couldn't tell me about your undercover work, but you could have told me who you were when you met me at the clinic."

She shivered at the hard note she heard in his voice. "I did what I thought best. Once you were on the island, I couldn't take the chance that you'd make a slip. If you didn't know, you'd treat me as a stranger."

"Hardly a stranger. So many times I thought there was something familiar about you, that we'd met before. How did you change your appearance so much?"

"It's not as big a change as you might think," she said, unable to keep a tremor out of her voice. "Contact lenses, hairstyle, hair color. The only thing that's really different is my nose. It needed some plastic surgery five years ago. I broke it escaping from the terrorists who kept me prisoner."

Rob's face changed. "You were hurt? Nobody would have blamed you if you'd retired."

"I had to prove that I hadn't lost my nerve."

"You don't have to prove anything to me, Diana," Rob said gently.

"I know." Her throat tightened, and she wished she could take his hand. Instead, she pressed her head against his chest. "I'm sorry, Rob. For everything. For all the lies."

He was silent for a long moment. She could feel the rhythm of his breathing, the steady beating of his heart near her cheek. Then he asked, "Was it all a lie, Diana? What happened between us, was that a lie?"

She knew he meant their lovemaking. "No," she said softly. "It wasn't all a lie. I care about you. I tried to keep you safe. I'm sorry I couldn't. That's why I work alone, so that no one is endangered if things get sticky."

"You can't spend your whole life alone."

She sucked in a sharp breath, pain gripping her heart in a vise. "We've been through that. When this is over, it's goodbye. Just as it was before."

"It doesn't have to be," Rob said stubbornly. "We're different people now. We can work something out."

"It would be like before, each of us with our separate lives, the absences tearing us apart. I won't live like that again."

"Was that what made you ask for a divorce, my being away so much? You didn't say anything. You had your studies, and I had my work. I thought we were happy."

"We didn't even know each other," she said, with a bitterness she thought she'd rationalized away years ago.

"But why just then? Do you know that I was ready to ask for assignments closer to home when I came back from that trip to the Far East?"

Diana thought for a long moment. Despite Joubert's threats, she didn't accept that they might die. Nick would realize something had happened to her and contact Bouchard on his own. They would be freed. But she knew from past experience that much could go wrong. Joubert could decide to shoot them as soon as the crates were loaded and dump their bodies at sea, or just leave them in the remote reaches of the caves.

She had to tell Rob. She owed him that much. Keeping her voice determinedly steady, she said, "I had a miscarriage. Just before you got back."

His eyes widened. "You were pregnant? We were so careful."

"Not careful enough, it seems."

"You never said anything." Pain etched stark lines on his face. "Did you think I wouldn't care? It was my baby, too. Or didn't you want me to care? Yeah, I think I see it now. You're afraid to let anyone care about you, and to love them back, because to you that implies weakness."

She bent her head. "Yes, that's true. But it wasn't only me. Something happened on that trip, didn't it? Something you never wrote about, something you couldn't talk about. You were so withdrawn. And then you went away again, without a word about coming back."

He ground his teeth in frustration, aching with the need to hold her. "I saw an orphanage filled with children deliberately burned to the ground, all for a political statement.

The next assignment was already booked, a dangerous one. I wanted to do it, to forget the screams of the children. There were times I hoped I wouldn't come back from it. But, strangely, it was a kind of therapy. I could have talked to you when I got back. But you'd moved out, and the next thing I knew your lawyers served me with divorce papers. We wasted all these years, Diana."

"Did we?" she said sadly.

"The sparks were there," he said positively. "I think they still are, if you'll have faith in us."

Chapter Nineteen

Mohammed Kurtz and Cedric Blackwell strode into the cavern, followed by a man with a rifle in his hands.

"I was wondering when he was going to show up," Rob muttered. "I figured there had to be a connection."

The man they'd last seen near Makrino, driving the steel-gray Mercedes, walked over to them, his lip curled in a sneer. "We meet at last. Mr. Minardos, you have more lives than a cat."

"So I was the target, was I?"

Blackwell sent the man a look of distaste. "Jimmy here followed you to Makrino. He thought in his feeble brain that he should prevent you from coming to Pagoni. By the way, who was that blond woman?"

Diana smiled tightly. "I guess my cover was better than I thought."

Blackwell nodded. "So it was you, Diana. Jimmy didn't know you. But I recognized you from the first moment I saw you in Joubert's house. Who are you working for this time? Interpol?"

She returned his gaze coolly. "Indirectly, I suppose. I'm puzzled, though. You didn't expose me to Joubert."

"Let's say I had my own agenda." He reached into his pocket and pulled out a pistol so small it looked like a toy.

A chill ran up Diana's spine. That gun was capable of firing bullets that could blow one's internal organs to bits.

He didn't point it at her, however. Instead, he deftly plucked the rifle from Jimmy's hands. The surprise on the man's face was comical. Petro, belatedly remembering he was in charge of the prisoners, came toward them. Before he could assimilate the situation and react, Blackwell had aimed the pistol at his chest. "Drop your gun, Petro."

Petro's cigarette fell from his gaping mouth, and his gun clattered to the floor.

Standing at the far end of the cavern, Joubert had noticed nothing amiss. Only four crates were left, waiting for the return of his men. No one remained to defend Joubert if Blackwell was bent on taking over.

Diana wasn't sure what to make of this turn of events. She knew only that no one was paying attention to her or Rob, and that they were free. She held her breath, bracing herself to take advantage of the slightest opportunity.

Joubert turned and saw the gun in Blackwell's hand. "What's going on?"

"We have a traitor in our midst."

"Petro?"

"No, not Petro. Your sometime partner, Mohammed Kurtz."

Beside Blackwell, Kurtz made a strangled sound. His face turned as pale as the stalagmites at Diana's back.

"And his bungling assistant Jimmy here tried to help by running Minardos's car off the road. You mentioned to Kurtz that you were thinking of granting Minardos an interview weeks ago, didn't you? Not very wise. The last thing Kurtz wanted was any kind of publicity for you. You made a mistake trusting him, Joubert. He found a buyer for the goods, and he was going to cut you out."

"And now you're taking over." Joubert appeared perfectly calm as he reached toward his jacket pocket.

"Keep your hands away from your sides," Blackwell said in his cultured voice.

"I'm only getting a cigar," Joubert said mildly. He flipped open his jacket, showing the gold case in the inside pocket.

"Okay, but no sudden moves." Blackwell's hard eyes took in the others grouped in front of him. "I've got another man coming in, so don't anyone try to be a hero."

Joubert put his hand inside his jacket. The flat report of a pistol resounded through the cavern, and Kurtz fell, clutching his shoulder.

Diana didn't wait to see more. She squeezed Rob's arm, giving him a quick kiss. "I'll be back."

She thought she heard him say something. It sounded like "I love you," but she wasn't sure.

Keeping in the shadows, she ran into the passage through which she and Rob had entered the cavern. She heard a shout behind her, but before anyone could gather his wits to follow, she ducked down a narrow adjoining tunnel. Darkness closed around her like a smothering shroud.

She paused, gasping for breath. She felt hot and cold at once, clammy sweat breaking out on her skin as if she had a fever. Closing her eyes, she prayed for strength to fight the darkness and her own terror.

For Rob. And for herself.

He had faith in her. The thought wound through her in a silken thread of hope. Rob had changed the way she saw herself. In her mind she heard again the soothing cadence of his voice, the words he'd offered the last time they'd make love—words of reassurance, strength, love. The terror began to recede.

She lifted the bottom of her pant leg and took a tiny penlight from a hidden pocket in the inside seam. The bulb cast only a thread of light, but it was enough to help her should she need it. Switching off the light to save the battery, she started down the dark passage, Nick's map displayed in her mind.

She trailed her hand along the damp wall. Its rough stones were worn to smoothness by aeons of trickling water. Her breath rasped loudly, the only sound except for the faint squeak of the rubber soles of her sneakers on the wet surface.

She reached the fork marked on the map and took the tunnel to the right. It was narrower than the one she had been following, but still high enough for her to stand upright.

She was surprised at her own calmness. The action of walking, automatically putting one foot ahead of another, was completely different from the scene in her nightmare, in which she was confined helplessly in the dark, unable to move more than a couple of inches in any direction. And during her imprisonment, her underground cell had been so small that she could only take three paces in any direction.

Renewed confidence surged up in her. She would make it. She had to.

Her courage ebbed again when the passage began to shrink. She had to walk sideways, her back scraping the wall behind her. Then she found she could no longer stand upright. She continued in a sort of stoop, hunching her shoulders to get around outcroppings and holding her breath as she squeezed through narrow spaces.

Once she became stuck. Her arm, extended to protect her head from bulges in the low ceiling, caught in a rough fissure between two slabs of stone. She jerked at it and felt her sleeve tear.

She closed her eyes, and white dots spun against the backs of her eyelids. Her head felt as if it were filled with helium, and her breath labored in and out of her lungs with an audible wheezing.

She heard a sound, her own groan, and wondered where she'd found the breath to make it. Her throat was dry as she twisted to free herself. The light-headed feeling worsened, and she stifled a scream. The ceiling seemed to be sinking lower, suffocating her. She was back in the cell, inhaling the musty odor and hearing the scuttling of tiny insect feet, the clicking of minute jaws that would strip the flesh from her bones.

She must have fainted, for she found herself huddled on the damp floor, her cheek lying on something that bit painfully into the skin. Moaning, she shifted her head until it rested against the rough wall at her side. She floated in mindless oblivion, strangely at peace, no longer frightened. The darkness remained, but it held no terror. She was so tired; she could sleep, never dream, never awaken.

A low rumble came faintly to her ears, as if a train were passing far beneath her. She lay still, breathing shallowly, precisely, as she waited for the telltale quivering of the earth . . .

With a sharp cry, she pushed herself up, crouching in the dark as she fumbled to bring the penlight into position. Her hand was cramped from the desperate grip she'd kept on it. She clicked the switch. The thread of light reassuringly strafed the rock above her.

Blinking, she turned it off. Her arm was free, although as she raised it warm liquid trickled from her elbow toward her shoulder. Sweat. Or blood. It didn't matter. She had to get out of here, had to get help.

She licked her lips, moistening them, tasting salty sweat and the tart-sweet flavor that was Rob's. Rob. He'd said he loved her.

Her mind swam with the sweetness of his words, the hot tenderness of his lovemaking. She couldn't love him, but the nights they'd spent together had been so good. She didn't want to give them up. Perhaps she could pretend. For a while. Except that she would hurt him. Again. Still, wasn't it better to love for a time than not to love at all?

It occurred to her that she had spent most of her life pretending, had been pretending for so long she often wasn't sure what was real and what was part of the facade she had to present to the world. She'd pretended to belong to the families she lived with, to blend in with the secure, loved children who were her classmates at school. Later, she'd pretended to be tough to protect herself on assignments in dangerous places, with dangerous men who'd tried to talk her into a temporary oblivion of cheap wine and cheaper sex. She'd stood apart from them, and she'd finally been excluded.

She'd even pretended with Rob, during their brief marriage. But during these past days, their second chance, she'd been unable to pretend. Perhaps that was why he scared her. No, not him. It was her reaction to him that scared her. And the effortless way he had of seeing through the pretense to the real her. Wasn't that where the problem lay? She had been afraid he would find only an empty shell.

To him, she wasn't an empty shell. It struck her all at once that he never said anything he didn't mean. And he hadn't been angry at her deceit; he'd understood her need to do her job, and to protect him.

He did love her. And it wasn't the facade he loved. He'd destroyed that the moment he'd removed her hat and looked into her soul, nakedly displayed because she was too startled to cover up.

Courage. That was what it took. She smiled suddenly in the dark, narrow tunnel. She'd found the courage to go through this, to defy the nightmares that had haunted her all her life. It would take even more courage to love him, but she could find it. With time and his patience and his love, she could find it.

With a faint thud, she hit what seemed to be a dead end. She paused, groping to turn on the flashlight. Had a cave-in blocked the passage? If that was the case, would she be able to find another way out?

Before she could use the light, she smelled it, a new pungency over the dusty odor that swirled up when she disturbed the dried moss and fine sand on the cave floor. Smoke. Wood smoke, advance guard of the brushfire.

Not wanting to click the light on and perhaps give away her presence, she edged around a sharp bend. She stifled a shout of elation. Daylight. Ahead of her she could see a patch of daylight.

"I made it, Rob," she whispered. "I made it."

The light turned out to be an illusion. Dawn was still hours away, but the fire had painted the night sky in lurid shades of tangerine and crimson. The distant crackling of flames was no longer only in her imagination as she dashed across the meadow. Pine trees beyond the little plateau were blazing, and burning resin sent plumes of inky black smoke into the sky.

She found Nick at the edge of his garden, shirtless, wetting down the shrubbery with the garden hose. Tenacity. Even in the face of the fire, he was trying to protect his property—not that the feeble trickle of water would do much good.

He looked up, startled, water running unnoticed over his bare feet. "Analise, where have you been? I expected you sooner."

"You can call me Diana. Everyone knows." Her chest heaved as she fought to catch her breath.

Nick frowned. "Robert, too? He's regained his memory?"

"Everything." She urgently laid a hand on his arm. "Nick, we have to get back as quickly as possible. He's a prisoner, and he's hurt. But first I have to phone Bouchard. The lines aren't down, are they?''

"Still okay, last time I checked. I was ready to call him myself when I didn't hear from you." He led her into the house, pointing to the phone on the wall. "The fire's worse."

"So I see," she said as she dialed. "When are the extra fire fighters due?"

"As soon as it's daylight. And about time, too."

The telephone was ringing in her ear. Two times. Three. "Come on," she muttered, pounding her fist against the wall. "Answer." The number was a local one, no doubt a guest house where everyone would be asleep.

On the sixth ring, a sleepy voice answered. "Bouchard?" Diana said, breathless with relief.

"Oui."

She switched to French so that there would be no mistakes in communication. She explained the situation as concisely as she could, ending with "You'd better notify the coast guard at once, or the boat will be gone."

"I have them standing by. Cove number three, you say?" Months ago she had given him a detailed map of the island's coast, with landmarks indicated in simple code.

"Yes. But you'll have to come in through the estate. I'll have Nick wait at the gate to show you the way."

"Fine, but where will you be?"

"I have to get back to the cavern."

"Just be careful," Bouchard said.

Diana smiled, for the first time noticing that her cheek felt tender. "I will. Good luck, Monsieur Bouchard."

She hung up the phone, catching sight of her image in the mirror over the sink as she turned toward the door. She looked a sight, she thought dispassionately, covered with green slime, hair tangled like a banshee's. On her cheek, almost obscured by mud, was an angry red scrape.

She shrugged. Bath and a bandage later. First she had to get back to Rob, although a glance at the clock told her that less than an hour had passed since she'd left him.

Her face grim, she muttered a quick prayer. *Please let him be okay. Don't let me be too late.*

Nick was waiting for her outside, fully dressed, with sturdy boots on his feet and a bag slung over his shoulder. In his hand he carried a heavy, old-fashioned revolver, which he gave to her.

She took it, frowning. "You know I don't like guns."

His mouth turned up in a brief grin that reflected the recklessness he'd been known for in his youth. "Never mind. They're all heavily armed. This might even the odds."

He coughed harshly. The smoke was denser now, making it painful to breathe. Diana's throat felt dry and raw, and her eyes were stinging. Thunder rumbled, and she glanced at the livid sky. Impossible to tell if clouds hung overhead. "If it rained . . .

Nick made a quick sign of the cross. "Go with God. And get Robert out of there."

SHE MADE IT to the little beach without incident. The only living creatures in the garden were the peacocks, their incessant cries shredding the smoke-filled air. Their shrieks faded as she crept up to the cave entrance.

A small powerboat rested on the sand, not the one the crates had been loaded onto. She thought she saw lights flickering out at sea, but the dense smoke—or perhaps it was the approaching storm—cut visibility to almost nothing. Thunder crackled at intervals, and lightning sizzled across the flat surface of the water.

Surprisingly, the cave appeared dark. The lanterns the men had set in the passage were gone. Sweat broke out on her spine, trickling down under her shirt. Was she too late?

Tense with new apprehension, she crept toward the cavern, the revolver a dead weight in her hand. She didn't dare use her light, in case Joubert or Blackwell—whoever now had the upper hand—had left a guard.

Loud voices alerted her that they hadn't all fled. She slowed her steps. Joubert's angry voice echoed from the rock walls. "You'd better decide, Tamara. Are you coming with me?"

Diana stopped at the edge of the large cavern. Only two people were visible, spotlighted by powerful battery lanterns. Joubert and Tamara.

The girl stood pressed against a wall, her arms wrapped defensively around her waist. Joubert gripped a small pistol in one hand. In the other, he held the ever-present cigar. His cold eyes blazed with anger, and the madness of a powerful man who had been thwarted.

Diana's breath hitched in her throat. Was he planning to shoot Tamara?

A faint moan came from the shadows beyond Joubert. Rob? No, it was Kurtz, lying where he had fallen. He wasn't dead, although blood stained the floor beneath him. His chest rose and fell with his breathing, and she saw his eyes open, skitter around, then close once more. Wise man, to keep out of it.

A movement drew her attention to the shadows on her right. Rob stood on his feet, out of sight of Joubert. He looked shaky and pale, but she saw he wasn't about to collapse. Keeping out of the illuminated circle, she edged closer, catching his eye when she was almost within reach of him.

She smiled grimly. With Joubert's attention focused on Tamara, and none of his men apparently within earshot, she had a chance. She could take Joubert; by this time the coast guard should have stopped the boat.

It would have worked, if Rob hadn't stepped forward. She almost groaned aloud. She might have known—the male instinct, misguided in this case, to protect a woman.

"Why don't you give it up, Joubert?" Rob said in a taunting voice. "You can't win. You've got no one left, and Blackwell's long gone with the boat."

Joubert jerked his hand around and fired, but Rob had melted back into the shadows, his wounded leg apparently not slowing him down. Diana felt his hand on her arm and turned sharply, prepared to knock him over, if necessary, to stop him from getting himself killed.

"Come on," he said, his eyes bright and reckless. "We can take him. He's already rattled."

"So rattled he could kill us," she whispered harshly, her jaw tight with anger. "I told you I'd handle it. It's my job. Just stay out of my way and let me do it."

Instead of obeying her, Rob spoke again. "Well, Tamara," he said, in an aggressive tone Diana had never heard from him before. "Whose side are you on in this?"

The girl shook her head from side to side. Diana could see the trembling that racked her body; the short, flippy skirt she wore swayed as if moved by a breeze. Her face was dead white, a ghastly contrast to her dark hair.

"Minardos, you're a fool," Joubert said, blowing out blue smoke that drifted toward the ceiling, as ephemeral as gauze.

Stepping forward, Rob bowed mockingly. "You're the fool, Joubert. And a poor judge of character. You continued to work with Kurtz, even when you suspected he might be planning to double-cross you. You should have been suspicious when you saw him teaming up with Blackwell. As for Diana, you were starting to reveal the more critical parts of your business to her. Even if you didn't suspect her real purpose, did you think she would condone your activities once she realized what was going on?"

Joubert shrugged, his arrogance plainly undiminished. "It worked in the past. I've never seen a human who couldn't be bought."

"Your philosophy," Rob said, his voice as smooth and hard as polished steel. "The same philosophy that made it easy for Blackwell to bribe your men to go in with him. Even Petro decided that Blackwell might be a better deal, since he had the goods and you were left with nothing."

"I still have my business," Joubert retorted.

"Not if you're indicted for murder. Why did you shoot Kurtz? Blackwell was the leader."

"Because he got Blackwell into this. I knew Kurtz was up to something when I caught him snooping in the main computer on his last visit."

So that was why the computer had been down, Diana realized. Paul had deliberately disabled it until he could change the codes.

"No one betrays Paul Joubert," he went on. "No one. I'll find Blackwell, too, once I take care of you."

"Then why don't you kill us and get it over with?" Rob said, goading him. "Why wait?"

"You have about fifteen minutes to live, Mr. Minardos. I still have one man who's bringing a boat. You'll have an accident when you're at sea, and I'll be in the clear." His eyes shifted momentarily from them to Tamara. "Tamara, go see if Dino's coming yet."

She said nothing, standing as if in shock.

"You mean Dino's working for you?" Rob asked. "Was that him haunting the beach in a robe one night?"

Joubert inclined his head. "Probably. He was quite taken by the ghost story, and we wanted to keep people away from the beaches."

"What about the rest of the film people? I don't see George, so I presume he's innocent."

"He had nothing to do with it. But since I was financing his documentary, he didn't question the extra crates on the yacht. The filming gave me an excellent cover." He turned his eyes back to Tamara, the look in them hard and glittering.

"Tamara," he snapped, "go down to the beach and wait for Dino."

She shook her head. "I won't. There's no light in the passage, and I hate dark places."

A red flush of anger crept up Joubert's face. "You've got a flashlight. Go."

The girl didn't move. With a jerky movement, Joubert tossed his cigar on the ground. "Tamara—"

"Now!" Rob rushed forward. He would have made it, too, if his leg hadn't collapsed just as he reached Joubert. With a cry of dismay, Diana ran out of the shadows.

It was too late. Joubert stood with his pistol against Rob's head. Diana could only watch helplessly, her own gun raised but useless.

Joubert smiled thinly. "A standoff, Diana? Will you sacrifice your friend Robert for the successful completion of your work? You can shoot me, but he'll die first. What's it to be, Diana, you or him?"

She said nothing, nausea churning in her stomach. She prayed desperately for a noise, men's voices—hadn't he said Dino was coming?—anything to distract him. All she needed was an instant. Rob would drop to the floor, and she would get Joubert.

"That was your mistake, wasn't it?" Joubert said silkily. "You began to care for Rob." He tightened his grip on the pistol, pressing it against Rob's temple. "But it's too late now."

Diana stepped forward. She let her hand drop, the gun dangling from her fingers. "Is it? Maybe you're right. The work I've been doing is dangerous. The pay isn't that great.

How about if you let Rob go? We'll talk, see if we can come to some sort of agreement.''

She heard Rob make a sound of protest, but continued walking, slowly placing one foot ahead of the other. She almost smiled when she saw that she'd correctly judged Joubert's monumental ego. He was actually thinking it over.

What he would have decided, she never had a chance to find out. The sound of men's angry voices echoed down the passage from the sea. Dino strode into the cavern, his face set in its usual sullen lines, and Tamara's friend Adoni was right behind him. Their shadows moved up the wall and across the ceiling in their wake.

"I didn't know anything about this—I would never have agreed to take you out in the boat!" Adoni yelled at Dino. "And that night you dressed up like the ghost and had me pick you up from the beach, that was really stupid. I don't know how I could have been dumb enough to go along with it."

Dino shook off Adoni's hand. Diana heard a happy cry as Tamara flung herself into Adoni's arms.

Dino, with supreme disregard for Rob or Joubert's gun, stopped in front of Joubert. "I quit," he said. "This whole thing has been a waste of time and energy. What good is ten percent of nothing?"

Joubert's eyes flashed in anger. He swung the pistol around to cover Dino, giving Diana the chance she needed. Dropping her own gun, she shoved Rob out of the way and slashed at Joubert's wrist with the side of her hand. Joubert cried out, and she deftly caught his gun before it could hit the ground.

"That's it." She grinned in triumph, meeting Rob's eyes. He grinned back, holding up her gun, which he'd picked up before Dino could get any ideas.

Dino had none. "I'm out of here," he said.

"I don't think so," said a new voice from the cavern entrance. Bouchard. He was followed by Nick and a man Diana recognized as a Greek customs official. Nick immediately went to check out Kurtz's condition.

"How is he?" Diana asked, without taking her eyes off Joubert.

"He'll live," Nick said briefly.

Bouchard snapped handcuffs on Joubert, and Diana gratefully put down the pistol.

Joubert scowled and cursed. "I have the best lawyers in the world. You won't convict me."

"With Diana's evidence, we have a strong case, Monsieur Joubert," Bouchard said. "We'll get an expert to investigate your computer files, as well. I'm sure we'll find plenty to interest us. You won't be smuggling art for a long time to come."

Joubert switched his glare from Bouchard to Tamara. "So you didn't give up that boy when I told you to. This *shepherd*." He spit the word out as if it were an epithet.

"Adoni is studying to be a lawyer," Tamara said, with more spirit than Diana had ever seen her display. "I'm going to marry him. And if you think you can forever dictate what I do, you're even sicker than I think you are. I know you gave me a place to stay when I needed it, but you didn't have the right to take over my life. I can make it on my own."

"You're giving up your career for good?" Joubert roared. "I planned a dramatic comeback for you."

"I don't want it. I've had enough of that life, of everyone trying to manipulate me. You, too, since I've been here. But it's over now. I'm going to live simply. You can't block my income, and the trust fund will be available to me next year. With that, we'll be comfortable."

"So it's your money that Adoni loves."

Tamara turned her face up and received Adoni's kiss. "Not everyone is interested in money, Paul. Adoni doesn't care about my money. And he had nothing to do with the art thefts or the smuggling."

"Come to think of it, Adoni," Rob said, "how did you pay for that Alfa?"

"I bought it for him, as an engagement gift," Tamara said. "I cashed in a bond that matured. And I had a hard time making him take it."

Two men in the white uniforms of the coast guard came into the cavern, carrying a stretcher. They laid Kurtz on it and carried him away.

Bouchard watched dispassionately as the custom official led Joubert, still shouting, out of the cavern. "He can hire all the lawyers he wants," Bouchard said, rubbing his hands together. "But he may have difficulty paying them, if it turns out that some of the businesses he controls are merely fronts for smuggling. Quite a story for you, Minardos."

"You can be sure I'll follow it up," Rob said. "I want this smuggling to stop just as badly as you do."

Bouchard turned to Diana. "You'll be pleased to know we got Blackwell. He took the time to remove a couple of items from Joubert's house." He shook his head. "I think he counted on the fire to delay us."

Rob wrapped his arm around Diana's waist. "How is your leg?" she asked.

He shrugged. "A bit numb, but it's stopped bleeding. I'll live." His body shook as he burst into laughter and hugged her close. "You really did it, didn't you, Diana? You made it through the caves."

"Of course," she said complacently, reveling in her newfound confidence. "Did you ever doubt me?"

OUTSIDE, they were in for a surprise. Dawn had come, but without the usual blazing sun. A soft rain fell from a gray, leaden sky. The air still smelled of soot and smoke, but a water bomber roaring ponderously over their heads told them the fire would soon be contained.

On the bluff above the beach, a Land Rover drove down a rough track through the pines, carrying away the prisoners. A familiar figure stood next to a second vehicle.

Rob limped up to the man, extending his hand. "Venetis, it's good to see you."

"At least the circumstances are more pleasant, Kyrie Minardos," said the Corfu policeman. "I trust you've made a full recovery."

"From the accident, yes."

"Good, good..." Venetis's gaze slid across to Diana. "And this lady proved invaluable in your recovery?"

Rob laughed, hugging Diana close to his side. "You can say that again."

He and Diana gratefully accepted a ride down to the house, where Bouchard was waiting to take a written statement from them. The rain gently settled on their hair, washing away the clay and dirt of the cave. Around them, the shrubbery steamed, releasing the rich, pungent odor of wet earth and blooming flowers refreshed by the moisture.

"You are going to marry me again, aren't you?" Rob said as they got out of the car behind the house.

"Am I?" Diana asked.

"Of course you are." He paused and plucked a sprig of jasmine from a vine cascading over the wall. She inhaled the sweet fragrance as he tucked the flower into her tangled hair. "Beautiful," he said.

Diana made a face. "Covered with mud?"

"Any way I can get you. You haven't answered my question, but I already know the answer."

"What else do you know?"

His eyes gazed into hers, clear as the silver rain falling around them. "That I love you."

Diana smiled. Her insecurities had evaporated, lost in the darkness of the cave. He loved her; she could not do anything but return that love, accept him as he had accepted her. "And I love you, Rob. For always."

Harlequin is proud to present our best authors and their best books. Always the best for your reading pleasure!

Throughout 1993, Harlequin will bring you exciting books by some of the top names in contemporary romance!

In July
look for
The Ties That Bind by

JAYNE ANN KRENTZ

Shannon wanted him seven days a week....

Dark, compelling, mysterious Garth Sheridan was no mere boy next door—even if he did rent the cottage beside Shannon Raine's.

She was intrigued by the hard-nosed exec, but for Shannon it was all or nothing. Either break the undeniable bonds between them... or tear down the barriers surrounding Garth and discover the truth.

Don't miss THE TIES THAT BIND ... wherever Harlequin books are sold.

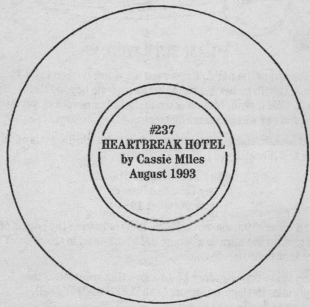

**Relive the romance...
Harlequin and Silhouette
are proud to present**

by Request™

A program of collections of three complete novels by the most
requested authors with the most requested themes. Be sure to
look for one volume each month with three complete novels by
top name authors.

In June: **NINE MONTHS** Penny Jordan
Stella Cameron
Janice Kaiser

**Three women pregnant and alone. But a lot can
happen in nine months!**

In July: **DADDY'S HOME** Kristin James
Naomi Horton
Mary Lynn Baxter

**Daddy's Home... and his presence is long
overdue!**

In August: **FORGOTTEN PAST** Barbara Kaye
Pamela Browning
Nancy Martin

**Do you dare to create a future if you've forgotten
the past?**

Available at your favorite retail outlet.

HARLEQUIN® Silhouette

Fifty red-blooded, white-hot, true-blue hunks from every
State in the Union!

Beginning in May, look for MEN MADE IN AMERICA!
Written by some of our most popular authors, these
stories feature fifty of the strongest, sexiest men, each
from a different state in the union!

Two titles available every other month at your favorite
retail outlet.

In July, look for:

CALL IT DESTINY by Jayne Ann Krentz (Arizona)
ANOTHER KIND OF LOVE by Mary Lynn Baxter
(Arkansas)

In September, look for:

DECEPTIONS by Annette Broadrick (California)
STORMWALKER by Dallas Schulze (Colorado)

You won't be able to resist MEN MADE IN AMERICA!